GUARDIAN

CATHERINE MANN

BERKLEY SENSATION, NEW YORK

THE BERKLEY PUBLISHING GROUP
Published by the Penguin Group
Penguin Group (USA) Inc.
375 Hudson Street, New York, New York 10014, USA

Penguin Group (Canada), 90 Eglinton Avenue East, Suite 700, Toronto, Ontario M4P 2Y3, Canada
(a division of Pearson Penguin Canada Inc.) • Penguin Books Ltd., 80 Strand, London WC2R 0RL,
England • Penguin Group Ireland, 25 St. Stephen's Green, Dublin 2, Ireland (a division of Penguin
Books Ltd.) • Penguin Group (Australia), 250 Camberwell Road, Camberwell, Victoria 3124, Australia
(a division of Pearson Australia Group Pty. Ltd.) • Penguin Books India Pvt. Ltd., 11 Community
Centre, Panchsheel Park, New Delhi—110 017, India • Penguin Group (NZ), 67 Apollo Drive,
Rosedale, Auckland 0632, New Zealand (a division of Pearson New Zealand Ltd.) • Penguin Books
(South Africa) (Pty.) Ltd., 24 Sturdee Avenue, Rosebank, Johannesburg 2196, South Africa

Penguin Books Ltd., Registered Offices: 80 Strand, London WC2R 0RL, England

This is a work of fiction. Names, characters, places, and incidents either are the product of the author's
imagination or are used fictitiously, and any resemblance to actual persons, living or dead, business
establishments, events, or locales is entirely coincidental. The publisher does not have any control over
and does not assume any responsibility for author or third-party websites or their content.

GUARDIAN

A Berkley Sensation Book / published by arrangement with the author

PUBLISHING HISTORY
Berkley Sensation mass-market edition / September 2012

Copyright © 2012 by Catherine Mann.
Excerpt from *Protector* by Catherine Mann copyright © 2012 by Catherine Mann.
Cover art by Dan O'Leary.
Interior text design by Laura K. Corless.

ISBN: 978-0-425-25099-0

BERKLEY SENSATION®
Berkley Sensation Books are published by The Berkley Publishing Group,
a division of Penguin Group (USA) Inc.,
375 Hudson Street, New York, New York 10014.
BERKLEY SENSATION® is a registered trademark of Penguin Group (USA) Inc.
The "B" design is a trademark of Penguin Group (USA) Inc.

PRINTED IN THE UNITED STATES OF AMERICA

10 9 8 7 6 5 4 3 2 1

ALWAYS LEARNING   PEARSON

To Joseph. Welcome to the family. Love you, son!

ACKNOWLEDGMENTS

As a longtime fan of the TV show *JAG*, I have always dreamed of penning a book about a female military lawyer. I'm thrilled to say *Guardian* offered me the right vehicle for just such a character. Once Sophie stepped up to question her witness, aviator David "Ice" Berg, the story took wings!

Many, many thanks to my editor, Wendy McCurdy, for her fabulous insights. I'm eternally grateful to my longtime agent Barbara Collins Rosenberg. As always, I count myself blessed to have the best critique partner in the world, Joanne Rock. Writing is for the most part a solitary job, and I know I'm a lucky author to have such a stellar support network!

Last, but never least, thank you to my four quirky, amazing, utterly lovable children—Brice, Haley, Robbie, and Maggie. (See, Brice and Haley, I finally named characters after you!) And to my air-force-hero hubby, who surprised me with chocolate-covered strawberries as I struggled to meet my deadline. I love you!

ONE

★ ──────────────────────────────

Major Sophie Campbell had wanted to be a JAG since she lost her father in elementary school. That didn't mean she always enjoyed her job.

Today, she downright hated it.

But come hell or high water, she would get some useful nuggets of information out of the witness for the defense—cocky aviator David "Ice" Berg.

"Major Berg, you are aware that the fire control officer on your test team, a man under your command, made a serious error firing from an AC-130 aircraft into a private citizen's home?"

"Ma'am, I've seen the tapes from the test flight," Berg drawled, his South Carolina roots coating each word. "It's tough to miss the flames. But Captain Tate didn't screw up."

Of all the test directors to be in charge of this particular mission, why did it have to be Berg? Sexy as hell, with a sense of humor and unflappable calm, he managed to charm his way through life.

Not today.

"Let me rephrase the question." Sophie flipped through the pages of her legal pad.

Stalling.

She didn't actually need further information. She needed to decide the best tact for extracting crucial evidence from the rock-headed aviator occupying the witness stand for the past two hours. Based on prior encounters with stubborn Major David Berg, Sophie prepared herself for a protracted battle.

"Major Berg," she pressed, dropping her paper on the walnut table in the military courtroom, "in the month leading up to the incident, your team was under incredible pressure to complete testing on the gun mount system on the AC-130—the attack modified version of the C-130. You were being pushed to finish ahead of schedule so the upgraded system could be used in combat."

"Objection!" Counsel for the defense leapt to his feet. "Is there a question?"

"Sustained," the judge, Colonel Christensen, monotoned. "Get to the point, please, Major Campbell."

"Yes, sir." She nodded.

Berg didn't so much as blink. He'd earned his call sign "Ice" honestly. The man truly was an iceberg under pressure, and today's stakes were high. Damn high. In order for a child to get justice, a young captain with a spotless record would have his life and career ruined with a court-martial conviction.

This case sucked on a lot of levels.

"I'll rephrase." A simple twist in wording would get the question before the witness and hopefully cast doubt in the jurors' minds. "Are you certain Captain Tate didn't cut corners on crew rest before the mission in question?"

Berg quirked a dark, lazy brow. "Asked and answered in my initial deposition. I am certain."

Sure, she was pushing the edge of the envelope with badgering a witness, but her options had dwindled in the past couple of hours. She needed to win this case. Too many people counted on her. Primarily, the child injured in the military testing accident. But also, her own child, who was dependent solely on her.

She refused to consider that Berg might be right. Not that she doubted his honesty. His pristine reputation at Nellis Air Force Base was highly respected. Well, as much of a reputation as anyone could garner working in the top secret field of dark ops testing. He was known as a by-the-book aviator with nerves of steel. Still, he must have missed something or been misled by those who worked for him. Maybe he had to cut a corner in the testing process that led to Captain Tate making this tragic—and too damn high-profile—military accident.

"Major Berg, do you acknowledge that there was immense pressure in the month leading up to the incident in question?"

"Stress is standard ops in the test world."

"And why might the pressure be higher during wartime?"

"Troops in the field need the technology we develop."

"And in times of stress, you agree that sleep can be difficult?"

Sophie neared the raised wooden stand. Berg radiated such raw strength, she doubted any amount of months on the job would lay him low.

Banked embers within her were suddenly fanned to life.

Her steps faltered.

Heat?

The slumbering numbness that had invaded her emotions for the past year eased awake with a burning tingle. An almost painful warmth spread through her, begging to be fed by . . .

Major David Berg? David? Ice? No frickin' way!

What could have snagged her attention now, after she'd known him for at least a year and a half? Something about him today seemed different.

His *mustache*, she realized abruptly. He'd shaved his mustache, unveiling a full, sensuous . . .

Sophie blinked once, twice. Had he noticed her lapse? A honking-big, unprofessional lapse.

She cleared her throat along with her thoughts. "Did Captain Tate receive the full eight hours of crew rest?"

"Twelve hours, ma'am," Berg answered smoothly. "Regulations state crew rest is twelve hours long, something I know, my crews know, and I'm sure you know as well."

"Of course, twelve hours." Well, it had been worth a try to trip him up and create a reasonable doubt. Moving on to plan B.

Sophie closed the last two feet between them, stopping just in front of Berg. Air-conditioning gusted from the vents above, working overtime to combat the Nevada summer heat. Her uniform clung to her back, the blue service coat about as thick and stifling as a flak jacket right now.

Her nerves must be frazzled from the insane year of restructuring her life as a single mother. She needed to concentrate on her job, not . . . him. Since Lowell's death, she didn't have the time or energy for anything other than caring for her son and paying off the mountain of bills her husband had left behind.

She pressed ahead, placing an evidence bag with a scheduling log inside on the witness stand. "If it's twelve hours, then I'm confused how you fit in the missions and required rest without a single minute being off."

He picked up the schedule, scanned it, and placed it back on the stand. "The numbers are tight, but they work. Yes, we were on a deadline. A tight one with no wriggle room, not even a minute. That's what we do, year in and year out. When has the military not been overworked and undermanned?" Berg's drawl snapped with the first twinges of impatience. "So in essence, the crazy-ass schedule we work is actually standard."

Trained to watch for the least sign of weakening in her witness, Sophie rejoiced over the almost imperceptible clench of his jaw. Berg's pulse throbbed faster above his uniform collar, the reaction so subtle, she felt certain only she noticed. She ignored her own quickening heart.

Time to press the advantage, if she dared.

A quick glance at the judge's bench reassured her. The jowly presider looked in need of some crew rest himself. She had to move fast.

"Major, you can't be with your testers twenty-four/ seven. So it's actually impossible for you to say with complete certainty that Captain Tate received the required amount of rest prior to his mission. I mean really, did you walk with him every step of the way?" Her words fell free with a soft intensity that curled through their pocket of space. "Eat with him? Follow him to the bathroom?"

If she could just piss off Berg enough, she sensed he

would snap and slip, say one little thing wrong that would enable her to secure a conviction. It wasn't like he would go to jail—although somehow she knew he would rather take the punishment on himself than see anyone in his command suffer the shame of a court-martial.

"Ma'am, I'm not required to watch my testers sleep. Although I did see Captain Tate drive away, in the direction of his home, after dinner—which I did watch him eat." His steely eyes glinted like the flecks of silver dusting his brown hair. "However, I didn't follow him into the bathroom, since we're not a couple of junior high girls."

Sophie snapped back a step.

Chuckles drifted from the jury and the handful of observers in flight suits sitting behind Tate. Even her boss, observing from the very back, brought a hand to his mouth to cover his grin. Damn it. Of course Berg played well to a crowd. In a military proceeding, the accused could choose between a judge or jury trial, and just her luck, they'd gotten a jury.

"Order!" The judge's jowly cheeks shook like a basset hound's. His gavel resounded through the military courtroom.

Part of being a successful attorney involved knowing when to retreat with grace, recouping for the next advance. Having foolishly depended on her husband for so many years, after his death, she now struggled with the concept of relinquishing control, of not delivering the last shot.

"Thank you, Major, for that . . . enlightening . . . information about the personal-hygiene habits of your unit. I only wish you could be so forthcoming with the rest of your testimony." Sophie turned to the bench. "Withdrawn."

The judge darted a censorious glare her way. The jury and Berg's fellow flyboys laughed again, but this time she didn't mind.

He moved forward, his shoulders and chest seeming to enlarge, filling the witness stand with his muscular chest full of military ribbons—a Distinguished Flying Cross, a Bronze Star, and almost too many air medals to count. Each oak-leaf cluster signified ten more combat missions. He didn't just put his ass on the line testing the newest equipment in the inventory. Berg served overseas, sometimes the first to use those new systems outside the test world.

Rumor had it he'd received that Distinguished Flying Cross in Afghanistan. As the fire control officer in an AC-130 gunship, he'd held off hundreds of Taliban fighters attempting to capture a pinned-down SEAL team. His plane had circled and circled, with Berg staying in the fight well past daylight, dangerous for the aircraft. He'd shot so precisely, so effectively, his ammo had lasted until a helicopter could arrive with pararescuemen to scoop up the injured SEALs.

She accepted the inevitable. Any shot she could deliver here today wasn't going to rattle a man who'd spent hours flying over hundreds of Taliban fighters lobbing potshots and aiming rocket launchers his way.

"Nothing further." Sophie affected her most efficient walk, heels tapping back to the table. Her boss, Lieutenant Colonel Vaughn, nodded approvingly from the back. She pivoted on the toes of her low pumps to face the judge again. "We reserve the option of recalling this witness."

After two hours of cross-examination, she'd scored more than a few points.

At what cost?

She and Berg had run into each other during early depositions. And even before that, they'd first met in a past investigation, but she'd still been married then. He'd been in the middle of a messy divorce. She hadn't looked at him—hadn't really seen him—the way she did today.

Regardless, stakes were too high for her to worry about David Berg. If she won the court-martial proceeding, that cleared the way for the young boy injured in the accident to move forward with a civil suit.

The judge rested his fist on his jowly cheek. "You may step down, Major Berg."

Sophie averted her gaze from the witness, pretending to jot notes. With an hour left until court recessed, she didn't want to risk jack. No doubt when she saw Berg next the unexpected attraction would have left as abruptly as it had arrived.

Annnd, she looked at him anyway. *Damn.*

Her nerves sizzled.

Tucking his wheel cap under his arm, the major circled to the front of the stand. His uniform fit his lanky body perfectly, accentuating each athletic stride.

She studied him from a more personal perspective. Sexy, with brown hair, but not handsome per se, she decided. Not in the conventional sense. His angular features defied so mundane a label.

Deep creases fanned from the corners of his silvery blue eyes, attesting to a combination of years in the sun and ready laughter. His skin was a hint lighter where his mustache had been, drawing her attention back to his mouth. He wasn't smiling now.

Berg exuded the confidence of a man comfortable in his skin, his appeal making her distinctly uncomfortable in her own.

Sophie resisted the urge to tuck her thumb in the waist-band of her skirt. Already snug, her uniform tightened as he narrowed the distance between them. She resolved, yet again, to eliminate midnight ice-cream sprees until she could afford to buy a larger size. He probably didn't even know how to count fat grams.

The hungry heat returned . . . and she didn't crave a pint of rocky road.

The last thing she wanted was some obstinate aviator cluttering her mind. She finally had her life on track, and she didn't intend to risk her hard-won independence simply because of a fleeting bout of hormonal insanity.

Level with her, Berg hesitated. His six feet four inches dwarfed her five feet three. Five four if she added the minimal lift of her shoes.

Even when not in uniform, she'd always disdained high heels, maintaining they gave her the look of a child playing dress-up. At that moment, she would have plea-bargained two *gallons* of rocky road for a pair of Tina Turner spikes.

Steel-blue eyes pinned her for one slow blink before Berg shoved through the swinging wooden rail and out of the courtroom.

* * *

Major David "Ice" Berg cared about two things above all else: his daughter and his job.

Steamed by more than the Nevada sun, David leaned against the exterior wall by the front entrance of the courthouse. At least Haley Rose was settled with his sister for the afternoon.

Five minutes alone with Major Sophie Campbell to straighten the facts, and his world would be in order. With one of his tester's careers in the balance, he couldn't just walk away.

A hand clapped him on the back. He jolted, hard and fast.

Two buds from his test squadron stood behind him—Jimmy Gage and Vince Deluca. Last week, both had returned from a six-month rotation overseas taking the test unit's newest modifications to the spy drone fleet. So they weren't a part of the test project in question; however, they'd both come over to lend their support in court.

Vince grinned. "Need help going to the bathroom?"

The bulky, tattooed biker looked scary as hell, even in his flight suit, but was the biggest marshmallow in the unit. However, his humor wasn't welcome at the moment.

"Shit, not funny, Deluca."

"If you're you, maybe, but for us?" Vince punched Jimmy Gage on the arm. "Funny as hell."

Jimmy was the unit's all-around good guy, the kind of bud who could be counted on to back you up in a bar fight. "I see a call-sign change in your future. Instead of 'Ice,' you could be 'Charmin.'"

"Or 'John.'"

"What about 'Whizzer,' like 'Wizard'?"

Vince snorted. "There's a reason we always send you to buy the keg while the rest of us choose the names."

"Jackass," Jimmy muttered.

Vince thumped his chest, right over his heart. "I feel the love."

David wished he could be as easygoing about this, but his thoughts just stayed with the kid that had been injured from the accident. This couldn't be a random accident, because then it could too easily happen again. He needed a cause and he needed for that cause not to be one of his people. "Thanks, dudes, I appreciate your support in there today."

"We'll be celebrating the end of this nightmare soon. We'll have a big party to welcome Tater back on flying status."

"Roger that," David said. "Beer's on me."

Jimmy adjusted his hat. "Sounds like a plan." He turned to Vince. "Let's catch up with Tate over there before I head out."

Caleb "Tater" Tate stood under a palm tree with his lawyers, military and civilian. The young captain hung his head, listening to whatever his dream team was telling him.

Vince glanced at David. "Wanna come along?"

"Can't, but thanks," David answered. "I need to finish up some business here, then I need to get home to the munchkin. Catch you later."

He watched his two crew-dog buddies cross the parking lot to Captain Tate. Even when they cleared his name—and they would—the fallout from this would follow him. Somehow, the test process had to have gone wrong. But God, a test project often took years to complete. The boss had tapped Berg to step in to oversee the project four months ago, only a month before the accident happened. And yeah, he'd been sent in because the program wasn't moving along as quickly as higher-ups wanted.

Sophie Campbell had been right on that point. But she was wrong in believing he would condone any corner cutting. And he'd been working his ass off reviewing every old record on the test to find any error—be it from the civilian contractors or military testers.

Which meant more late hours when he already didn't see his kid enough.

He brought home any paperwork and files that weren't classified. But there just weren't enough hours in the day.

He glanced at his watch, impatient from waiting in the heat, drier than his South Carolina home state's humidity, but a scorcher of a day all the same. He still had to pick up Haley Rose from his sister's. Single parenthood left him with little time to waste.

What's taking the lady JAG so long?

Jumbled voices swelled through the opening doors. Masses poured out and divided, easing down the courthouse stairs like the gush from an emptying aqueduct. Bluebirds feeding on the patchy lawn scattered, clearing a path. No sign of her.

David pushed away from the warm wall and jogged down the steps, exhaling his frustration. He would have to take a long lunch tomorrow and track her down, which would make him late picking up his daughter for the second time in a week. Crap.

He cut a path across the scraggly lawn. He glanced back just as Sophie stepped through the door with one of the other lawyers from her office. Her boss maybe? A kick of possessiveness shot through him. Unwanted. Unwelcome. And damn stupid. It wasn't as if they were acting like a couple. She paused for a moment to put on her hat before the other guy took off, leaving her standing alone.

Yeah, he was relieved and staring. He braced for the inevitable whammy—that wallop to his libido that came every time he looked at her.

Long ago, he'd learned to harness his reaction to her. From the first time he'd come across her, eighteen months ago during a deposition on another case, he had wanted her. The glint of her wedding band had sparked regret.

Not to mention he'd been in the middle of a hellacious divorce.

Her marital status may have changed along with his, but her posh lakeside neighborhood remained the same. He didn't need any further incentive than that to resist her. Encounters focused solely on work offered security from temptation.

Sophie hurried down the steps, her pencil-straight uniform skirt hitching higher up her leg. Her legs had driven him close to crazy during his stint on the witness stand. And when his eyes traveled upward to the best set of curved hips in the free world?

A man could lose himself in her softness.

Her sun-streaked blond hair was swept back into some kind of twist. Not for the first time, David imagined pulling out the pins and sliding the silky texture between his fingers. Her light hair contrasted with her golden glow, deep brown eyes, lightly tanned skin.

Tan lines.

Shit.

He knew the minute she saw him. Her gaze went from open to distant in a snap.

"Major Berg," she acknowledged before charging past.

Ego stinging, he watched her hips twitch in her brisk walk as she left him in the dust. His whole body throbbed from viewing only two inches of skin above her knee, and she barely noticed him. Her dismissal bothered him more than usual because he really needed to speak with her.

A good swift reality kick reminded him of his reason for seeking her out, and he resolved to take comfort from the chill of her greeting.

"Major," David called, catching her in three strides. "Wait a minute."

"I haven't got a minute." Sophie tossed the words over her shoulder without meeting his gaze.

"Make time."

She took two shorter, quick steps for his every long stride. "Call my secretary for an appointment."

"Hold on!" He gripped her arm and tugged her to a halt. "If I'd wanted an appointment, I wouldn't have spent the last hour waiting."

The combined force of her sudden stop and spin to face him brought them a whisper apart. The simple act of touching her for the first time sent blood surging well below the belt.

Down, boy.

David unclenched his hand, allowing himself a brief trail down Sophie's sleeve as he released her. A bubble of privacy wrapped around him, as it had during the moment on the witness stand when she'd leaned a bit too close.

A hint of uncertainty crossed her face before she stepped back. "This better be important."

"It is."

"You have exactly two minutes." She checked her watch, late-day sun glinting off the faceplate. "I'm late picking up my son."

He gestured toward the corner of the building, away from the crowd. "Let's step over here in the shade."

Following her, he almost cupped his hand to the middle of her back. Sophie stopped to face him just in time to prevent him from making *that* colossal mistake. Sophie Campbell was a JAG, an officer in the same air force he served. The Bronze Star on her uniform proved she was more than just someone sporting a bunch of "I was there" ribbons. Right now, he wanted to know how she'd gotten that Bronze Star as much as he wanted to know the taste of her.

"One minute left, Major Berg."

Right. "We need to talk about your line of questioning upstairs."

"Do you have something to add to your testimony?"

"No."

"Then we have nothing to discuss." She moved to dart around him.

David braced a hand against a sprawling eucalyptus tree, blocking her escape. "I feel bad for that injured kid—Ricky—and for his family, too. Aside from how damn tragic the whole thing is, Dr. Vasquez has got to be swamped with his son's medical bills on the salary of an untenured assistant professor. I'd like to help the kid win a hefty settlement, but I can't. You're on the wrong track."

"Major Berg . . ."

"Cut it out, Sophie. We're not in the courtroom." So much for keeping matters impersonal.

"This isn't accomplishing anything. If you have something concrete to discuss, come to my office, and we can meet in a more . . . professional setting." Her gaze skittered away from his. "David, I really can't do this today."

He concurred on that point at least. "Am I supposed to wait around until you can fit me into your schedule?"

"I'll be in touch."

"No good. I don't feel much like playing tag team with your voice mail."

Sophie watched undisguised frustration wrinkle David Berg's brow as he barred her exit. She needed to leave. Now. Rather than diminishing, the tingling she'd felt earlier had increased to something resembling a third-degree sunburn.

Much longer with him and she might launch herself at him like a sex-starved woman. Which, of course, she was, even if she hadn't realized it until an hour ago.

Sexual attraction. That's all it is, just a natural, physical reaction. After a nap and some ice cream, she would be fine. The reasonable explanation calmed her. As a normal, healthy woman, of course her body would inevitably react to enforced abstinence. She could push aside the unwanted attraction long enough to talk with him, for the good of her case.

"All right, I would like to go over a couple of points in the incident report. But I honestly don't have time this afternoon."

David's hand pressed to the tree trunk brushed mere inches beside her cheek. His heat reached to her like a furnace blasting on an already hundred-plus-degree day.

He shifted, his knee bent, his shoulders angling closer. "What if I meet you tomorrow for lunch?"

The offer tempted her. Hell, the man tempted her. She tried to focus on his tie instead of the flecks of steel in his blue eyes.

The rows and rows of tiny rectangular ribbons on his uniform jacket drew her eyes. An image of her father in his uniform came to mind, so vivid she could almost smell the flowers in the funeral parlor when she'd seen her father wearing it for the last time.

Time to leave before she did something totally off the chain—like cry. "Your two minutes are up. Stop by my office after court tomorrow."

Sophie ducked under his arm in an attempt to escape his appeal.

Two cracks sounded.

David slammed into her, tackling her. Her briefcase flew from her grip.

Another pop. A gunshot? No time to question. Her head smacked the rocky earth as David Berg's body blanketed hers.

Two

★ ────────────────────────────────────

Sparks flashed behind her eyelids, her head throbbing from smacking the ground. Sophie gripped David's uniform jacket as if holding him tighter could make them both less of a target. Shots and sirens blasted through the air, rivaling the sound of her heart hammering in her ears. Or was that David's pulse?

Or even theirs combined, linked like their bodies tangled up together.

Machine gun fire sounded, followed by an explosion that reverberated like a hand grenade. The acrid scent of shots and smoke stung her nose. Only a few months ago, an airman had opened fire on a hangar full of deploying troops. Could lightning be striking twice on this same base?

Her world darkened by the press of him around her. David's honed muscles tensed against her as she braced herself for another shot to rip through the air. To tear into her body. And at that moment, everything else faded but thoughts of her son. If something happened to her, he would be orphaned, with no one but her elderly grandmother to care for him.

She'd been all too aware of the possibility since the day Brice was born—she wore a military uniform, after all. She could protect herself. But she'd always thought if the worst happened, it would be in combat. She'd originally planned to make a career of the air force. But after her husband died, she'd put in her paper to get out once her commitment was up. Finally, she was only weeks away from being a civilian.

Their mixed heartbeats seemed louder as her mind allowed her to close off the battle sounds in the distance, to rein in her fear. Her senses went on high alert, taking in David's crisp scent that pushed away the sting of smoke. The heat of him blanketed her with total *man*. And how completely insane was it to be scared as hell and turned on all at once? Her hunger and fear feasted on the adrenaline surging through her.

His warm, rangy body stayed pressed against her. Too easily, she could savor all those buried yearnings. Was it her imagination, or did David inch his face closer as if he might . . .

She felt David shift over her. Looking? Assessing? She couldn't see past the bulk of his shoulders.

"Shit," he hissed, levering upward. "They just started an exercise down the street."

An exercise?

Of course it was. Security cops had stepped up practicing for unexpected attacks on a base, and it wasn't as if such exercises only happened during nine-to-five timelines.

Relief all but melted her into the sandy ground.

Now that David had inched upward, she looked past

his broad shoulders and saw the signs posted two blocks away announcing the exercise—what appeared to be practice storming a building. At least she wasn't the only one who'd freaked out. At least a half dozen other people had run for cover and were now easing from around trees and back to their feet.

Even knowing others had been surprised as well, she still wondered how she'd missed the alert signs when she was talking to David. Although he hadn't noted them either, and that unsettled her even more than her own distraction.

If he felt the same attraction . . .

"Uh, David?" she whispered his name, then damn, damn, damn, realized she should have called him Berg, or Major, to establish distance. And was that funny as hell considering how close they were now? His leg pressed intimately between hers, a sweet pressure against a deep ache. "Do you think you can get off me now?"

His blue eyes went stormy for a second before he blinked all expression away.

"Yeah, right." He rolled to the side and sat up. "Are you okay?"

"Fine, thanks." She breathed deeply to chase off a lightheadedness that had little to do with hitting the ground and everything to do with the man beside her. She sucked in another gasp and realized . . . Oh God. It was too easy to breathe deeply. Her hand shot to her waist and . . .

Damn it.

Her too-tight skirt had popped a button. The absurdity of it all hit her. She laughed. And laughed more, letting the laughter just flow as she sprawled on her back staring up at the Nevada sky. Yeah, she was on the verge of hysteria, strung too tight from a year of sheer hell.

"Sophie?" He gripped her shoulders and eased her up to sit. "What's wrong?"

Other than just about everything in her life?

Her laughter faded. She swallowed back the urge to cry and focused on how to get to her feet without losing her skirt or having to fess up to popping out of her clothes. She pressed a hand to her waist, winged a prayer, and stood.

Thank God, the zipper held.

Her knees, however, didn't. David caught Sophie by the upper arms. His fingers wrapped around as he kept her from melting to the pavement. She let him help since everything around her still blurred together, certainly not because his touch felt impossibly good. She must have hit her head harder than she'd thought.

"Easy now." Frowning, he glanced over his shoulder at a bench. "Maybe you should sit. Are you all right?"

"I'm fine," she lied, her head throbbing. "And you?"

"Not a scratch."

"Good. Thanks for the quick thinking, even if it was a false alarm." Her deployments, as well as years as a military brat, provided her with ample real-life scenarios to draw upon.

"You hit your head pretty hard." David led her to a bench shadowed by a palm tree.

Arguing with his stubborn jaw would drain more energy than she could scavenge. "Thanks."

"No problem." He tugged his jacket and straightened his tie, wincing as if it was too tight.

Humvees filed down the road along with a caravan of security police cars, lights flashing, all converging on the building under "attack" for the exercise.

"David, I'll be fine after I sit for a minute and catch

my breath. Thank you for your help, but I don't need an oversize babysitter."

His thumb stopped twitching. "I'm not leaving until I'm sure you don't have a concussion. Period. So stop arguing. We're not in the courtroom. You would do the same for me—or for anyone."

"Of course." She nodded, which sent the world spinning again. Sophie hung her head to stop the welling nausea. She rubbed a hand over her hair and discovered a warm dampness oozing from the base of her head. Grimacing, she stared at her fingers, sticky with blood.

"Damn it!" David crouched in front of her. "Why didn't you tell me you were hurt?" He prodded the back of her head with a firm touch.

"Ouch!" She dodged his hand. "If I wasn't before, I am now."

"Sorry, Counselor." David stood, his height towering like the palm trees clustered in groups of three on either side of the lawn.

He radiated such vitality and strength, her mouth went dry. "I'm really . . ."

David touched her again, gentler this time, silencing her. His hands smoothed over her hair, soothing until her head lolled forward again.

"Stay with me, Sophie." His voice rumbled from somewhere deep inside his chest, the husky timbre hinting of intimacy.

She forced herself to count the buttons on his service jacket instead of wallowing in the light tug of his fingers sliding through her hair. "How does it look?"

"You might need a couple of stitches." His hands slid away. "I can run you to the emergency room."

"No!" She yanked free.

"What?"

"I mean, I don't need to go to the hospital." It would take a lot more than a bump on the head to get her in a hospital with all the memories just waiting to knock her feet out from under her. "Someone around here is bound to have antiseptic and a Band-Aid."

"You could have a concussion." His strong jaw jutted. "I don't have to spell out how dangerous that can be."

She sagged against the bench. He was right.

Of course she couldn't take a chance with her health. Her son and grandmother counted on her. "I'm sorry for snapping. Aftershock, I guess. I'm just worried about getting home to relieve Nanny."

Her grandmother was starting to slow down, age making her joints ache. She should be enjoying retirement rather than taking care of a kid.

"Your son's *nanny*?"

Why was he hung up on who watched her son? Her head throbbed too much for her to sort it out. "Yes, he's a bit of a handful for her lately."

He nodded briskly. "Sit tight and I'll bring my car around. If it turns out you have a concussion, I can drive you home as well."

The sooner she got her head checked, the sooner she could get home, regroup, and establish the control she would need before seeing him again.

"Sure, thanks." She hated giving in but simply didn't have the energy to battle that stubborn jaw. The ice cream would have to wait. "I wouldn't want you to go to any trouble."

"No trouble. I feel responsible since I was the one who

slammed you to the ground. I mean it, though, when I say it's no trouble. It's on my way home."

Home. Where he didn't have a wife any longer. Was there someone else waiting for him?

Undoubtedly, his single status combined with his rumpled appeal would keep his calendar packed. Not that she was interested. She just wasn't in the market for a relationship full of dates and front-door good-night kisses.

Wait a minute. How did he know where she lived?

★ ★ ★

"Slider" studied David Berg damn near hitting on Sophie Campbell over by the bench outside the court hearing. The poor bastard didn't stand a chance at tapping that, though. She was one cool bitch. Like now, she was bleeding from a head wound and still perched on the edge of the seat like she was sitting at attention in a briefing.

He pretended to listen to what the rest of the folks were saying as they gathered outside the courthouse a few yards away from Campbell and Berg. The training exercise farther down the road had rattled the hell out of the rest of them. Some idiot had waited until the last minute to post the warning signs. He glanced down at the practice run—one of about a dozen such exercises since the base had come under attack by a lone gunman six months ago.

He'd been so damn sure no one would notice how he'd played fast and loose with the rules in order to pocket some extra money from testing programs. He understood his flaws, his weaknesses, but he'd never doubted his intelligence, his ability to outthink an opponent. Although even he had never expected gunfire to launch straight into a civilian's home. Talk about raining fire down on his plans as well.

Still, he'd expected the incident to be swept under the rug. This was the kind of high-profile cluster-fuck that smart people preferred to bury as deep and fast as possible. No such luck. Someone with a fucking conscience decided to press for a military trial. This kind of scrutiny could too easily uncover his side dealings.

He wouldn't hesitate to kill anyone who stood in his way. A firearms "incident" on base would be easy to explain away. Hopefully, it wouldn't come to that. Regardless, he could not allow anyone to uncover the true cause of that accident. He would skate by and live to fly another day.

But he didn't intend to leave it to luck.

He'd worked too hard to achieve all he had in his career field. People had underestimated him when he was a kid, but that had just made him stronger. He hadn't been the fastest or the strongest, so he'd simply outsmarted them. Now, he just needed to get past this unfortunate incident, shift people's focus long enough to bury the evidence deeper. Most of all, he needed to shift Berg and Campbell's attention.

And he'd learned something vital from the testing accident. The best way to rattle people?

Target a kid.

★ ★ ★

David needed to get home to his daughter, Haley Rose, and no doubt Sophie must be ready to see her kid.

He checked the wall clock in the ER waiting room while Sophie signed the release papers. Spine rigid, she stood as if in the middle of a court negotiation rather than finishing up treatment for a concussion. Head bleeding and uniform askew, she still maintained an air of control, freeze-dried energy. A warrior in her own right. He couldn't think of a woman less in need of help, yet the lingering rush of protectiveness still coursed through him.

Protectiveness? Is that what you're calling it these days?

David winced. He couldn't suppress the nightmarish image of how bad it could have gone in a real-time war scenario rather than some practice run. He'd seen more than his share of dead in uniform—men and women. The list never ended and neither did the memories.

But something different was going on here. He hadn't dated much since his divorce, and they'd all been civilian women. Other than Sophie, he'd never faced the frustration of attraction in the workplace.

Sure, there was nothing keeping him from asking her out. They weren't in the same chain of command and there were no rank issues to consider. Although she was investigating someone in his unit, which could be sticky. He worried about the impact a potential relationship could have on the case, a case crucial to his career and peace of mind.

Shit.

When had he gone from being attracted to her to thinking about asking her out to dinner and just . . .

Shit.

Once he drove Sophie home, he would have his life back in order and could focus on work, on finding out what the hell had gone wrong with that gun turret, so Caleb Tate's file could be cleared. No matter what the prior test records indicated, there had to be a flaw in the product—which meant more than Tate counted on him.

Everyone who would be using that technology in combat depended on him. Time was damn short, though, to figure out exactly what went wrong before Caleb's trial ended and the new modification was used in battle.

Maybe he could wrangle some conversation with Sophie about the trial during their ride to her house, just to see the case from a different angle.

Her heels clicking closer snapped his focus back to the present. Her sharp, efficient walk gave him all of ten seconds to prep himself for the latest assault on his senses.

"Berg," she fished her cell phone out of her purse, "you really didn't have to wait around. I'm going to call a cab."

God, she was argumentative. "Is it my aftershave?"

"What?"

"I gargled this morning." David lifted each arm slightly in turn. "I'm a firm advocate of deodorant, especially in this 'air you can wear' hot weather." He lowered his arms. "So?"

She gawked at him as if he were a couple of bullets short of a full magazine. "Thanks for the update. But I think I gathered more than enough info on your daily hygiene back in the courtroom."

"What can I say? I couldn't let it pass when you fed me the perfect opening with that bathroom line." He appreciated a good challenge, and Sophie made a worthy adversary. If she hadn't attacked his professional reputation, a fact that still made his jaw clench, he might have enjoyed their sparring, with its flirtatious edge nudging them into dangerous territory. "You delivered a final parry. Let's call it even."

"Fair enough. I'm going to get the cab now. Thanks. You can go."

He didn't move.

Her shoulders slumped. She dropped the phone back into her bag. "You're taking the chivalry thing to a new level here."

He ignored her frosty dismissal. "We've determined it's not my aftershave, deodorant, or mouthwash. So why turn down a perfectly good offer for a ride home?"

"Don't you ever quit?" She blinked slowly.

"Give it up, Sophie. You're weaving on your feet."

She pressed her fingers to her head again. "I've been shot at before. I don't know why today's incident shook me up."

Of course she was rattled. He should have realized that rather than barking out orders. She just needed gentler handling right now, something he doubted even she knew.

He touched her neck lightly, just beside the butterfly bandages. God, her skin was soft. "How's the head?"

"Hurts," she admitted through gritted teeth, then straightened. "No need for stitches, though."

"Glad to hear it." Her tousled look tugged at him, so he softened his words with a smile. "Come on, Blondie, let's go."

"I'd argue sexual harassment if I had the energy."

Her half grin packed a full-size wallop.

David resolved to get her home, fast, no chitchat after all. He would settle for stopping by her office the next day—a neutral, professional setting. He still had an evening of fifth-grade fractions to tackle with Haley Rose before he could think about sleep. "I'm not too enamored with your behavior either, Counselor."

He cupped her elbow, just to steady her while leading the way to his car, or so he told himself. He guided her through the sliding glass doors and out to ER parking. The sunset brought cooler temps. Although the drier desert heat didn't bother him as much as it did others. He'd grown up with the thick South Carolina humidity, played golf in weather that had caused more than one observer to pass out from heatstroke.

They reached his car—a vintage Harvester Scout, soft top. David dropped Sophie's elbow like a steaming iron. "Here we are."

He tried to help her in, but she'd already managed the leap up. The butterfly bandages taped low on the base of her head peeked through strands of hair. For a moment, he relived that instant outside the courthouse when he'd tackled her, his objectivity blown to bits. His urge to protect her surpassed normal job requirements, and that shook him more than the role-playing gunman.

David steadied himself with routine, easing his jacket off and folding it in half lengthwise. Old habits had ingrained themselves in him after years of long hours and a lot of travel. He draped his coat along the backseat, securing it with Sophie's briefcase flung over the top.

He slid into the driver's seat, ready to get her home and out of his mind. "Do you need me to put the top up?"

The drive to the hospital had been short, but they had a solid half hour to drive to her place. And then finally he could head home, sit with his kid, and help her with math homework.

"Don't bother." She finger-combed her silky hair into place. "The wind might help my headache. How do you know my address?"

"My sister lives in the same lakeside neighborhood as you. She watches my daughter after school. I was spending so much time running back and forth from my condo to my sister's place, we decided I might as well move into the guesthouse."

"You *live* in my neighborhood? How did I not know this but you do?"

To give himself time to think, David pulled off his tie and rolled it around two fingers into a pinwheel ball. He leaned to open the glove compartment.

The cooling breeze felt good against his neck . . . until David realized it wasn't the wind, but Sophie's breath. His stretch had strategically draped his torso over her legs in much the same casual fashion as his jacket resting along the back.

If he dropped his hand to caress her calf . . .

She would probably club him with her thickest brief.

David grabbed the steering wheel and tugged himself upright. He was past ready to put some distance between them.

"I saw you on my way out to work one morning. But I guess you didn't see me. As for why I never mentioned it before, it just never came up," he explained curtly, leaving out the part about how just one look at her as she'd driven past had sucker punched him right in the libido. "Let me show you this great shortcut I know."

* * *

Sophie lost all sense of time as she leaned back in the seat and let the fifty-mile-an-hour wind wreak havoc on her hair. David wove through traffic, the bumper-to-bumper flow an ever-annoying constant in their tourist community.

Gaudy neon billboards whizzed by one after the other, casinos, live shows, golf resorts. The same signs repeated themselves, counting down the miles to life on the Vegas Strip.

Exhausted as hell from work and the concussion, Sophie studied David through heavy-lidded eyes. Currents of air channeled through the neck of his blue uniform shirt, filling it in rippling blasts. What would it be like to tunnel her hands underneath and explore that defined chest she'd felt earlier?

Her toes curled in her shoes.

He lived in her neighborhood. He'd been that close, and she hadn't known it. The exclusive lakeside community was outside of most military paychecks. Waterfront anything was pricey in a desert state like Nevada. She only lived there because her husband had owned restaurants and casinos. Or rather, as she'd found out after he died, he'd owned highly mortgaged restaurants and casinos. She'd been left with no choice but to liquidate most of his assets and pray she could keep her head above water. Holding on to the house until the local market turned around was damn near crippling.

Her chest tightened with panic and she shoved aside the worries she couldn't control. Distraction was welcome, and the hunk beside her provided plenty. David changed gears, his long legs working as he downshifted around a corner with only a slight drag and whine of the engine. But then David Berg did everything with ease.

He personified military professionalism, with a driven edginess in his world, and she respected him for it. She just didn't plan to tangle her life or her son's world with a father who thrived on danger ever again. She was better off on her own, blending into a calmer civilian life.

Sophie looked away.

David slowed the Scout as they approached the gated Lake Las Vegas community. Her husband had insisted on the high-end house with all the trappings, elite all the way for his family. Except after a while, she'd realized he really wanted all of that for himself, appearance, flash, live for the moment and worry about the mortgage tomorrow.

Now, she was stuck busting her butt paying for that tomorrow.

She twisted at the waist to grab her briefcase and pull out her ID . . . except wait. He had one.

God, her head was fuzzy.

David lifted his hand to greet the uniformed attendant as he waved them through. He frowned when she stayed silent. "Something wrong?"

"Nothing." The last thing she wanted was to sound like a wimp. It was just a bump on the head. She was a trained warrior, for heaven's sake. For now anyway.

David turned at the corner, driving past the row of looming stucco houses along the shore of Lake Las Vegas. "So this isn't my kind of neighborhood. A little too rich for my taste." He shrugged. "I'm more of a middle-class-condo sort of guy."

"That wasn't what I was thinking."

"Then what were you thinking?"

She blurted, "I was wondering where your ex-wife lives."

Where had that come from, a question that hinted at interest, even jealousy?

His fingers thumped the steering wheel. "She moved to Colorado."

"I didn't mean to pry." She tried not to sound defensive. And failed. "*You* asked what I was thinking."

His lean fingers drummed faster. "My ex-wife, Leslie, moved back to Colorado after our divorce."

The laid-back aviator who stored ties in his glove compartment and drove an old-school Scout faded in a snap. The steely glint in his eyes, the brace of his shoulders shouted subject closed.

Sophie gestured to her driveway. "This is my house."

Although he already knew that. How close was his place?

David pulled off the road. The vehicle's idling rumble filled the silence.

As he'd questioned her thoughts moments prior, she wondered what rattled around in his hard head while he stared at her home with such a bland expression. The two-story beige stucco home with a three-car garage looked much like the other houses lining the finger of the shore.

Big.

Pricey.

Exclusive.

He scratched along his jaw. "Nice little place you have, Counselor."

Why the edge of scorn? He'd said his sister lived in the same piece of exclusive lakefront property. She'd heard he'd played in the semipro golf circuit before joining the air force, so he likely had a nice cushion padding his bank account. He could probably afford to disdain such luxuries, having been given a choice. Her family hadn't had much, especially after her father died. Sophie planned to make sure her son enjoyed the security she'd never known as a child, financial and emotional.

Brice had already lost more than any ten-year-old should. With a mama-bear ferocity that scared her at times, she renewed her vow to keep him safe.

Absorbed in her reflection, she didn't notice David

crossing to her side of the Scout until he stood beside her with an outstretched hand. Sophie accepted his help since it was faster than arguing. The minute her feet hit the ground, her vision swam.

David steadied her. "Take it easy. I'll help you up the steps."

His support felt too good. She shook her hand free. "Don't worry. I really can walk. And once I get inside, Nanny will smother me with attention."

"Oh, right. I keep forgetting about your nanny." He passed her briefcase, holding it like a shield between them. "Okay, then. Don't think a bump on the head lets you off the hook for our appointment tomorrow."

"In my office." She wrapped her fingers around the supple leather while he held firm.

"After court." He let go. "Good-bye, Blondie." Shooting her a wave, he circled to the driver's side.

"David!"

He paused, half in, one foot still touching the ground. "Yeah?"

"Thank you."

They stared at each other across the humming engine. The air between them crackled with memories of that time they'd spent tangled up on the ground together. Of what it felt like to be intimately close to someone again. Even beyond that, what it would be like to have someone with whom to share life's burdens. Because of her husband's secrets and betrayal, she'd never really known.

"No worries." David thumped his chest. "It's what we do for our brothers and sisters in arms."

He eased behind the wheel but didn't back away until she'd made it safely to the top step of her home.

Home. Where she could relax with a late dinner . . . and try yet again to pretend if she worked hard enough, she could fill the void in her son's life left by his father's death.

Pretend she still couldn't feel the sensual touch of David's fingers in her hair.

THREE

★ ──────────────────────────────────────

David nailed the accelerator.

Sophie Campbell was an open invitation to an encore performance of having his life shredded. And he had only himself to blame for the way his marriage to Leslie had played out. He should have known better. Leslie's *first* ex-husband had warned him. But he'd been so sure things would be different.

Wrong.

Leslie hadn't just walked out. She'd torn apart their family. He'd brought up her son as his own, and then when she'd decided she didn't want to be a mom anymore, there'd been nothing David could do. Her son had gone back to his biological father. Haley Rose lost her mother and her half brother.

David didn't want to think about what he'd lost. He needed to focus on the present, the future, his kid.

He parked in his sister's driveway and slumped in his

seat. Some days sucked the life right out of a person. He just wanted to gather his daughter, go home, and forget about Sophie Campbell tucked against his chest.

His sister gripped the second-floor balcony railing in the middle of a Pilates stretch. David allowed the inevitable smile to cut through his fatigue.

Not for the first time, he considered how Haley Rose would one day look like her aunt Madison. The dominant genes of the Berg family couldn't be missed. Madison wore her standard Lycra workout clothes, her lengthy rope of dark hair trailing forward over one shoulder.

He stepped out of the Scout and shouted up to her, "Sorry I'm late, Mad. I tried to call . . ."

"Do you see a watch anywhere?" Madison linked her hands and stretched her arms over her head, a tangle of silver bracelets sliding to one elbow. Who wore bracelets with workout clothes?

His sister.

He climbed the concrete steps that led up to the sunning deck on the second floor. "If you ever owned a watch, you lost it."

"Only on purpose." Barefoot, she rolled up her yoga mat and tucked it under her arm.

Her free spirit frustrated the hell out of him at times, but he had to admit she'd saved his hide the past year by providing child care and even a place to crash. With Leslie's lack of interest in Haley Rose, he needed all the help he could get. Madison's easygoing manner soothed his high-spirited daughter.

What kind of parent was Sophie, with her nanny and big house?

David shook free from his thoughts of Sophie and met Madison at the base of the stairs. "Where's the runt?"

"Playing with her new little friend at his house." She held a single finger to her lips before he could interrupt. "Yes, I did a thorough check on everything from his family to his blood type before letting your child play with him. He's a nice kid. Good manners. Does his homework and eats all his vegetables."

"I trust your judgment."

Madison snickered. "Since when?"

"I'm glad she's making friends. I worried about uprooting her to move here just because I didn't want to drive the extra miles."

"You moved so you could spend more time with her and so I didn't have to hang out at your gross bachelor apartment."

"You're a lot nicer now that you're grown up."

"Suck-up." She swatted him with her yoga mat before opening the French doors. "Brice is the perfect playmate for your tomboy. They're just working together on a science project for the fair. It's not like we have to worry about their hormones yet."

"I'd rather not think about my daughter, hormones, and boys." David shuddered.

"I told you. He's a good kid." She lifted her brother's wrist and looked at his watch. "I should probably go over and pick her up before they wear out Nanny."

"The nanny?"

"No, her name's Nanny. The boy's great-grandmother. His mom's a lawyer on base."

Ah hell.

* * *

After a quick wriggle into a shirt and pair of shorts, Sophie stalked along the shore to retrieve her son before the sun finished setting. When would this day end? Not any time soon, apparently.

At least he hadn't officially "ditched" Nanny this time. Nanny knew exactly where Brice was—off playing with the daughter of a nice, young, *unattached* flyboy who just moved to the neighborhood.

Sophie hadn't needed even a single guess to determine who bachelor number one might be. Grandma Anna, Nanny, wouldn't let up until she marched her only granddaughter down the aisle again. Sophie didn't intend to march anywhere except down her stretch of the lakeside and home. And what do ya know? Now she had *his* address.

Ten minutes later, she charged along the shoreline, and as the house in question came into view, she saw David in the distance. Tall, lean, and too damn sexy, he stood on the balcony talking with a super-skinny woman wearing Lycra workout clothes.

The kick of jealousy made her mad.

Then she remembered that he lived with his sister.

The rush of relief made Sophie madder.

She struggled to remember the woman's name. It had been so long since she'd attended neighborhood functions at the clubhouse. Grief and work had almost consumed her whole.

Finally, her mind latched on to a name from a Christmas party nearly two years ago. Madison Palmiere. Madison's husband was a bigwig at one of the major airplane manufacturing companies.

No reason she should have guessed Madison was related to David, since they had different last names. Too bad she hadn't thought to make the connection earlier. She wasn't surprised so much as frustrated. Beyond the professional realm, his presence now invaded the haven of her home. She'd worked hard for peace after Lowell's death.

His *death*?

The word sounded too benign. *Death* didn't come close to describing Lowell's stupid, careless stunt. Sophie didn't want to hate the husband she'd loved, but the contradictory emotions spiraled inside her all the same. No man with a wife and child should fly under bridges for thrills. Stubborn and reckless, he'd done it again in spite of his promise and had died, leaving her to face everything alone.

She thought she'd forgiven him for throwing away his life, theirs together. In the hollow silence of endless nights, she'd learned to accept fate's arbitrary twists.

Until one too-sexy-for-his-own-good flyboy had opened the floodgates.

Her sandals slapped against the muddy bank with drumming force, the water lapping at her feet. Trying to hold back the flood of anger proved futile. She wanted to crank the clock back to a time before that moment in the courtroom when some unnamed quality about David Berg had challenged her awake.

Numb was better.

Sophie glared at David and closed the last few feet separating them.

* * *

"Nanny?" David gulped.

Madison nodded. "The lady's a real dynamo for someone in her midseventies, but . . . Is something wrong?"

David shook his head. "The Man upstairs has a wicked sense of humor today."

Divine proof stomped into sight with a vengeance. Arms pumping, a determined Sophie stormed down the shoreline, closing in on Madison's house. She'd obviously recovered from any ill effects from the bump on her head.

Sophie neared the dock, slowing to a more sedate pace. She plastered a polite grimace of a smile on her face. David wondered why even a counterfeit symbol of happiness from her stirred him. He loped down the stairs, his sister's slower pace echoing softly behind him.

Damn, but Sophie looked hot in jean shorts and a well-worn T-shirt that looked as soft as her skin. He realized he'd never seen her in anything other than her uniform before now. She looked . . . more approachable.

David stuffed his hands safely away in his pockets.

"Hello, Madison." Sophie's smile faltered as she stopped a couple of feet away from him. "David."

"Hey, Sophie . . ." Madison gestured between them, her bracelets jingling. "Hey, wait. David, this is the Major Campbell you've been . . . uh . . . talking about from the case?"

Sophie lifted one eyebrow. "Talking about?"

David stayed diplomatically silent, because yeah, he'd griped about what a pain in the "briefs" she'd been more than once.

Madison laughed softly, too damn knowingly. "I didn't realize you two knew each other."

Simultaneously, David and Sophie agreed. For once.

"Just base business."

"Only through work."

Madison quirked a delicately arched eyebrow. "Okay."

His thoughts shot back to that moment at the courthouse when they'd been tangled up together on the ground, his body revved by the feel of her soft curves against him. The fire had been stirred all the more by the cheap thrill of touching her afterward, when she'd been disoriented. And how pathetic was that?

A flash of awareness sparkled in her eyes for an unmistakable moment before she turned to Madison, giving David a full view of her back, *her narrow waist, the curve of her hips.* "I understand my son wandered down this way."

If she thought she could brush him off, she could think again. David frowned. "I thought they were at your house."

"He's not here?" Sophie paled under her tan.

All too well David understood the wayward nature of parental imagination. Worst-case scenarios could script themselves with little real provocation. She didn't need more stress after their afternoon.

Madison fidgeted with her bracelets. "They were working together on a science project for the fair. They know not to walk along the water by themselves, so they must be on the sidewalk."

The sound of youthful squeals carried on the gritty desert wind before the children came into view.

Sophie sagged, then stiffened. "David, I don't want Brice to know about my concussion."

Madison gasped. "Concussion? What happened?"

"I just fell, nothing big as far as I'm concerned. But since Lowell's death, Brice is afraid something's going to happen to me."

"Oh, honey." Madison leaned closer. "Have you taken him to see a psychiatrist? I can give you the name of a really good family counselor I saw after my second divorce."

"Thanks, I'll let you know. Right now, I just want to get my son home."

"Of course." Madison backed off. "He's your kid."

"Yes. He is."

Sophie's full lips curved into the first uncomplicated smile he'd ever seen from her. Maternal pride illuminated her face with the timeless beauty of a mother's love for her child. She was so damn gorgeous, he felt like he'd been blindsided by a missile strike.

The roaring need to see her smile for him drowned out anything else.

Then she turned away to greet her son, leaving David more unsettled than ever.

Two bedraggled children raced into sight. Sophie walked up the driveway to meet them. Wind lifted her golden hair, exposing the vulnerable curve of her neck. She hooked an arm along her child's shoulders just over his backpack. A silky curtain of hair slid forward and blocked her face as she listened to Brice.

David had the answer to his question regarding Sophie's parenting. Her ease with her son was evident.

He would have been better off not knowing.

Madison elbowed him in the side. "Just base business, huh?"

Haley Rose catapulted forward, saving David from responding to a question he wasn't sure he could answer.

"Hi, Dad!" She flung aside her backpack and locked her arms around his waist.

"Hey there, runt. Missed you today." He tugged her trailing dark braid.

David patted her back and felt the same kick of love he'd experienced the first time she curled her tiny fingers around his.

He'd thought his daughter was happy. But now as he watched her with Sophie's son, he couldn't help but think how his daughter was aching to replace the half brother she'd lost. Leslie couldn't be bothered to get her kids together, and her first husband thought a clean break was better and to hell with how many times Haley Rose cried herself to sleep.

"Ouch, Dad. You're squeezing too tight." Haley Rose wriggled out of his hug.

"Sorry, kiddo. Did you get much work done on your project?"

Haley Rose snatched up her backpack and hitched it over her shoulder. "Me and Brice made a bunch of notes. Can he and his mom stay for supper so we can show you?"

He looked fast at Sophie and found awareness quickly replaced by panic in her eyes that said, *No way in hell.* He couldn't agree more. And he hoped Sophie fully grasped how important it was not to let the kids misunderstand. He didn't want either child to get matchmaking ideas.

His daughter was too fragile to take another disappointment right now. Sophie needed to hear just why it was so important. The sooner, the better. But not here where the kids could overhear.

He would broach the subject in private. And if he could wrangle some time to address the subject of Caleb Tate's trial? Then all the better.

* * *

After tossing and turning all night, then court all day, the last thing she needed was extra paperwork in the office. At least the building was quiet after hours. She would make it up to Brice with a mother-son video-game tournament on Saturday—thanks to her military training on the firing range, she could actually hold her own, something her son liked to brag about. She pushed aside questions about what David and his daughter did for bonding time on the weekends.

Focus on work. The man had already stolen enough of her concentration this week.

Sophie sat at her desk, searching through Captain Caleb Tate's deposition for something she must have missed. She'd already reviewed Berg's deposition and statements made by others who'd flown with Tate that day.

An empty to-go box held the stain of the taco salad she'd quickly downed for supper, along with two cups of coffee. A fresh cup of java steamed beside a photo of her son winning last year's science fair.

Right now, her case straddled the fence. Tate had chosen a jury. Most likely betting on having another aviator on the trial who would sympathize with him.

Granted, for her, the burden of proof wasn't as tough in a military court. The rules of evidence weren't as strict as in a civilian trial. That didn't mean she could—or ever would—slack off.

She could read the depositions on the computer, but for this kind of brainstorming, she preferred printouts and government contracts, using colored pencils and highlighters to draw connections and graph notes.

Thumbing through pages, she scanned past the questions about his name. His address. His time at the location. She paused at the part about his job information.

CAMPBELL: State your occupation for the record.
TATE: I am an AC-130 FCO—fire control officer.
CAMPBELL: On that day, what type of sortie were you
     flying?

TATE: We were flying an operational test mission of the new cannon mounting system.

CAMPBELL: And what does that entail?

TATE: The current gun mounting system on the AC-130 is from the Vietnam era. It requires a lot of maintenance to keep it running and a lot of crewmen to fire it. The system we were testing updated the stabilization gyros and aiming systems of the gun and took tasks that were manual and made them automatic.

Sophie reached for her coffee and sipped, shutting out the echoes of footsteps in the hall as people left for the day.

CAMPBELL: Such as?

TATE: The old gun was loaded by crewmen opening the breech and jamming a new shell in. The new system has an autoloader.

CAMPBELL: What kind of round are we talking about here?

TATE: It's a cannon shell.

CAMPBELL: What's the difference between that and a bullet?

At that point in the deposition, Tate's face had gone tight, his irritation showing through. Anger could be a good thing, since it made people slip up. She hoped maybe there was something in this next part she may have missed in earlier reviews.

TATE: You don't know the difference between a bullet and a cannon shell?

CAMPBELL: For the record.

TATE: The difference is a bullet kills with kinetics and a cannon shell blows things up.

Then, Tate's lawyer had silenced him, reminding the young captain to keep his cool.
Did he have a quick temper?
She jotted "Quick to anger?" in the margin.

CAMPBELL: On that day, the system under test fired a round that landed off the range, causing damage to a house and injury to a six-year-old boy. Correct?
TATE: That is correct.
CAMPBELL: Describe to me your actions from the firing of the last round on the range to the firing of the round which caused the mishap.
TATE: After the last round on the range, I placed the master arm switch to *Off* and verified the safe light was green, showing the gun was disarmed. We received clearance to exit the range, at which point I verified again that the gun was not armed. And we exited the range and headed back toward Nellis Air Force Base. Approximately ten minutes later, there was a very loud sound that came from behind me, which apparently was the cannon firing off a round. I verified again that my switches were all in *Safe* and reported the incident over the radio to Nellis Command Post.
CAMPBELL: So you're telling me the gun just went off on its own. You didn't touch any switches, turn any dials, push any buttons, nothing, nothing at all?
TATE: I just said that, didn't I?

CAMPBELL: Would there be a way to prove that you didn't pull the trigger on that gun by mistake? Any printouts? Any recording that would show that?

TATE: Yes, ma'am, if we were on the range, we would have had all of that. But because the test was complete, we had turned off all the data recorders that would have shown that information.

Her eyes halted on the middle of the page. Hairs on the back of her neck rose along with the sense that she was being watched. It was late. And she was almost certainly alone. Uneasiness settled over her and she checked out of the corner of her eye.

David Berg filled her doorway. Silently, he stood watching her. God only knew how long he'd been there. Anger stirred—at him for not announcing his arrival and at herself for even caring.

Well, he could just wait until she was ready to talk.

★ ★ ★

David stood in the half-open door of Sophie's office. After the way she had raced to leave his place yesterday, he figured he might not be welcome here. But he had to address the bad, bad idea of their kids hanging out together. He needed to have that talk away from his daughter's little listening ears. He also wanted her to take a second look at Caleb Tate's training records, to fully grasp his top-notch aviator skills.

All the same, he intended to keep a solid thirty-six inches between himself and Sophie at all times. No standing close enough for him to catch a whiff of her shampoo. He'd already determined her perfume only had a radius of twenty-four inches as long as the ceiling fan didn't swirl the air around too much in her little office. He spent a lot of time analyzing every detail of how Sophie affected him so he could do his best to resist.

With her prestigious diplomas on the wall, including a law degree from Duke, she could have worked at a high-powered firm and instead she'd chosen to serve in uniform. He had to respect that, even if she was on the opposite side with her current case.

Maybe she didn't need the money, if her husband left a hefty estate. She radiated the perfect image of simple refinement, one he burned to muss.

Her hair was pinned up in a twist, no doubt to hide the bandage beneath. What other surprises did Sophie have hidden under that cool facade? The glimpses of her with her son still rocked his preconceptions of the killer shark of a counselor.

Thirty-six inches apart. David rapped a knuckle against the door.

Sophie held up a quick hand for him to wait and finished reading the paper in front of her. "Be right with you."

A scattering of books and folders littered her desk, proclaiming productivity without chaos. She restacked the sheaf of papers and set it aside.

The leather chair squeaked as she shifted to face him. "Hello, Major Berg."

She spoke with a professional tone he appreciated, needed.

"Major Campbell."

Rolling back her chair, she motioned for him to sit in one of the two chairs across from her desk. A full desk between them. Good.

"I'll get to my questions about Captain Tate in a minute. But first, we need to get something else out of the way." He needed to move this visit along faster before he did something stupid, like haul her in for a kiss and to hell with the consequences. "I don't think our kids should play together."

Her eyebrows shot up. "And your reason why?"

"Because I don't want my daughter to get hurt."

"It's not like they're dating."

"If only it was that simple." He scrubbed a hand over his jaw. He didn't particularly relish trotting out his crappy personal life. "Haley Rose has been really, uh . . ." He searched for the right word. "She's been really fragile since her mom left."

Sophie's shoulders relaxed and genuine sympathy lit her eyes. "I'm sorry to hear that. I understand how frustrating it is wanting to cushion a child from the harsh realities of life."

"Amen to that."

"Berg . . . David . . ." She leaned forward on her desk. "I'm not interested in a relationship. So your daughter is safe from thinking I'm going to step into her life."

Whoa, wait. She thought he was here to make sure they didn't have a *relationship*? "It's more complicated than that." He was going to have to spill it all. "My ex had a son from her first marriage. Haley Rose grew up with him, but when my ex left, Hunter went back to live with his biological father. It's not healthy for my daughter to use your son as a substitute brother."

Pushing away from her desk, Sophie exhaled hard. "I didn't know. I am so sorry," she said, leaving her desk and taking the seat beside him. "I can see where you would be worried. I'll talk to Brice."

Her brown eyes turned warm and compassionate. She even swayed toward him sympathetically. Shit. She was twenty-four inches away and the air-conditioning was blowing the air around full blast.

Who the hell was he kidding? He'd come here for himself as much as his child or Caleb Tate. All day at work, he'd been looking forward to seeing her. He'd even counted down the hours like a sap.

A frown puckered between her eyebrows.

He reached toward her. "How is your head feeling today?"

"Better." Her answer came out breathy, with a hitch.

His fingers hovered close to her shoulder, close enough to touch . . .

Footsteps padded down the carpeted hall. Sophie blinked and pulled back. His hand fell to his lap. He looked fast behind him.

Sophie's boss, Lieutenant Colonel Geoffrey Vaughn, stopped in the open doorway. "Are you almost finished for the day?"

Sophie pressed a hand to her waistband. "Soon, Geoffrey."

"Major." The attorney nodded to David.

"Colonel." David stood.

The man's blues were crisply pressed. This guy didn't store his ties in the glove compartment.

Wiry and just under six feet, Vaughn lounged against the door frame and rubbed a hand along the back of his neck. "Do you mind locking up behind you when you're done? I'm heading out to meet the gang for drinks. I can wait if you want to come along."

"Not tonight. Thanks, though." Sophie moved behind her desk again. "I appreciate your sitting in yesterday."

"You're still the boss on this case," Vaughn declared graciously, although he was at least ten years her senior. He stepped into the hall, then ducked back in the room. "I'll be by for Brice after lunch Saturday."

"Thanks. He's been breaking in his new baseball glove all week."

"No problem." Vaughn pulled his hat from his brief-case. "He's quite a kid."

"Yes, he is."

That special, unreserved smile returned, the one she saved only for her son. Leslie never looked at Haley Rose like that.

"Good night, Major." Vaughn tucked back into the hall, for good this time. His measured footsteps faded.

David's jaw went tight. "I don't want to keep you two from any plans."

"Plans?"

"With Vaughn." He should be relieved. His life would be simpler if Sophie had an ongoing relationship.

"Geoffrey and me?" She laughed.

David didn't.

"He's an old friend of Lowell's—my husband. And he's my boss. Geoffrey's helping Brice with pitching." She flicked a fingernail against the edge of a folder, the repeated clicking growing louder. "As much as I try, there are some things I can't do for my son."

"I understand that too well."

"Adults are supposed to take care of kids." She slapped a file into her briefcase, slammed it closed. "I guess that's what frustrates me most about this trial. Damn it, why doesn't someone own up to hurting that boy? Why isn't anyone responsible for harming Ricky Vasquez?"

She walked around her desk with heavy, angry

footsteps until she stopped just in front of him. Her head came to just under his chin. She tipped to meet his gaze straight on. Height didn't matter. She could have faced down a mob without any backup.

"Ricky shouldn't have to question each second of every day and wonder if grown-ups have done their job. It's my responsibility to make sure he's safe, to make sure Brice never gets hurt again by someone too caught up in his own selfish needs to think about his son."

Brice? "You mean Ricky?" he asked gently.

Her eyes widened. She pressed the back of her wrist over her mouth. "*Ohmigod.*"

"Sophie." He reached for her arm.

She snatched it away. "No. I need to . . ."

"Give yourself a minute." He cupped her shoulder, only her shoulder, careful not to spook her. But he couldn't stand by and do nothing to comfort her. He'd heard about Lowell Campbell's accidental death. The guy wasn't military, but any aviation accident in the area was going to warrant attention from the base.

The man had been a damned fool.

"No, I . . ." She blinked fast, her eyes sparkling topaz.

"It's okay." David squeezed her shoulder, rubbing like he would for anyone else. Right? Just until she calmed down.

Sophie didn't relax, but she didn't push him away, either. She didn't cry or rage. She merely stood, stiff and unrelenting, while he patted her shoulder.

This was *not* smart, touching her, but he couldn't make himself step away. He could hear the occasional catch in her slow breaths, could feel her restrained emotion.

Then she turned to look at him and he caught the scent of her hair, a flowery perfume like the jasmine in his home state of South Carolina.

Jasmine? He was thinking of flowers, for God's sake? He was screwed. Totally screwed.

Sophie blinked once, swallowed hard, the composed counselor returning. He would have thought she was completely unaffected, except she refused to look at him.

She crossed to her desk and braced her hands on the edge. "If you'll see yourself out, I have some other files to gather."

The lady wanted space? Fine. He needed space from her. Perfect combination. But first he had a couple of things to say. "I also came here to talk about Captain Tate." He dug into his flight bag and pulled out a stack of papers. "These are copies of his flight training records, all the way back to the beginning of his time in a simulator. Perfect scores. Perfect performances from the start. Just look at them. And if you've seen them already, look again. I highlighted some praise by his former instructors that you may not have fully grasped."

"Fine, Berg." She met his eyes full on again, her barriers clearly in place. She extended a hand that trembled. "I'll review them tonight."

He passed over the printouts and should have been pumped over getting the hell out of her office.

Yet even when he turned away, he couldn't shake the image of her French twist pulled up to reveal a vulnerable neck with those butterfly bandages over her cut. Five minutes in her office, and he'd forgotten all his reasons for staying away from her *and* her son.

Damn straight. He was so screwed.

* * *

She turned her car off outside her home and didn't even consider going inside. The house was dark anyway, with only a low light on in the kitchen, the one Nanny left on for nights Sophie worked late.

Throwing open the car door, she stepped out into the hot night air. She tossed her uniform jacket and shoes into the car—and what the hell—shimmied out of her panty hose as well.

A short sprint later and she was wriggling her toes in the cool mud. One at a time, she yanked the pins from her hair and flung them into the water, watching each sink slowly out of sight. Wind-chime tunes carried along the breeze, dancing a tinkling path out into the dark. Nanny and Brice both slept inside the house, so she could walk as long as she wanted—as long as she *needed*. And she would need a damn long walk to sort through that moment in her office when David had touched her. Just a simple hold on her shoulder, but she'd wanted more.

And she saw in his eyes that he knew it. Even worse, he wanted her, too.

Sophie shook her hair free until strands whipped against her cheeks. Barefoot, she stumbled against a root jutting from the water, her blouse fluttering loose from her waistband. Wind blowing off the water drifted around her, slipping underneath. Each gust teased her skin with whisper-warm brushes like a lover's kisses.

Married at twenty, pregnant by twenty-two, she wasn't innocent. She had been widowed. Gone to law school. Served her country. She'd even deployed to the Middle East. But now her life was focused completely on her son. She'd understood what she was giving up by choosing to remain alone after Lowell had died. No relationships, especially not when her son still wore that haunted lost look. She hadn't questioned her decision to stay alone.

Until tonight.

David. An aviator like her father. Fearless like her husband.

Even knowing this to be true didn't stop her from wanting him. People didn't always want what was right. Hadn't she learned that lesson already?

Flashes of those needy moments in her office taunted her. She'd been so proud of herself for maintaining professional distance . . . And then she'd let her emotions get the better of her, and she revealed too much when she'd slipped and called her client Brice. God, even she hadn't fully realized until that moment how much Ricky's case resonated with her because of her own son. As a lawyer, she was supposed to be in control of her words and still she'd blundered into such a massive Freudian slip.

Then David had touched her. She hadn't pulled away. Her body still pulsed with a need that almost washed away reason. Almost.

He was an aviator like her father and a risk taker like her husband. The repeated knowledge became her mantra as Sophie trudged through the shallow water. Each recitation strengthened her determination to protect herself.

Resolute, she turned back. She ignored her tear and let the wind claim it as it brushed her with the haunting music of wind chimes. Sophie focused on her home, a haven. Stepping from the water, she walked along the shore, each step settling her.

Squinting, she caught a glimpse of her curtains fluttering. A light knifed through the darkness as someone slipped out of her front door. Fear snaked down her spine. The shadowy figure vaulted over her porch banister and tucked into the darkness.

FOUR

Brice and Nanny were alone in the house.

Sophie's heart thudded in time with her feet as she raced across the muddy bank. All thoughts of being protected fled. No one would touch her family. She scanned the yard for signs of the intruder returning. Nothing but a black void where the night had absorbed him. Or her? Or maybe more than one?

She yanked her purse from the car in case she needed to unlock a door. Had the intruder gone in through the window?

Panting, Sophie reached the bottom of the stairs. She flung her arms forward, gripping the banister to pull herself up the steps faster until she reached the deck. Splinters stung her fingers.

The front door was slightly ajar. So much for needing a key. She touched the cracked wood around the jimmied lock. Recklessly, she threw open the front door. Cool air from inside chilled the sweat beading on her brow.

A fresh well of fear bubbled within her. Her sprawling living room was empty, illuminated by the eerie moonlight streaming through the window wall.

Outright pandemonium would have frightened her less.

Nothing was broken, torn, or missing. Still the room had undoubtedly been searched. Everything looked skewed, as if her well-ordered world had been shifted ever so slightly to the left. She set her purse down.

How far had the prowler invaded? *Brice.*

Determination focused her fear. Sophie slid open one of the small secretary drawers. She wrapped her fingers around a letter opener. The cool brass seared her palm. She would have preferred to have her 9 mm, but it was locked away in a safe in her room—past Brice and Nanny's rooms.

A distant part of her brain prodded her to call for help, even though she'd seen the intruder leave. The stronger voice urged her not to waste a second more before checking on her child.

Sophie padded along the hardwood floors of the darkened hall. Her damp, gritty feet slipped. She braced a hand against the wall.

"Oh God, oh God, oh God . . ." Sophie barely realized she chanted the prayer as she nudged her son's door open. Her grip tightened around the letter opener.

She peered in and, thank God, Brice slept on his back, arms flung wide as he sprawled on the bottom bunk. She sagged against the door frame. With the help of a galaxy night-light, she could see the blue plaid bedspread rise and fall with each reassuring breath of the boy beneath.

Unlike the living area, Brice's room looked untouched, simply bearing the normal signs of childish housekeeping. A sock hung from a drawer. The toe of a Rollerblade peeked from under the bed as if it couldn't be stuffed any farther.

Sophie crept inside, dodging planetary systems and rocket ships dangling from the ceiling. She checked every shadowy corner and the closet before stopping beside his bunk bed. She brushed back a lock of Brice's hair, sighing the end of her prayer.

As she turned to leave, her toe caught on the strap of his backpack. She pulled the schoolbag from under his bed and looped it over the doorknob on her way out.

Nanny slept farther down the hall, away from the living room, so Sophie approached it with less fear. Thank God, apparently there had only been one intruder. A simple look into her grandmother's room confirmed her hope. The old woman slept soundly, a slight snore whistling through the silence. Watching her grandmother sleep, Sophie gathered the tatters of her shredded self-control.

She eased the door closed and retraced her path down the hall to the telephone. She dialed 9-1-1 on the home phone, stated her name, address, and that she'd seen an intruder. The dispatcher told her to stay on the line . . .

As she waited, her eyes fell on her cell phone peeking out of her purse a simple hand's reach away. Without even stopping to question why, she thumbed through her neighborhood directory and dialed Madison Palmiere's number to look for David.

* * *

Madison Palmiere bit her lover's shoulder to keep from crying out as her third orgasm of the night pulsed through her. After a string of crummy relationships that had left her thinking she was frigid, she was enjoying the hell out of her footloose single status.

Or at least that's what she thought at moments like this, with bliss shimmering through her and her lover gasping damn near desperate praise against her ear.

Her cell phone rang by the bed.

"Shit," she moaned.

"Let it ring," he hissed through gritted teeth, his hips pumping as he rode the last waves of his own release.

She grappled along the bedside table and thumbed the silence button on her telephone. Her hands found him again fast, gripping his arms, biceps rippling under her fingertips. She rocked her hips against his fluidly, finishing him, as delicious anticipation licked through her because she knew he was far from done for the night.

Captain Caleb Tate was fifteen years younger than she was. But since she was at her sexual peak, they synched up in bed a helluva lot better than she had with her last husband, who'd been twenty years her senior. Or her first husband, who'd been a selfish lover when he was sober and a fumbling non-finisher when he was drunk, which had happened most of the time in their last year together.

Or her high school boyfriend who'd thought it was cool to slap her around and she'd been too insecure to walk away.

This new relationship with a younger lover was definitely the way for her to go. She was in control, satisfied, and *free*.

Caleb's final shout echoed through her room, deep and carnal and delicious. He rolled from her onto his back, panting, his wrist over his eyes.

Madison flung her arms wide, replete. For now. She let her eyes rove unabashedly—from his buzzed fair hair to his tanned skin glistening with sweat. Six feet three inches of big blond man sprawled, taking up more than half the space in her king-size bed. She'd been sleeping with him for two months but hadn't tired of looking at him yet.

She liked their clandestine meetings—keeping their affair a secret, at her request, from the start. Earlier in the summer, he'd come by the house looking for David one Saturday afternoon, but David hadn't been around. Caleb had looked so shattered about the accident and the upcoming trial, she'd invited him up to share a pizza and a glass of Merlot. He had *not* gotten drunk, and he'd been far from fumbling.

Exhaling hard, Caleb swung his feet to the floor, sitting on the edge of the bed. "I'm going to get a glass of water. Want something?"

He had the quaintest way of never saying he was going to the bathroom to ditch his condom, always couching it in a gentlemanly offer to get something for her. He was so damn sweet.

"I'm good. Thank you, though." She touched his back, scoring her nails lightly down his spine as he left her. Her eyes lingered on the flex of his taut butt as he walked across the room. She'd redone the room after her divorce, spent a fortune, and sent the bill to her cheating ex who'd "interviewed" his next trophy wife on their bed.

Forget traditional elegance, she'd gone for making a slamming statement in eclectic contemporary: yellow walls with brown and gold accessories. Most important, a brand-new chic platform bed.

She gathered up the down coverlet to her chest and reached for the phone to check the missed call. She thumbed through the directory and found . . .

Sophie Campbell?

"Madison?" Caleb stood in the open bathroom

doorway, so mouthwateringly naked, she almost pitched the phone to the floor. "Something wrong?"

"It's Sophie Campbell—her son has started playing with Haley Rose."

His face closed up tight. He scrubbed a hand over his jaw and pulled a half smile. "I didn't realize you were friendly with the enemy."

"We're not friends—the kids are. Haley Rose met the Campbell boy on the school bus last week." She pressed the phone to her chest. "I should call her back. It could be something about the children."

"Then your brother should handle it when he gets home from playing goofy golf with his daughter." He dropped a knee onto the bed and crawled back over her, kissing her stomach and plucking the phone from her slackening grip. "How about I distract you while we wait for my mojo to kick in again?"

"Tempting." Definitely. "But no thank you." She grabbed his ear and tugged him upward.

"Damn it, Madison, that hurts." He stretched out beside her.

"Then don't try to manipulate me." She snatched the phone back from him. "I enjoy helping with Haley Rose. She's like my one shot at motherhood, except I never have to change diapers or pay for college. Sweet deal for me."

"You could have kids."

If he thought this line of conversation would distract her from making that call, he was sorely mistaken. "I could. But I won't." She smacked his hip. "Now get out of here before my brother gets back and finds out I'm banging the brains out of one of his junior officers."

"We could tell him. We *should* tell him." He sat up and leaned against the headboard.

"That would take all the illicit fun out of sneaking around."

"Sure." His gray eyes went bleak. "And it's not like there's any benefits to dating a guy who could be in Leavenworth in a couple of weeks."

"Hey," she soothed, pressing her hand to his chest. "You're going to beat this bogus charge."

"You can't know that." His voice went ragged as the real world slithered in as it always did.

"And yet, I do. My brother's certain, so I believe in you, too." She kissed him, closemouthed but lingering, wishing she was as confident as she pretended to be. "Now scram, and be sure to use the side exit like a good, smoking-hot boy toy."

His smile was a big lie for her benefit, and she knew it. But he still tossed on his clothes and left. For a handful of heartbeats she considered going after him, thought about what she would say. And kept on considering until his headlights swept out of the driveway. For the best.

She clicked on the missed call and phoned Sophie back.

* * *

Someone broke into my home. Sophie's terse voice from the phone echoed in David's head as he drove to her house.

He'd pulled into the driveway with Haley Rose only to be met by his sister in her robe. She'd thrust her cell phone at him. *Sophie.* He'd passed over Haley Rose to his sister and jumped back into his SUV. He raced over those four blocks in half the time.

He jammed his foot against the brakes. The Scout jerked to a halt outside of Sophie's lake house. Where the hell were the cops? He flung aside the seat belt. He hefted his gear bag from the back where he'd left it after work and pulled out his 9 mm from the bottom.

She had sounded composed. He wouldn't have expected otherwise.

He tried to reassure himself by focusing on her calmly spoken words. Instead, he kept hearing the tiny hitch in her breathing, too like the moment she'd lost her composure in the office. She was scared. Damn scared. He wasn't too steady, either.

She'd said the intruder had left, that she was okay and had already called the cops. He should have just stayed on the phone with her—but he'd thrust the cell back to his sister and left without hesitation. He sidestepped footprints leading away from the house.

Adult footprints? Male?

David took the stairs two at a time. The lock dangled from splintered wood. Until that moment, he'd hoped she'd just overreacted to a limb thumping a window or an owl swooping by.

"Sophie?" He nudged the door until it creaked open an inch. "It's just me. David."

Waiting for her to answer gave him too much time to think. Had the perp come back? Was she hurt?

David stepped to the side, gun gripped in his hand and held low. He didn't want to startle her, but if she didn't answer in ten seconds . . .

Seven. Eight. David tensed. *Nine. Ten.* He pivoted around.

The door swung wide. "Hello, David. Thanks for coming over."

He sagged against the porch railing. Her casual greeting almost made him laugh. Then he noticed her mussed appearance. Tension pulled him upright.

A tangled mass of blond hair swirled around her face. Her uniform jacket gone, one shirttail hung free from her skirt. Her legs were bare, no stockings or shoes.

Had someone . . .

He couldn't even complete the thought, but had to consider the possibility. "Sophie . . ."

"Come in." She gestured with one hand, the other clutching a letter opener. "I hope you didn't rush. There's no threat here now. I just, well, uh . . ."

"Sophie." He slowly reached for the door. If he touched her, he knew she'd bolt.

Her hand clenched around the letter opener.

That small gesture shoved his objectivity into the lake. He reminded himself that she'd said on the phone she'd seen the intruder run away and no one was hurt. But she was still obviously rattled. Understandably so. David wanted to pull her into his arms. The thought of anyone touching her, hurting her . . .

He needed to punch a wall.

Another more daunting thought stopped him. Had she been forced to protect herself before the intruder ran off? He glanced at the letter opener. No blood. Thank God.

"Are you sure you're okay?" He kept his tone calm, steady, nothing short of a miracle given his grinding frustration.

"I'm fine." She blinked faster. "We should step inside so we don't let all the air-conditioning out."

"Uh, wouldn't want to run up your electric bill," David said wryly. "Sophie."

She spun to face him. "What?"

"Do you mind?" He closed his fingers around her hand clutching the letter opener, not because he cared about the weapon but because he needed an excuse to touch her. Her icy fingers warmed in his grasp. If only he could dispel the chill of whatever had made her stand in front of him shaking.

"Oh, I forgot about it." She stared at their hands joined over the weapon. "Silly, huh, when there's nobody here?"

"Not at all." Even the most hardened combat vets lost it sometimes. "Let's sit."

He placed the letter opener on the secretary by the door, then grasped her hand again. When she didn't tug free, he squeezed her fingers gently. She seemed content to accept comfort, even if she didn't acknowledge it. Like when he'd held her shoulder in the office.

David led her into the formal living room and settled beside her on the sofa, giving him a moment to pull his focus back where it belonged. His hand relaxed around the grip of the gun, and he placed it within reach on the coffee table. "You didn't give me much to go on with the quick phone conversation, other than he'd left and you'd called the police."

"Sorry about that. Honestly, I'm not sure why I called your sister looking for you." She combed her fingers through her hair. "When I came back from my walk, I saw someone leaving the house."

David scratched his jaw, almost afraid to hope she'd come through unscathed. "You weren't inside with the intruder?"

"No."

He swallowed heavily, pressing two fingers to his eyebrows. On the phone she'd said they were okay, but there were a helluva lot of shades to *okay*.

"Nanny and Brice even slept through it. I was out walking to unwind after . . ."

Her deep brown eyes flared with the memory of that

moment in the office when she'd lost it, when he'd touched her. Just a hand on her shoulder, for God's sake.

Yeah, he understood the need to walk off tension.

"I needed some fresh air after work and I saw someone sneaking out of the house." She looked down at her disheveled clothing and frowned. "You thought I was attacked? Oh, no! David, I'm fine, really. He didn't hurt me, and he didn't hurt my family. I wouldn't have called you, but I thought I should have some kind of backup while I wait for the police in case they took a while to get here—which apparently they are."

Forget punching a wall or holding her. He needed space and a few seconds to clear his head and formulate more coherent thoughts about this break-in. Had she been purposefully targeted? Had the perpetrator been looking for something specific, because otherwise, why not steal something? Had this high-profile case made her a target, or could she have enemies of a more personal nature?

David stretched away from her to the end table and turned on a lamp. The furniture polish gleamed in the lamplight. His nose twitched at the lemony smell.

For the first time since he'd entered her house, David allowed himself a look around. The rest of the decor matched the lamp, classy and pricey. Two striped sofas faced each other in front of a fireplace. Towering shelves held books, only a few knickknacks. Immaculate white walls surrounded furniture of muted blues, dark woods, and brass.

Not too different from his childhood home. A world apart from the cluttered condo where he and Haley Rose had lived before he'd moved into his sister's posh guesthouse.

"Really," she said, standing, "I'm feeling silly for

calling you. The police are on their way. You can go home."

Leave? Not a chance.

He stood. Only a few inches separated him from Sophie, not even close to his thirty-six-inch rule. She smelled like Carolina jasmine mixed in with a clean breeze rolling off the water.

Were her eyes red-rimmed? *Ah, man.* They were. He wasn't sure how much more of the vulnerable Sophie he could resist in one night.

She massaged the fleshy part of her palm where brown flecks dotted her skin, her thumb prodding at the tiny splinters.

"What happened here?" His hand slid under hers, her skin soft against his calluses.

"I must have snagged them on the stair rail when I ran inside to check on Brice and Nanny." Sophie scraped her fingernail against a longer sliver protruding through the skin.

David's frustration multiplied. "What were you thinking running in after a prowler on your own? You could have been hurt. What good would you have been to them then?"

She ignored him, picking at the splinters in her hand until David grabbed her wrists. The perp could have turned that letter opener against her, maiming her, killing her. "Why didn't you go to a neighbor's and call for help instead of charging inside half-cocked?"

"Would you have left your child inside without checking first?"

He should have known better than to argue with a lawyer.

Sophie tugged her arms free. "That's what I thought. I appreciate your looking around outside. Please, go home now."

He set his jaw and readied his next argument.

"Mom?" Brice called from the hall. "Why are you awake? Is something wrong?"

Sophie heard her son's voice and breathed a mental sigh of relief. Her nerves already on edge from the break-in scare, she needed to think before making any decisions. She wanted to leap all over his offer of help, leap all over the comfort he offered as well.

As frustrating as it was to sit here with David, it really was a good thing she had called Madison after phoning the cops—since the police still hadn't arrived.

She pulled away from David and crossed to her son. "Hi, sweetie. Sorry if we woke you."

"What's Haley Rose's dad doing here?" Frowning, Brice stopped beside his mother. "Is something the matter?"

"Everything's fine. Try to go back to sleep before we wake Nanny, too."

She missed the days when her little boy would ask for hugs and gift her with sloppy baby kisses. She needed to hold her son close, to reassure herself he hadn't been hurt while she'd been taking a moonlight stroll, mooning over David Berg instead of staying inside watching out for her child. Her throat went tight.

Brice shifted from one foot to the other. Eyes wide, he looked from Sophie to David. "Are you sure?"

His concern seemed so manly coming from a kid wearing nothing but an overlong adult-size T-shirt. Like every night since Lowell's death, Brice slept in one of his father's old shirts. Some days she longed to shred those T-shirts, constant reminders of a man she had once loved, but who hadn't loved her enough to live.

Brice's T-shirt sported the logo of a regatta Lowell had entered three years ago. The entry fee could have paid last month's mortgage.

Her son couldn't give up the security of his father's clothes. What would he do if they lost their home? She searched for reassuring words to calm a child with too many adult worries. "I'm positive, kiddo." *Liar.* "Everything's fine."

Brice scratched his knobby knee just below the T-shirt. "If nothing's wrong, then what's he doing here?"

Sophie silenced David with a slight shake of her head, then wished she hadn't turned to him again. He looked too good in khaki shorts and a polo shirt, bared long arms and legs attesting to whipcord strength. Dark hair sprinkled along his skin.

Bristle over strength, like the man.

She remembered well the comfort those strong arms could offer. That didn't mean he wanted to be her on-call bodyguard.

"Mom?" Brice stepped between Sophie and David, turning sideways, putting more distance between the couple.

"Oh." Sophie slid her gaze back to her son. "We had a prowler outside. He's gone now." Cupping Brice's shoulder, she gave him a reassuring squeeze. "Just to be safe, I called David, uh, Major Berg to help me look around until I can fill out a police report. Would you mind knocking on Nanny's door so I can talk to her?"

David waited until her son left the room before he

pinned Sophie with a determined stare. "Maybe you should pack a few things and stay somewhere else."

Sophie bridled at his take-charge attitude. Asking for help didn't signify an abdication of her own responsibilities, damn it.

She added another step to the space between them. "I think that's a little premature. I should hear what the police have to say first."

A siren wailed lowly in the distance.

David scrubbed a hand across his jaw. "And there they are. About damn time."

"Then you can leave now. I've got this." Sophie could still feel the heat of his touch on her shoulder from when he'd comforted her in her office. A deeper ache settled in her stomach, tingling lower still, making her want his hands on her again—without the barrier of clothes.

"Or I can wait for you to finish up." His stubborn jaw jutted.

And no matter how much she wanted to argue with him, she had to think smart and use the resources available to her. She had to know if someone had targeted her house in particular. If so, had that person been staking out her place the whole time? Had someone been watching her in order to slip in during the only time this evening when she'd been away from the house?

She hugged herself tighter against the chill seeping all the way to her bones and tried not to think about the warmth of David's touch.

FIVE

★ ─────────────────────────────────

Stifling a yawn, David watched the patrol car pull out of Sophie's driveway. It was pushing three in the morning and he had to work in a few hours. But he wasn't leaving until he had her buttoned up tight in her house.

What a night.

Prints had been lifted, casts made of the footprints. Nothing more could be done for now. Sophie didn't see any reason to leave the house, and David couldn't come up with a concrete reason to make her change her mind.

He stretched his arms over his head and worked the kink out of his neck. At least he didn't have to field angry calls from Leslie about a late-nighter at the base. Their marriage had collapsed under the pressure of his job—no great surprise since military service members checked in with one of the highest divorce rates in the country. The Berg union was merely one more sad statistic.

As downright pissed as he got with Leslie, he knew the breakup had hurt her as well. He never should have married anyone, and she'd been so young. Too young. She'd been overwhelmed by the stress of being a military wife with a kid and another on the way.

But how could he regret something that had resulted in Haley Rose? And as much as it hurt like hell not to see Hunter, David wouldn't trade the time they'd had as a family for anything.

The divorce had been messy, no question. But once he'd accepted Leslie wasn't coming home and only wanted enough money to start over, he'd written the check without a wince. Leslie's decision that he would be the better parent for Haley Rose had filled him with an almost nauseating relief over not losing his daughter, followed by a crushing grief that Hunter wouldn't be a part of his life.

Realistically, he understood he needed to make further adjustments for his single-parent status. Increasing hours in the operational test world made serious demands on his time. He couldn't take advantage of his sister's help indefinitely.

With his upcoming promotion to lieutenant colonel, he was slated to go to a desk job at the Pentagon. Not exactly his cup of tea, but hell, he would spend more time behind a safe desk and less time away from home. He often wondered if he could have traveled less, if he'd chosen a different career path in the air force, maybe his marriage might have stood a chance.

All regrets aside, he didn't love Leslie, and she didn't love him. She managed the part-time-parent role, so Haley Rose still had a mother. What more could he do?

Not repeat his mistakes.

He climbed the steps back up to Sophie's, his pace slower this time than when he'd bolted up two at a stride to get to her.

David nudged the front door open with his toe and looked around the empty living room. He could hear Sophie in the next room, her husky tones that somehow seemed at odds with her softer appearance.

Her voice lured him. He'd never simply listened to her, the force of their attraction distracting him. Her tone told him far more than her words, its low pitch hinting at a hard-won maturity. Being widowed so young would affect anyone.

David paused by a framed family portrait on the wall displaying toddler-aged Brice sitting on his mother's lap. Sophie was tucked under the arm of the sandy-haired man behind her as she smiled down at her son.

Murmurs drifted from the kitchen where the women spoke. Sophie's voice flowed over him, into him. David traced a finger along the frame.

David heard the older woman's laugh and stepped away from the Campbell family portrait. He needed to make tracks out—now.

"David, is that you?" Sophie called, the husky sound of her catching him in the gut.

"Uh-huh." He followed her voice into the kitchen. "I'm just finishing up."

He liked this room better than the rest of her house. School flyers littered the refrigerator. Some kind of school project made out of clay, shells, and pipe cleaners lay half completed on the bar separating the cooking area from the table. White walls and light blue curtains seemed airy rather than sterile like the living room.

A family lived here, making memories.

Nanny stood beside Sophie at the sink, working free the splinters peppering Sophie's palm. Sophie and her grandmother stood shoulder to shoulder in height. The older woman possessed a birdlike frailty with none of Sophie's softening curves. A wrist-thick braid twisted in a bun on her head seemed too heavy for her fragile neck to support.

Frustration steamed over him. Two women and a child, alone, without even a rudimentary security system. Apparently living in a gated community hadn't done shit for keeping her safe.

The older lady glanced up, smiling. "Hello, Major Berg. We sure are lucky you were close enough to call. You've been a real godsend."

Her smile. Sophie had inherited more than her height from Nanny. She also got her smile.

"Glad to help, ma'am. I've fixed your lock well enough for the house to be closed off again," not that the lock had stopped anyone tonight, "but you'll want to replace it. You should consider an alarm of some sort, too."

"I could," Sophie said noncommittally.

Because she didn't see the need? Or was there some other reason? He studied her for clues, some sense of what was going on inside her head, worried as hell about a woman who wasn't even his to worry about. Sophie stood beside him, her curtain of hair shielding her face. She fidgeted with Brice's project, something resembling a cross between an ecosystem and a swamp monster.

He dropped a loose pipe cleaner into the bowl with the other arts and crafts supplies. "Or you could stay with my sister until your place is locked down tighter. Madison has plenty of room *and* a security system."

"Thanks, but we're good. I don't think anyone's coming back tonight, and I'll take care of securing the house this afternoon." Sophie pushed the school project aside. "Nanny will be here to supervise."

He backed away from the table. "Okay then. Don't hesitate to call."

"Thank you again. I hope I didn't make things too difficult for you to work." Her eyes went wide. "You aren't on crew rest, are you?"

Her questions in court rolled over him, the way she'd questioned his professional reputation, insinuated he might be lying. His jaw flexed. "No crew rest. And if I had been, then the flight would have been canceled. That's how we do things."

"Of course." Sophie folded her arms over her chest. "I'm glad I didn't wreck your schedule."

She'd wrecked a lot more in his life than robbing him of a few hours' sleep. He'd fought the attraction to her for so long, he'd thought he had it under control. Wrong. The feelings had just been piling on top of each other, waiting for just the right time to blindside him.

Her touch affected him. Damn it, *she* affected him, a woman who was hell-bent on taking down his squadron.

He needed to get the hell out of this house.

★ ★ ★

Sophie stuck her hand under the faucet, trying to soak the splinters free. The lingering sensation of David's touch stung more than the slivers of wood.

Still, having him here had helped, something she didn't like to admit. The break-in unsettled her more than she wanted to admit.

He'd handled the immediate crisis, but she couldn't afford to let herself depend on him for anything long term. Too many other worries crowded her life. Such as how would she afford to have new locks installed? Her stretched budget already screeched in protest over a trip for burgers. But she was trying so hard to hang on to the house to give her son stability.

Nanny bustled around the kitchen with all the subtlety of a freight train. Her wind suit whistled a friction tune. People who saw her grandmother for the first time might mistake her as someone frail and elderly. For two seconds.

How could anyone have this much energy in the middle of the night?

Nanny held Sophie's hand over the sink and poured peroxide over all the splinter wounds. Sophie relinquished control to her grandmother, not that she really had another choice. Nanny had been her one stable port in a life full of turmoil, her mother figure for all intents and purposes, since Sophie's father and mother had never married. The result of a backseat teenage tangle, Sophie had grown up with her father and his parents. She considered herself lucky to have had them.

"Nanny, would you like for us to go to a hotel?" She stifled a wince as her grandmother pushed out the largest splinter. "I want you to feel safe."

"Hotels are pricey, and the money's better spent on a new dead bolt and security system," her practical grandma said, tearing off a paper towel and patting Sophie's hand dry.

"I agree, but I want to be sure. This break-in has me rattled. I would have worried less if he'd stolen things, or come in while I was asleep." Sophie looked around her house she'd fought so hard to keep so her son would be in the best and safest neighborhood. Not that the place had been all that safe tonight. "But the timing seemed so perfectly targeted for when I would be gone."

"Then I imagine we should all be extra careful about

double-bolting the doors, keeping a cell phone nearby, watching for anyone acting suspicious. With luck, though, the police will come up with something on those finger-prints and we'll have answers by tomorrow."

Her grandmother sounded so confident all would be well. She looked at Nanny's silver braid and thought of all the times she'd crawled onto her grandmother's lap as a child. Her earliest memories were of clutching that braid and tick-ling her chin with the end until she drifted off to sleep.

Such a simple solution to chasing away monsters in the night. But she wasn't a child anymore.

Sophie smoothed a hand over Nanny's coiled braid. "Are you okay? I wouldn't dare refer to your age, but this has been a stressful night."

Nanny grinned, riffling through the contents of a first aid kit. "I'm not moving so slowly I missed seeing what a nice-looking young man that major is."

This kind of help she did not need. Nanny would have out the *Bride* magazines if Sophie wasn't careful. "I've told you before. No matchmaking. I am not interested in Major Berg."

Nanny snorted while working loose another splinter.

"Okay, so I'm interested in him." She breathed in and out. Hard. A lingering hint of his aftershave sent a fresh shower of sparks through her. "But I'm not ready for a relationship. I'm not sure I'll ever be ready for anything serious again."

Nanny released Sophie's hand and grasped her chin. "You were a good wife to Lowell. You loved him. You mourned your husband's death. Now it's time for you to move forward."

Sophie wanted to believe her but knew better. "You didn't, after grandpa died."

"No one pushed me." Nanny's grip pinched. "As much as I love you and Brice, you can't take the place of having someone, a man, to share my life with. I don't want to let the same happen to you."

What was it with the men in her family checking out early? Why couldn't any of them stick around long enough for gray hairs?

Thoughts of skimming her fingers over the flecks of silver at David's temples caught her when she was too vulnerable to duck.

Nanny pulled two coffee mugs from the hooks under the cabinet. "Maybe you could just have an affair with him. He does have a damn fine backside."

If only life were that simple. Sophie clapped a hand over her forehead. "I am not going to discuss that man's butt with my grandmother."

"Your grandfather had quite a nice backside."

"Too much information." She held up a hand. "Conversation over. I need to catch at least a couple hours' sleep before I head into work."

The sobering stakes of the trial grounded her again. Winning her case would send one of his friends to jail and put a professional black mark on David's record. This wasn't the time to fantasize. Real life was about harsh realities.

And her reality? She couldn't afford the distraction of David Berg, but she'd closed off her life from so many people since her husband had died, she wasn't sure who else to turn to for help.

* * *

David's footsteps echoed in the cavernous airplane hangar.

Metal beams formed a skeleton overhead, the whole hangar gaping, like walking through the belly of a whale. A busy belly.

Aircraft mechanics crawled over a spindly gray Predator drone—unmanned craft. Three military maintenance guys in camo and two civilian contractors wearing coveralls worked to install a new camera system with upgraded sensors to record ground intelligence. The craft was cracked open—pieces of skin peeled back as they worked to wedge replacement pieces in there.

Work stands lined the walls with pieces of the project laid out. Master Sergeant Mason "Smooth" Randolph hummed along to the radio as he shaved a circular piece down with a metal grinder to make it fit, smooth-eyed the piece, then vaulted back up onto the nose of the Predator.

David itched to jump right in. The familiarity soaked into his pores, revving him up and soothing him all at once. He loved his job, the thrill of flying the latest gadgets in the military inventory, the mental challenge of creating new technology, testing and tweaking until it could be rolled out.

When it came to toys, his squadron's rivaled those of James Bond and Batman.

The better the technology, the smaller the human footprint in a deployment. Test projects made a hefty dent in the defense budget, but big picture? What it saved couldn't be quantified—relationships salvaged, thanks to fewer deployments.

Lives saved by placing fewer people in harm's way.

And all he had to do to make that happen? Strap his butt into an aircraft no one had flown before. And his squadron didn't just test new airplanes—like the hypersonic jet a couple of hangars over. They also tested modifications to aircraft already in the inventory—such as the gun turret modification on the AC-130.

He'd even been in on the development of unmanned spy craft the size of insects. Remote control flying those surveillance peepers to gather intelligence was a blast.

And the squadron wasn't just about pilots but navigators, sensor operators, gunners, and loadmasters—all the different crew positions. They were all aviators, all called to figure out new ways to cheat the laws of gravity.

In the air force, he was a navigator even though he had a civilian pilot's license, a rating that was tough as hell to find time to keep current, given the demands of his present job overseeing three different test projects at once.

He knew his time here was drawing to a close. He couldn't keep the kind of hours needed or weeks on the road to other testing ranges across the country. But he'd wanted to leave on his terms, not with this horrific screwup hanging over his head. The thought of that kid injured, a child who would spend the rest of his life with a limp and scar.

Not to mention the horror of being shot when he should have been safest—asleep in his home.

He rubbed the back of his neck.

Sitting on the Predator's nose, Smooth waved. "Morning, Major. You're in early. Did you bring coffee?"

David forced a smile. "Coffee and doughnuts, on their way."

Subcontractor Keith Nelson barked, "Can we cut the chitchat, girls, and get back to work?"

The old guy had a chip on his shoulder about flunking the physical to join the air force. He was an ass, no question, but a detail-oriented ass who was good at his job. Nothing got by him.

Smooth jumped to the ground. "Any more news on Tate? The trial? Gage and Deluca said you really tore it up in the courtroom the other day. Fed that JAG her lunch."

"Lawyers," Nelson sneered. "Fuck 'em. They always screw everything up, nitpicking every contract and document to pieces like we have a decade to waste waiting for them to process everything. How are we supposed to defend ourselves if whenever we come under attack, we have to consult the attorneys before we can even crank an engine?"

Smooth laughed. "Don't let the lawyers hear you say that."

Nelson scowled. "It's not like they're around to hear us." He checked over his shoulder. "Are they?"

More laughter bounced around like a football kicked into the rafters, and David wished he felt like joining in. "Coffee and doughnuts will be showing up shortly, just make sure you send some to us so we don't fall asleep in the teleconference."

He would be joined for that boring telecom by Jimmy "Hotwire" Gage, Vince "Vapor" Deluca, and Mason "Smooth" Randolph. They had been on his crew in the old days when he flew the tests rather than ran tests. They'd been through a lot together, and now they were the old guys.

Smooth hopped off the nose again and jogged over. "Everything okay, sir?"

"Sure. Why?"

"You just look tired."

"Neighbor had a break-in and I went over. Everyone's okay." He didn't know why he withheld just who that neighbor was. "Have you heard anything from Tate?"

Smooth and Tate had been hanging out lately since Randolph's wife was overseas for six months as a contract police force. "Part of him wants to return to flying as soon as possible. Another part of him is freaking out that the accident was his fault, and if you put him in the cockpit again . . ."

Some sentences didn't need to be completed.

"That's a damn heavy load to be carrying." David clapped Smooth on the shoulder as he left.

They needed to get this trial behind them for a lot of reasons. Where the hell was the evidence to clear Caleb Tate?

For the first time since he'd walked into that courtroom two days ago, his world steadied and he knew exactly what should happen. Rather than working against each other, he needed to work *with* Sophie Campbell. Starting at the close of business today, he had a whole weekend to work on finding those answers once and for all.

* * *

Slider was pissed.

The break-in at Sophie Campbell's didn't seem to have rattled her in the least. Even though she had to have been up all night, she'd been steadier than ever in court today. Crisp. Driven.

Sexy.

He wove through the cars in the parking lot, searching for hers. He just wished he could have been there to see her face when she realized someone broke into her house while her son was there. He'd paid a Vegas street junkie a couple hundred bucks to break in. The edge of how badly that *could* have gone for Sophie and her family added a bigger jolt than if he'd been the one jimmying

the door. Besides, he had to be certain he was not anywhere near the house when the B and E occurred.

Clearly, he would have to keep the heat coming.

Checking around the lot, he saw plenty of foot traffic,
so no one would think anything of him being here. But
no sign of Sophie coming out yet. Kneeling next to her
sedan, he let air out of her tire with a slow hiss. Not
enough air for her to notice, but enough for the tire to blow
out on her half-hour trip home. Sometimes the simple
tricks worked better than the fanciest technology.

And if she actually died in the accident?

Then the trial would have to start over, and he would
have the time he needed to redirect the fallout from that
accident. To be sure that when they pinned blame, there
would be no questions. No trial.

Game over.

* * *

TGIF didn't even come close to describing how relieved
Sophie was to see the end of this day. Stepping outside
of the building that housed the military proceedings, she
put her hat on, squinting against the sun.

Aside from being exhausted from no sleep, thanks to
the break-in, she'd found today's court experience had
been especially draining. The little boy injured in the
accident had been in the gallery with his parents and,
God, but it broke her heart in half every time she turned
around and saw them. The Vasquez family had stayed
away for the most part, not wanting to further traumatize
their son, and she could understand that. But all the players also needed to stay focused on how damn important
this case was.

She stepped back for the Vasquezes to come through

so they could speak outside, away from the packed halls and stuffy formality. Only six years old, Ricky struggled to handle the crutches, but he didn't give up. His shattered leg was in a cast. The uneven thump as he made his way outside broke her heart all over again.

He still faced two more surgeries. Doctors weren't sure if he would walk without a limp, or if he would be able to run, to play sports.

His parents stood on either side of him, Ricky's father speaking up first. "Major Campbell, we cannot thank you enough for all you are doing to get justice for Ricky."

"It's my job, Dr. Vasquez." Although doing her job would clear the way for more lawsuits. If only people did the right thing without being forced by the justice system.

Ricky's father was a music professor at a local university. His wife had taught in the same department but quit her job to be with her son through his rehab from the injury. They were struggling to make ends meet with their income cut in half and their child facing so many operations.

Mrs. Vasquez squeezed Sophie's arm. "Your job did not include you coming to our house a half dozen times so Ricky wouldn't have to answer deposition questions in a frightening office setting."

"Whatever I can do to make this easier for you. We all just want answers."

"Mrs. Campbell?" Ricky tugged the edge of her service blues jacket.

His mother put a hand on his shoulder. "Sweetie, her name is *Major* Campbell."

"It's okay." She knelt in front of him. "You can call me Sophie."

His wide, dark eyes stared back at her earnestly. "I drew you a picture, Major Sophie."

"Thank you, Ricky." She took the paper from his tiny hand. "I'll put it on the refrigerator at my house, right next to a picture my son drew for me in art class."

She looked down at the crayon drawing—and struggled not to gasp. It wasn't just some childish scribble of a playground or dinosaurs like her son would have made at the same age. Ricky had depicted his house with an airplane overhead and a large flash of light exploding outside his window. A fierce determination scoured through her. She *would* make sure this little boy got justice.

"Thank you," she repeated, sliding the picture carefully into her briefcase. She patted his face gently, then stood, shaking hands with his parents. She watched them walk away, her mind racing with thoughts, even though her exhausted body shouted for her to call an end to this day.

"Sophie?"

David's voice reached through her fog and jolted her. *Stirred her.*

She pivoted on her heel sharply and found him standing a few feet to the side, looking tall and invincible in his flight suit.

"David? Were you in court today?" Certainly she would have seen him.

"No, I've been out here waiting for you." He rocked back on his green flight boots.

A warm whisper of awareness rippled through her veins. "For me?"

"We need to talk about the case."

His words cooled the heat in a flash. "Why would you think that?"

"Rather than working against each other, we should work together."

"Do you really believe you can persuade me that your guy's not responsible?"

"All I care about is finding the cause. Period. So no more kids like that," he pointed to Ricky Vasquez being helped into the car by his parents, "get injured. All that matters is knowing what caused that accident. Isn't that what you want? The truth?"

Temper heated the ice inside her right up again. "Oh, right, I just need to *want* the truth. Why didn't I think of that before?"

"Funny. I get your point." He canted closer. "But you haven't heard mine. We need to look at the evidence together rather than just interrogating each other."

She eyed him suspiciously. "Are you trying to wrangle information out of me for your friend?"

He cupped her shoulder. "Sophie, I'm trying to find out what happened so it doesn't happen again. That's what a test program is for. If that means Caleb's guilty of negligence on the job, then that's something he and I both will have to learn to live with."

"And can you accept that?"

"We protect innocents. Now let's do our jobs." He squeezed her shoulder once, lingered, then let his arm fall away.

She couldn't miss the intensity, the sincerity in his eyes. "What exactly are you suggesting?"

"Complete immersion in the data. What those in the business world would call a 'deep dive.' Let's put our heads together and pore over all the information. One of the most important things I've learned in the test world?

Brainstorming with different people, in different combinations, can bring new answers."

Working together? She considered the ethics of that and quickly dismissed any problems. Anything she would share with him had already been seen by Caleb's defense in the interest of disclosure. And David might have new insights to shed on data she might not have fully comprehended.

His idea had merit, although she wasn't so sure what they would uncover at this late date. She shifted her briefcase more securely in her hand. "Let's make an appointment for Monday."

"Why wait? We have all weekend long to work together."

All weekend long? With David? "What exactly do you mean?"

"I'll come over to your place. The kids can play together while we work. I'll even spring for pizza so no one has to cook."

"I thought you were worried about the kids playing together?"

"Maybe I spoke too quickly. Playing with your kid may be helping her get past missing Hunter." He clasped her elbow and guided her toward her car as if it was a done deal. "What is there to argue with? Everyone's happy."

Happy? She wasn't sure about that. But she couldn't argue with his logic. Her case was teetering right now, with a verdict that could go either way without any real sense of certainty, of closure. They needed to uncover the truth.

And she couldn't delude herself into ignoring the flutter of excitement in her stomach at the prospect of spending more time with David.

* * *

David followed Sophie's gold sedan, weaving through the Friday rush-hour traffic. Would their weekend together actually bring him the answers he needed? And would those answers convict Caleb? Or implicate someone else?

He only knew that seeing Ricky Vasquez had swept away any reservations. This had to be done. It was the right thing, the only option left.

And it wasn't like he could act on the rogue attraction to Sophie anyway, not with two children and her grandmother underfoot. They would work all weekend long. Period. End of sentence. No more getting worked up over the scent of jasmine. For God's sake, he wasn't some out-of-control teen.

He clicked on his turn signal and changed lanes. Billboards littered the roadside with everything from casinos to alien Area 51 propaganda. Flying test missions in this area was actually easy with so many wack jobs eager to write off anything out of the ordinary as an outer space phenomenon.

If only he could write off Caleb's flight catastrophe to little green men.

Hauling his focus back to the present problem—a blond bombshell lawyer who drove like they were on the lawless roads of Iraq. He pinned his eyes on her car and stayed close to her bumper. Easier said than done between rush-hour traffic and tourists driving haphazardly. Even Sophie seemed to be weaving in her lane as she powered down the road. Was she still suffering ill effects from the bump on the head? She'd definitely missed most of last night's sleep.

Damn it, he should have insisted on driving her again. They were still fifteen minutes from home. He considered calling her cell . . . but that would be more likely to distract her.

The stoplight turned red just as Sophie cleared the intersection. Shit. He hit the brakes and watched her surge forward.

And swerve sharply.

Her back tire blew out, sending her fishtailing into oncoming traffic.

Six

Sophie snapped back in her seat, her vision full of air bag blossoming in front of her. Her car pinwheeled, then slammed into another car with the sickening crunch of metal on metal. Pain exploded through her hard and fast.

And then everything went still.

"Sophie," David's voice shouted from outside her car, on the passenger side. "Are you okay? Speak to me, damn it."

"In here. I'm all right." Sore, but everything moved and nothing was trapped. She pushed on her door, except it was bent inward and didn't budge. "I can't climb out."

"Hang tough. I'm coming in."

Smoke tinged the air. Panic stirred. "Is the car on fire? Is anyone hurt?"

"You're going to be fine, and as far as I can tell, everyone's stepping from their vehicles unharmed." His steady voice came through over the creaks and thumps on the passenger door.

She noticed he didn't say the car wasn't burning. What if he was injured pulling her from her crushed car?

Bile stung her throat. She shifted to kick through the passenger air bag to the door, to help, to do something other than be helpless.

The door groaned open. David filled the open space and she stopped short of kicking him. His arms thrust inside and he grabbed around her waist, hauling. A part of her brain registered it had to be bad if he wasn't taking his time. Her heart in her throat, she angled over and gripped his shoulders. In a bumpy, painful drag, she was up and out of the car.

Cradled against David's chest. She gave herself three seconds to sigh in relief before she looked over his shoulder.

Oh God.

The wreck was worse than she thought. A trio of mangled cars wrapped around one another like a bad game of Twister. Smoke poured from the hoods of all three. Cars were parked willy-nilly on the highway with people talking on cell phones and helping the others in the accident. A teenage girl stumbled from one car, cradling her arm. An elderly couple walked away from the other car, seemingly unharmed, but the chaos in front of her still scared her.

She'd caused this. She didn't know how she'd lost control of her car, but there was no denying her memory. She'd been at fault.

Her breath hitched.

David looked down at her, concern in his deep blue eyes. "Did I hurt you? Do you think you can stand?"

"I can stand." Her teeth chattered. "I'm totally fine."

"You look it," he said wryly, setting her on her feet by his Scout parked on the side of the road.

"You're a crappy liar." She held on to his hands to make sure she didn't stumble, the world still spinning.

"That was sarcasm." He stared into her eyes and checked the back of her head. "As soon as the police finish filling out their report, we're going to the ER."

Not again. She'd had enough of hospitals to last a lifetime—when her father died, then her husband. "I just want to finish here and go home." She turned back toward the car. "I should get my purse and my briefcase. They'll need my insurance information. And I don't want to lose the picture Ricky drew for me."

"I'll make sure they get them out before they tow the car."

"Provided it doesn't blow up, you mean."

He cradled her face in his broad hands. "I'm just glad you're okay, and I intend to make sure you stay that way. Your head has been bashed around twice now. We're not taking chances. Once the tow truck arrives, we're leaving for the hospital, and then you're coming home with me."

"*We* are going to the hospital? *We* are going home together?" Where the hell had he gotten that idea? She grabbed his wrist and pulled his hand away before she did something silly—like lean into him. "What makes you think you get to make these kinds of decisions for me?"

"And what makes you believe you're thinking clearly now? You've had a break-in and a car accident in two days."

"So I'm having a really crappy run of luck. I'll lock my doors better and take a cab to work." She bit her lips to keep from losing her cool. What was it about this man that got under her skin? "Thank you for your concern. But I'll be fine."

"Odds are, you're right and I'm worrying for nothing." He stepped closer, crowding her and heating her at the same time. "But are you willing to put your son and grandmother at risk based on odds?"

Her head snapped back. "You really know how to go for the jugular, Major."

"Maybe I should have been a lawyer, too."

And still his argument took root. Fear pushed through the numbed feeling she'd had since the accident. Her mind and her senses turned sharper. The scent of smoke on the air, the wail of sirens in the distance, all reminded her of how fragile life could be.

She couldn't afford to take chances, her son couldn't afford for her to take the risk. "Fine, you win."

Nodding tightly, he opened the passenger door on his Scout. "Wanna sit down before you fall down? You can chew me out all you want on the way to the emergency room."

* * *

"Thanks for letting us descend on you like this, Madison." Sophie dropped her son's overnight bag on the double bed four hours after the car accident. "Hopefully my security system will be in place by Monday and I won't have to impose long."

Everything between the wreck and now had happened in a blur—the police statements, EMS checking her over at David's insistence, then packing on the fly. She'd done her best not to frighten her son, but there was no shielding him from the fact that their car had been totaled.

As for why they were staying with Madison Palmiere? She'd told Brice there was a glitch in getting the security system installed and they were spending the weekend here until things could be sorted out on Monday. He'd accepted her story and shifted into excitement over hanging out with his friend for a couple days.

Now, here they were in this chic home that certainly didn't look like it had ever seen children's chocolate smudged fingerprints on the wall or coloring-book pages on the fridge. Madison's place was mostly black lacquer, white leather, and marble. Minimal clutter with high-impact art pieces. Splashes of color showed up in each room with a different theme. In here, the guest room for Brice, a mammoth Asian silk flower arrangement rested on top of the chest of drawers, a green marble Buddha underneath.

Sophie just prayed her son didn't break anything.

Madison settled into a black lacquered rocker. "No problem. It's not like I have anything going on in my life." She draped her other arm negligently along the curved wooden rest. Her bracelets collected along the top of her dangling hand. "David knows I'm not one for schedules or rules."

"Well, he really should have called ahead first." Unpacking Brice's jeans and shirts, Sophie slid them into an empty drawer.

"Nah, would have taken all the fun out of it."

"I should probably take a page from your philosophy book." But she couldn't escape reality. She did still have the case to focus on. Thank God they'd been able to retrieve her purse and briefcase from the car. The fire department arrived in time to douse the flames, forestalling any explosion.

Madison's bracelets sang like wind chimes with each gentle movement of the rocker. "So, do you and David have something going on?"

Going on? Only in her restless dreams. "No."

"Yeah, right."

"This is purely professional." Or rather, it had to be. "We're going to work on a case together this weekend."

"Oh well, have it your way." Madison brushed a hand along the green Buddha, dusting the immaculate surface. "Besides, I know how he feels responsible for the world. Part of being a bad-ass warrior, I guess."

"So he dumps strays on your doorstep often?"

"You're the first."

"Oh." A flutter of excitement threatened to fill the hollow space with a yearning far worse than any simple ache. Trying to lose herself in routine, she focused on the contents of her son's suitcase.

Madison nudged the figurine an inch to the left. "Wanna hear all about David's past?"

Sophie looked up sharply. "Excuse me?"

"Do you want to know all about his ex-wife?"

Desperately. "No, thank you."

Sophie lifted a folded pile of Brice's sleep shirts. The faded cotton folded on top proclaimed, "I lost my shirt in Monte Carlo." She stuffed the stack into the back of the drawer.

"Sure you do."

"Wait a minute." Sophie perched on the edge of the bed, hand resting on the open roll bag. "If I wanted to know about your brother—which, believe me, is a bad idea—aren't I supposed to pump you for information and then you tell me I'll have to ask him if I want to know anything?"

"Too predictable and a big waste of time." Madison fidgeted with the clasp on one of her bracelets. "Besides, he'd never tell anyway. David has some misguided idea that he shouldn't tarnish the image of Haley Rose's mother."

"Maybe I should respect that." In fact, she did respect that about him.

"You're not even curious?" Madison played with a long strand of hair, starting a tiny braid in front.

Sophie tossed a pair of Brice's socks into the open drawer. "No."

And she really meant it this time. She didn't want to know more about David. The more she learned, the more she liked him. She found "like" far more dangerous than lust, or even love.

"Honorable to the core. The two of you are made for each other." Madison flopped back with a disgusted frown. "So you and David really aren't a couple."

"I'm not in the market for a relationship." Sophie lobbed another rolled ball of socks into the drawer.

"Too bad. I'd like to see my brother happy." Madison's fingers mover faster down the braid, a frenetic anger radiating from her. "Leslie wasn't content with stomping his pride and wiping out his savings account. She cost him his stepson, a child he'd loved since Hunter was a toddler. She took David's ability to trust."

Sophie wanted to pummel Madison with a rolled-up pair of socks. "David told me about his stepson. I think it's heartbreaking and unfair, truly."

"Do you feel sorry for him yet?" A twinkle lit her gray-blue eyes so like her brother's. "Because I really want David to be happy again."

"Maybe I'm a little sorry for him." Years of loving the wrong kind of man gave her a heaping dose of empathy for David's marital problems.

"He's a good person." Madison stilled, all humor erased by the intensity of her words. "He deserved better."

"I hope he finds it." She closed the empty overnight bag and zipped it shut with a yank. "Just not with me."

Sophie zipped her defenses up just as firmly. She had to. She stood a fighting chance at resisting David, the cocky flyboy. But holding firm against the image of the vulnerable man he tried so hard to hide from the world? That would require a hefty dose of self-control.

*   *   *

A week ago, David never would have guessed Sophie Campbell would be living under his roof.

Okay, technically it was his sister's roof. But still, his life was upside down. Sitting on the upper deck with his laptop, David scanned the shoreline, making a quick head count. He wasn't taking anyone's safety for granted, not with the hellish image of Sophie's car accident so fresh in his head.

Ten yards from shore, Haley Rose and Brice pedaled a small paddleboat around in the shallows, the full moon and dock lights illuminating them. Madison supervised from the pier, talking on her cell phone.

The hum of the electric ice-cream maker droned softly behind him. The world seemed so peaceful—eerily so considering they still didn't have a single lead on who'd broken into Sophie's house or what had gone wrong with her car.

The French doors opened behind him and he looked over his shoulder. *Sophie.* The sight of her sucker punched him in a way he should have gotten used to by now.

She'd showered. Her blond hair hung loose around her shoulders. She just wore a simple cotton sundress and

flip-flops, but she had that kind of Marilyn Monroe classic beauty and could make anything look sexy as hell.
His body hardened in response as adrenaline from the
close call earlier fired through him. Thank God he was
sitting, or she would see just how much those soft curves,
her creamy skin—her smile—made him ache to pull her
in for a kiss.

She held two glasses of his sister's Southern sweet tea
in her hands, offering him one before taking the recliner
next to him. Sipping her drink, she stared over the rim
of the glass. "Is your sister seeing someone?"

"Not that I know of. Why do you ask?" He closed his
laptop.

Sophie lifted her glass and gestured out toward the
dock. "Look at how she's cradling the phone. If I didn't
know otherwise, I would assume she's talking to somebody special. I just would hate to disrupt any plans she
has for the weekend."

"Her divorces have left her relationship wary." Which
he understood one hundred percent.

Sophie stayed silent, sipping, but her eyes shifted to
the children.

"I know. Relationship failure runs in the family." And
days like this reminded him all the more how much that
bit. He'd really wanted it all, kids playing, family gather-
ings. Hell, even family bickering. He'd wanted normal.
Apparently single *was* his family's norm. "Makes me
wonder if she and I have a defective gene, like a test
project doomed from the start because there's this one
weak part that sabotages everything else."

"You don't really believe that about yourself, do you?
It takes two to make or break a marriage."

If she thought she could spout a line that sounded like

it came out of a *Cosmo* article and he would feel better about his crappy marriage, she could think again. His irritability ratcheted up a notch.

"I thought we were here to review testing data, not my personal life." He leaned forward on his elbows, openly letting her read in his eyes just how damn bad he wanted to lean her back on that chair and peel away her clothes with his teeth. "Unless you have something else in mind."

She moved back fast and chewed her bottom lip.

He laughed softly, darkly. "That's what I thought."

* * *

Sophie couldn't sleep. No big surprise. Her whole body ached from the wreck, and yes, from undiluted sexual frustration.

She stared at the ceiling and tried to focus on anything other than David a few walls away. She rolled over onto her side and hugged the fat pillow, satin sheets tormenting her skin with every sensuous slither. Why was it that even the decor seemed to shout sex? The mostly white room, splashed with hints of black trim and a red leather chair in the corner. Minimalist for the most part, the only piece of art was a painting of a naked woman wrapped in a red sheet. Her face was hidden, but from the long dark hair it was easy to guess Madison was the subject.

Thank goodness Brice was sleeping in the green Buddha room rather than in here.

She flopped on her back, exhausted and still wide awake. Giving up, she flung aside the covers and gave in to the allure of leftover ice cream since she couldn't feed her primary craving.

Madison *had* told her to make herself at home.

Sophie padded quietly from her room to the spacious kitchen. Gleaming granite counters with stainless steel appliances looked unused—except the coffeemaker. She buried her head in the freezer full of neatly stacked single-serving meals and scavenged for the good stuff. Behind a carton of butternut squash soup, she found the container of leftover ice cream David had made earlier.

"Find anything you like?" His voice rumbled through the dark, raising goose bumps along her skin.

"What?" Sophie almost smacked her head ducking out of the freezer. She expected to see him lounging in the doorway but instead found him in the gathering room, where he lay stretched on the sofa. "I thought you slept in the guesthouse?"

"I'm no help to anyone a house away. The bedrooms here are full with the five of you. This seemed to be the safer option if something goes wrong." His raspy, sleep-heavy voice filled the space between them. A black satin comforter was draped haphazardly over his midriff, leaving the rest of him bare. Surely he had on shorts.

Still, he looked like a male model rather than a seasoned combat vet.

She hugged her ice cream to her stomach and grabbed a spoon. She still thought the threats weren't related. But she refused to risk anything more happening, to run the chance of her son's world being upset. The past year, she'd worked damn hard to help him feel secure again. Sure, he thought this weekend was a fun adventure, a chance to spend more time with his friend, but she knew far too well how fragile her son was. The pain of losing a parent didn't just go away. Only a month ago, Brice was still sneaking calls on his cell phone in the school bathroom to make sure she was okay.

Sophie scooped a creamy bite out of the Tupperware container and felt a little calmer. Silently, they stared, David with his hands laced behind his head, Sophie spooning ice cream as she stood in the archway.

David nodded toward a chair. "Sit down. I promise not to think you're after my body if you walk into the room."

She liked that he could make her smile, ease the tension coursing through her right now. She liked a lot more things about him than she would have thought. She wanted to curl up in that chair and talk with David, not about work but as two adults having a regular conversation. Reminding herself of their sleeping chaperones, she decided to take a chance.

Flagstones cool under her bare feet, she closed the gap between them and eased into the white leather club chair, nudging aside the mocha pillow—desert theme for this room, the stark white broken up with brown accents and two towering Joshua trees.

David's bare feet, crossed at the ankles, were just an arm's reach away. "Pretty sure of yourself, aren't you, Major?"

"Pretty sure of your self-control, Counselor."

If only he knew how tempting he looked, long, lanky, and sleepy-eyed. Sophie reminded herself that nothing would happen, not with two kids, his sister, and her grandmother asleep a few yards away. Somehow that didn't ease the coil of lazy longing deep inside her.

She scraped a heaping spoonful from the side of the carton. "You're lucky to have a family home to visit."

"I guess so." Their voices stayed low, confidential whispers guaranteed not to wake the others.

"You really shouldn't take it for granted." The house

she'd grown up in had been sold long ago, Nanny being Sophie's only tangible link to those early years.

"It's just a house. Sure it's familiar, but it's not my home, since I grew up in South Carolina."

"How did Madison end up here?"

"We're not close to our parents. She'd just gotten a divorce, so she came out here and met loser husband number two."

All right, then. So much for conversation.

She dipped back into the ice cream as his eyes tracked her. The cottony pajama-shorts set had seemed modest enough when she'd packed. But now her breasts felt heavy and bare swaying ever so gently against the fabric with her least movement. He had to notice.

The blanket had scrunched up on one side, unveiling his running shorts. His bare chest rose and fell with each steady breath. Those few moments against the courthouse wall, she'd listened to his heart thud as he'd stretched over her. What would it be like to curl beside him on the sofa and listen to that reassuring rhythm through the night, tangled up together under that black satin comforter?

David arched his feet, stretching and circling them until they popped through all the kinks. "I'm glad to have her here for Haley Rose. Especially now. I don't have all that many family memories from growing up. I want it to be different for my kid."

"Seems to me like you're doing a great job."

"I'm trying to be different from my parents. It's not like they were bad, just indifferent. If we brought home good grades and didn't act up, Dad was happy and shelled out the cash. Simple."

"Sad." The things he left unsaid were almost more

revealing than the words themselves. She saw the picture of a parent more concerned with success than love.

"Could have been worse. The problem was, I got complacent, too much, too early, and I started feeling entitled." He scratched his chest, his eyes taking on a faraway look. "I didn't do anything earth-shattering. Just petty stuff, enough to get in trouble and piss off my old man."

David a troubled teen? She wouldn't have guessed. Yet, it made sense, a kid doing whatever it took to get a distant parent's attention. "And what did your father do?"

"The old man would grease the wheels, smooth things out, until the next time when I pushed a little further. He would have ponied up the cash indefinitely to keep it hushed." David shifted, staring past Sophie with an unfocused gaze. "Except I caught the attention of a crusty old colonel who'd started a second career teaching at my high school. Colonel Reaves chewed me out in a way my dad never did. He got my attention and gave me direction."

David turned the power of his crinkle-eyed grin on her. Sophie smiled with him, just for show, but she understood well David had finally found the father figure he'd needed.

He sat up, the comforter twisting around his waist. "Now the colonel spends his time down at his retirement condo in Arizona golfing. We still exchange Christmas cards."

"The colonel sounds like a wonderful man."

"He is." David swung his feet to the floor, leaning forward, elbows on his knees. "You asked why I feel responsible for you and your family. Reaves is the reason, even my old man to a certain degree. This is what I do, the whole call to serve. It's the only way I know how to make sense of the world."

Oh God, she was in worse trouble here than she thought. He wasn't just hot, he was even more deeply honorable than she'd realized. She set her ice-cream carton on the coffee table.

"Sophie."

She glanced up, realizing they were both too raw from the revelations they'd made to each other. What would he do now? At the end of the sofa, he sat so much closer to her than she'd realized. As she perched on the edge of the chair, her knees almost bumped his.

He stroked a loose strand of hair behind her ear. "You're quite a woman, Sophie Campbell. Taking on the world, doing your best to set wrongs to right again."

In spite of the logical lawyerly voice in her head shouting for her to haul ass back to her room, Sophie smoothed her fingers along the silver flecks at his temples. "Thank you."

She waited for him to pull away. Neither one of them moved.

He caressed his thumb along her jaw, his touch gentle, seductive. "This is a bad idea."

"I know," she whispered. She couldn't walk away if she tried. She didn't even try.

"You should tell me to stop."

"I know, but I can't." Unable to resist, she curved her hand around the back of his head, threading her fingers through the close-cropped hair. All the tamped-down desire seemed to mist around them.

"This thing between us can't lead anywhere. I can't do long term." He tipped her chin, his finger brushing along her jaw.

"I know that, too. Me either." She pulled his face to hers anyway.

Their mouths met, open, greedy, seeking to take as much as possible from a single kiss. She touched her tongue to his, tempting, luring him past her lips. Then he plunged deeper, sweeping away her ability to think with the bold touch of his tongue. She gripped his shoulders, her fingers digging in as she held tight to keep from sinking.

God, David was a great kisser, and she loved to kiss. She soaked in the moment, needing to fill the void in herself after so many long nights without the touch of a man, of even the simplest brush of lips as a morning greeting or good-night farewell. An ache swirled low within her, while familiar, also somehow different, desperate.

Ravenous.

David slid his hands down her back, hauling her onto the couch until she stretched out on top of him.

And they really kissed. Passionately. Crazy. Out of control. The kind of frantic and sure touches that came from experience. He rocked her hips against his with guiding pressure, the hardening heat of him searing her.

She spread her legs to straddle him, bringing the core of her against the rigid heat of him. Desire pooled within her, bringing a moist heat where her body met his. She whimpered with need, her hungry hands urging his mouth more firmly against hers.

One strong arm secured her while he tunneled under her shirt and upward in a tingling path along her side. She prayed he wouldn't stop, her breast already anticipating his touch. He cupped her, his thumb circling gentle brushes that sent sparks of almost painful intensity sprinkling through her. If only they could stay like this and say to hell with the rest of the world and responsibilities.

"Sophie." He pressed his forehead to her shoulder.

Gasps of air flowed between them. She forced her lids open and stared into his eyes. Quicksilver flashes gleamed in the moonlight streaking through the window.

She saw . . . responsibilities.

They weren't teenagers content with a lengthy unconsummated make-out session in the back of a car. Their bodies demanded release, a natural conclusion to passions denied, then ignited.

That left only two choices: stop or finish. Really no choice at all for her.

Sophie melted against him, her face nestling against his shoulder. Even as she inhaled the warm, scented crook of his neck, she already distanced herself—in her mind if not her body. He rested his chin on her head while they steadied their breathing.

His hands moved lightly up and down her back. "Remember when I said I was offering to protect your family, not take you to bed?"

"Uh-huh." She willed her galloping heartbeat to slow.

"I lied." His hands went still, his breath warm against her ear. "Unless you want to take me up on the offer, you need to go back to your room."

She should have panicked, would have even the day before, but she'd begun to understand him. He wouldn't take her right there on the sofa when his daughter could walk in. He must be trying to chase her away.

Why?

She wasn't brave enough to find out. With more than a little regret, she peeled her body off of his. She needed to run, run far and fast from this honorable, lanky man who already tempted her more than she wanted to admit.

Sophie picked up her empty ice-cream carton and backed away from him all the way into the kitchen without taking her eyes off him. He stared back, his hand on his chest, his eyes at half-mast with a smoky heat that seared her. Turning, she set her empty Tupperware carton in the sink and made tracks back to her room.

If only she could toss aside her new insights on David as easily, because right now, she wasn't sure if she could hold out through the night.

SEVEN

Childish squeals floated up to the porch from the sun-baked shore, enticing Sophie. But work didn't disappear, even on weekends. She reclined on the beach lounger with a legal pad, brainstorming a list of questions for cross-exam on Monday, while David swung a golf club, hitting practice balls along the shore.

On her other side, the children played tag football with Madison and Geoffrey Vaughn. Her boss had been surprised at her change of locale for the weekend but expressed concern over the car accident. He'd agreed it was better to be safe than sorry, and if she needed somewhere else to stay, to consider his house available. Geoffrey had been flexible about adding Haley Rose to his plans to play catch with Brice—except Madison couldn't catch, so they'd swapped to tag football.

And David had been adamant about not discussing the case in front of Vaughn. Which seemed silly considering any information she had, her boss could access.

But they'd plowed through files this morning. She needed time for the information to shuffle around in her head until it slid together to form a complete picture.

So she let herself think and stare off—where David happened to be.

Sun gleaming down on him, David whipped the golf club again, muscles rippling. She'd heard single women whisper around the watercooler when he'd become a bachelor again, about how he'd played the semipro circuit for a while before going to college. She'd didn't know much about the sport, but he sure appeared top tier to her.

Not that he'd looked her way this morning. He had barely spoken to her all day, instead quiet and irritable. He must have depleted his store of words the night before.

At least the grump would be easier to resist than the man of moody confidences. "David, would you please quit glaring at Geoffrey."

"If your boss touches my sister one more time, I'm going to cuff him to the dock."

"She's an adult. Don't you think the overprotective brother routine is a little silly?"

He grunted. *Swack.* Another ball went flying down the shore.

Yet in spite of his grouchy mood, he'd filled the electric churn with more ingredients for homemade ice cream—lemon this time. Had David decided to make more after noticing her midnight kitchen raid? The possibility of such thoughtfulness touched her.

She peered over the rims of her sunglasses. "Maybe now you'll quit asking if he and I are dating."

"Funny, Sophie, very funny." David's arms flexed as he swung the golf club again. His polo shirt stretched across his broad shoulders.

Then he reached for more practice golf balls, his khaki shorts showcasing that fine butt and long legs. Given half an opportunity and a bonfire, she would burn every pair of his shorts.

And he wasn't even looking at her.

The sun warmed her legs below the hem of her shorts. Watching David warmed the rest of her. A contrary corner of her ego made Sophie want to stretch.

Instead, she drew her legs up and tucked her chin on her knees. Who was she kidding? Her legs weren't model long. She was happy in her skin, damn it.

Sophie studied the grumpy jet jock fluidly *swacking* golf balls. Twenty-four hours of make-believe family time had provoked a melancholy longing. She had wanted a life like this for her son, for herself. The shared laughter of a core family—man, woman, children.

While the ideal family picture was a dream, it wasn't worth risking what she'd fought so hard to build the past year.

David tapped another ball in place, lining up his drive. "Vaughn already spent the day here. Why do we have to feed him, too?"

"You're the one who wanted everyone to stick together." She knew he meant well, but she still resented his controlling attitude.

Sophie had already decided Brice shouldn't leave the house with Geoffrey. David hadn't given her a chance to speak. Just as he hadn't discussed the call he'd made to the auto shop this morning until after the fact. The mechanic had not looked over her car yet, but David said he'd alerted the guy to be on the lookout for anything suspicious.

All of which Sophie could have handled on her own.

They were supposed to be working as a team this weekend. Why couldn't he have discussed it with her first? His intentions were honorable—just a bit heavy-handed. "What's the harm in having Geoffrey here?"

"So he pitched a ball around with our kids for an hour," David grumbled. "I don't have to give him my sister in exchange."

She dropped her notepad to the chair and swung her legs to the side of the lounger. "Madison is only being polite. Even if she likes him, so what?"

"Military marriages are tougher than most. My sister doesn't need to set herself up for failure." *Swack.*

Did that mean David intended to spend the rest of his life single? Or just the rest of his career? And why did it even matter to her?

She couldn't deny he was hot. Last night had proven in no uncertain terms how attracted they were to each other. Yet in spite of their kiss and heated tangle on the sofa that had stopped a hair shy of consummation, David hadn't made a single move on her all day. Her body felt languid with longing, the close quarters having added a familiarity to their relationship. From behind her sunglasses, Sophie looked at his bare feet dusted with dried sand. What would he do if she brushed her foot along the top of his?

Sophie pulled away and crossed her legs yoga style, the electric churn beginning to labor behind her as the ice cream thickened. She needed some space to reestablish objectivity. Now. They still had two more nights left in the same house. She would stay away from that refrigerator—and the man behind the homemade ice cream—even if she had to lock herself in her room.

Sophie nudged her sunglasses. "I should have my new locks in place by Monday afternoon."

"Good." He jabbed his golf club back into the bag and jogged over to the ice-cream churn.

"Complete with a state-of-the-art security system." Which would leave them eating peanut butter into the next century.

Once the Vasquez case ended, she would have a better handle on her finances. Then she could set a stable plan into place for herself, Brice, and Nanny. Her first responsibility must be her son's security.

David dipped out a dripping glob of lemon ice cream. "Will you taste this for me?"

Life wasn't playing fair today.

Knowing she should take it from his hand didn't stop her from pressing her palms on her knees and leaning toward him. Slowly, she closed her mouth over the spoon. Her eyelids fluttered shut as the tart flavor slid over her tongue. She couldn't have suppressed her moan if she'd tried.

David watched Sophie savor the lemon ice cream, her tongue peeking out to steal the creamy dab left in the corner of her mouth. He almost groaned right along with her. Keeping his distance, honoring the fact she didn't want a relationship, was just about to kill him. He didn't think he could stand another cold shower. He couldn't decide which was harder, him or that leather couch he'd slept on last night.

At the moment, no real contest.

All this together time was really ratcheting his bad mood to an all-new high, reminding him of how he'd failed his daughter, his stepson, too. He'd failed to hold the family together, and now both kids had lost a mother and each other. Then Vaughn had to show up. Even his sister fawned all over the guy.

Shit.

He looked back at Sophie and damned if her eyes weren't focused on the beach, too, on the image of the children playing together. Then she looked at him again. There was no missing the hunger in her expression. Memories of last night's kiss hummed right there between them. He honest to God hadn't intended to do that, had only meant to talk a little, put her at ease so she would relax and open up during their work discussion. Instead, all the chitchat in the dark had just wrapped around them until he reached for her.

The connection he felt to this woman scared him shitless.

So he'd done what any man does when he wants to get rid of a woman determined to pick at his soul. He'd hit on her, which, of course, made his torment worse.

Thank heaven Monday and the installation of a new security system would mark an end to playing house. Sophie could move back into her fancy home, and he would return to his Spartan lifestyle.

Absently shoveling another spoonful of ice cream, he counted the hours until Monday morning. The ice cream melted in his mouth. He would miss her, miss the noise of a family. He swallowed and set aside the bowl, appetite ruined.

* * *

Watching the sun sink, Sophie propped her elbows on the dock railing and listened to the roaring of boats. Lights blinked in the distance. This whole day had been frustrating on too many levels. She wasn't used to feeling so out of control. And then, to add heartache to frustration, she'd been tormented with family scenarios all day. She couldn't miss her son's happiness or how her quiet boy came out of his shell.

She tugged her hair tie off and put it on her wrist. Wind tore at her and she tipped her face into the night air, relishing the sensation. She surrendered to the awakening. It was time to reclaim her life, not the same one she had before. But then this year had changed her.

She wouldn't allow herself to be swept along as she had during her marriage to Lowell. But she couldn't fight the tide as she had for the last year.

Time to swim. She needed to give up her house, move someplace she could afford, and show her son how to respect the past without clinging to it.

The even tread of footsteps echoed along the planked walkway. Not bothering to confirm with a look, she recognized David's loping stride. He eased beside her, resting his elbows by hers. David shifted his weight forward to one knee until he stood shoulder to shoulder with Sophie. Her bare feet almost touched his running shoes.

A fish jumped from the water below her, then plopped in again leaving circles widening along the surface. "Don't bother preaching about safety. I know I shouldn't be out here alone."

"We all need space sometimes." David stared at his hands clasped loosely in front of him. "Besides, I seriously doubt you're going to get in a car wreck here on the dock," he joked, even though she knew as well as he must that the threats were larger.

But she appreciated his attempt to ease the strain all the same.

She gestured out over the water, sun sinking fast. "Those kids on Jet Skis over there look ferocious."

He laughed along with her.

Definitely an intoxicating day.

Was that why he'd come out here? For more? For her?

She glanced back at the house. "Is Brice all right?"

"Just fine." His arms rested beside hers on the dock railing, as close as he could be without touching her. "He and Haley Rose are playing video games with your grandmother."

"With my *grandmother*?"

"She's not too shabby."

His face was close, near enough that if she arched up on her toes, she could kiss him. She watched his mouth move as he spoke, a hunger stirring in her belly.

"Madison is in her room, doing her Pilates or yoga or meditation. I'm not sure but the music is definitely . . . unique."

She wanted to kiss his smile more than she wanted air. She also wanted to tear his clothes from his body and have him here, in the water or even on the dock—if it was a little more private.

What the hell was going on with her?

She wasn't the rip-a-man's-clothes-off type. She was more the candlelight-and-flowers sort, sensual romanticism, not gritty passion. Making a change in her address was one thing. Taking on an affair with this man was a different matter altogether . . . if she dared.

He turned toward her, and her hand settled on his chest, her fingers gripping the warm cotton of his polo shirt. She felt his heart beat faster. Touching him, angling into the kiss was beginning to become such a natural thing . . .

A squeal sounded behind them. Sophie jumped back. David straightened, his shoulders rolling.

Haley Rose raced down the dock, an oversize shirt from summer camp drooping off one shoulder, her knees still covered with sand. "Dad, we have a question."

Brice walked after her, slower, his feet dragging. Nanny watched from the balcony until the children stopped beside them, then she tucked inside again.

The children stopped side by side. One so fair, one so dark, both so precious. Haley Rose was a great kid. David had done a good job on his own, and she knew how tough that was.

Curious furrows trenched in Haley Rose's forehead as she looked from Sophie to David, then back again. She brushed a tangle of plastic bracelets up her arm in a clear imitation of her aunt.

Finally she elbowed Brice in the side. "Ask her."

Brice stuffed his hands in his pockets and nudged Haley Rose none too gently with his shoulder. "This was your idea."

"Aw, Brice, come on. Just try." She hip bumped him.

Sophie leaned back against the railing. "Just try what, Brice?"

"It's just a kiddie amusement park. No big deal."

Guilt kicked in. She'd been so immersed in the court case—and David—she'd forgotten about the school fund-raiser with the amusement park offering a percentage kickback to help pay for the new gym.

Haley Rose yanked her father's hand. "Can he go? Can we go?"

Her syrupy smile could have slathered a stack of pancakes. The little manipulator even turned in her toes, the tips of her shoes touching. "Dad, please talk to Sophie.

You promised *I* could go, and I can't leave Brice behind, but he says his mom doesn't have the money . . ."

Sophie gasped and David cut her short. "Haley Rose . . ."

Sophie interrupted. "It's okay. She's just repeating what she heard."

Brice pulled himself upright. "Sorry, Mom."

Sophie brushed Brice's sandy hair off his forehead. "I just wished you'd talked to me."

Her son looked so much like Lowell, her heart twisted. But he wasn't like her carefree husband. Brice was a worrier. All the more reason to get her life in order.

Brice ducked from under her hand and grabbed Haley Rose by the elbow. "Come on. Let's go back inside. I'm gonna beat your Wii bowling high score."

Haley Rose exhaled a martyred sigh. "I guess that means we're all stuck here in the house together for the whole entire evening."

The whole entire evening. Together. In the house. David's gaze slammed into Sophie's. They stared at each other for a blink.

Sophie chewed her lip. "Do you think going would be, uh . . ."

Safe. She left the word unsaid but his eyes clearly registered.

He nodded slowly. "We'll be in my car, in a very public place."

Which helped on a number of levels, like giving them a buffer rather than sitting together here all night turned inside out with wanting each other and not knowing what the hell to do about it.

She pulled the hair tie off her wrist and scraped back her hair into a low ponytail. "We could eat supper at the amusement park."

Footsteps echoed on the dock and Sophie looked over fast. Madison walked toward them, looking sleek as ever in black Lycra pants and a tank. Her hair lifted in the wind, held back only by a headband. How had she slipped up on them? She had such an airy way of moving.

"Are you four ready for supper yet? I have a stack of take-out menus to choose from."

David's hand fell on Sophie's shoulder. "Mad, we're heading over to the amusement park. Want to come with us?"

She scrunched her nose. "Too much cotton candy and caramel apple temptation. I think I'll pass."

Haley Rose linked fingers with her aunt, bracelets and long, dark hair giving Haley Rose a mini-me look up next to Madison. "There's other stuff to do there besides eat. You'll have fun."

Madison smoothed her hand over her niece's head. "I think I can figure out something to keep myself entertained. Go enjoy your outing with your parents."

Haley Rose scrunched her nose in Brice's direction. "I hope nobody thinks you're my brother."

He rolled his eyes. "Who cares what people think? It's not like we're a family."

Family? Sophie looked up fast at David.

Panic tingled in her veins. Only a few hours spent together and things were spiraling out of control. An affair would be easy.

But family? That was a whole other matter.

* * *

Madison fed lemon ice cream to her naked lover as they stretched out on a white faux-fur rug in front of the fireplace. She'd cranked the A/C to counteract the fireplace crackling . . . romantically? She shied away from the softer image that word created.

Not romantically—sensually. Her encounters with Caleb were about sex. They both agreed on that point from the start. She'd been hurt too many times in the past, expecting more from a man only to have him take everything she offered and give nothing of himself back.

With Caleb, everything was out in the open, the ground rules were clear. This man wasn't going to have the chance to divorce her for a trophy wife. Caleb definitely wasn't like her first husband who'd left her unsatisfied, then blamed her for being frigid.

And her abusive boyfriend back when she was in high school? She would kill any man who ever dared to slap her around now.

She dipped another bite of ice cream and offered it to Caleb.

He cleaned the spoon, then kissed her wrist tenderly. "Are you sure we're alone for the evening? It would be embarrassing as hell to have someone walk in on us."

"The grandmother went to a friend's house until ten. The amusement park is open until one a.m. I figure we're easily safe until nine thirty. Which gives us twenty-five more minutes. Think you're up to some speed sex?"

He lifted a lock of her hair and stroked the full length. "I would just hate for anyone to walk in and see you, anyone other than me, I mean." He squeezed her hip gently, his palm calloused and perfectly masculine against her skin. "Because you are the most amazing woman I've ever been with, and I'm not liking the idea of sharing."

"Feeling possessive is against the rules." She gripped his wrist and pushed his arm away.

"Are you seeing someone else?" he asked casually, too much so for the heat in his green eyes.

"You mean am I sleeping with someone else?"

"Are you?" His voice went hard.

She didn't know whether to be irritated or flattered. Then she reminded herself of how crummy his life was right now with the trial, the possibility of losing his career, even his freedom.

She set aside the bowl of ice cream and cradled his face. "I'm not seeing or sleeping with anyone else. Believe me, you're all the boy toy I can keep up with."

He smiled tightly.

"What? Did that upset you?" She stroked down his deliciously taut six-pack until she cradled the weight of him in her hand. "Isn't sex all men think about?"

"All I think about is that damn trial—except when I'm with you." He went harder in her hand.

She stroked him, circling her fist down and up again. "Then let me help you really forget."

A flash of relief shot through her that she could lose herself in this, in being with Caleb, in exploring all the fantasies and sensuality that had been denied to her in her previous relationships. Here, with Caleb, finally she was in control of her pleasure.

And his.

Angling over him, she took him in her mouth. Groaning, he sagged back onto the rug as she worked him with her tongue and her hand. As hard as he was, he should be finished well before those twenty-five minutes were up. Even now, his whole body went rigid.

Abruptly, he grabbed her by the waist and hefted her away. "Someone's outside."

A car engine grew louder, pulling into the driveway. She jumped up quickly and ran to peek through the dining room curtains she'd pulled closed in preparation for naked time with Caleb. Outside in the horseshoe driveway, Nanny sat in the passenger seat of a strange car with a man around her age. They were talking, which bought a few more minutes.

Madison turned on her heels to him again.

"Damn it. Sophie's grandmother is back." She grabbed Caleb's clothes off the floor and sofa and everywhere else they'd fallen as she and Caleb had flung them. She pitched his pants to him, then yanked on her sports bra and leggings. "Get dressed, fast."

He pulled on his jeans, slowly, watching her with heated eyes. "So your brother finds out I was here. What's the problem with that? Maybe it's time."

Was he crazy? Once they started meeting families, having dinners together at a table full of relatives with curious eyes, poorly veiled expectations, everything would change. She would lose control again, become that weak, needy woman dreaming about damned picket-fence promises—and that was unacceptable.

"When we started this, we agreed to a no-strings affair. You didn't want complications during the trial, and I've had enough failed relationships, thank you very much." She willed her voice not to shake over how much those past betrayals had hurt. Every man she'd ever loved cheated on her. Her self-esteem could only take so many hits, damn it. "I'm here for you during a tough time in your life. I'm your distraction from a freaking big problem, but that's it, Caleb."

He stayed silent so long she feared he would win the point by default once the front door opened. Finally, he shoved his feet into his deck shoes, no socks. His beautiful green eyes with the crazy-long lashes went chilly. But that was better than fake promises and vows that never lasted.

"Fair enough." Fastening his fly over his erection, he winced. "Do you see my shirt?"

She scooped up his concert T-shirt from a black marble abstract cat. Pressing the wadded cotton to his chest, she lingered for an instant to savor the rigid muscles. "I do value what we have here. Escapes from reality are special."

"Right. Whatever." He shoved his arms through his T-shirt and yanked it over his head in a tight fit.

The band logo stretched across his chest and she didn't even recognize the name. Her forty-two years suddenly felt ancient. Her hand went to her throat, over the hint of wrinkles starting under her chin.

She followed Caleb to the back entrance off the kitchen so he could slip down the side stairs undetected. At the last second, she twisted her fist in his T-shirt right over an image of a skeletal guitar and yanked him in for a kiss. "I'll see you soon. Really."

He left without a word, and *damn it*, she hated the squeeze to her heart. Turning, she padded barefoot back to the dining room and monitored the driveway. Nanny was still in the car, chatting with her friend and only a mere flash off to the side gave any hint of Caleb leaving. The distant rumble of his motorcycle provided the final reassurance he'd made a clean getaway.

She sagged into the armless chair at the table and shifted uncomfortably. How could a padded chair be so hard? She thumbed away a smudge on the glass top on the coffee table and tried not to compare her life to her brother's.

Tough to do with all his paperwork splayed in front of her. He and Sophie tackled their save-the-world jobs while juggling family demands. She lived off alimony from a man who'd never cared about her in the first place. He hadn't even bothered to argue about the divorce or spousal support. He'd told her he wouldn't miss the money any more than he would miss her. After all, he had a twenty-three-year-old, knocked-up showgirl for a wife now.

Madison slumped back. She spent her days picking out marble statues and reinventing the Kama Sutra with her boy toy.

She thumbed a stack of papers, schedules, and charts alongside a legal pad with notes . . .

Out in the open.

For anyone in this house to see.

Even Caleb.

Her skin went icy as a horrible possibility whispered insidiously to life. Her affair with Caleb had started after the trial. He'd said he wanted to go public, but he'd never argued overlong when she insisted on keeping it private. Her eyes went back to all that information about the trial spread out in front of her.

Could Caleb have been tempted to look at Sophie's notes? Had he been alone long enough to sift through?

And an even more insidious thought whispered through her mind. Could he have started this whole relationship to get an inside look at trial information her brother might have? It seemed crazy. David was on his side, after all. But she also knew David would never lie for Caleb. If something bad came up, he would reveal it to the prosecution . . .

Every other man she'd slept with had lied to her, used

her. She'd thought Caleb was different, that she was in control this time. Now, she wasn't so sure.

★ ★ ★

Sophie strolled beside David as he finished the last of a smoked turkey leg. Content to lag behind the children, she watched Brice and Haley Rose sprint ahead to the log ride. Safely in sight, while giving her a breather.

Heat from the asphalt radiated up, warming her calves. The breeze mingled scents of sticky tar and sweat. The faceless crowd pressed around them. She and David walked side by side in an easy silence that offered a different kind of intimacy, no less compelling than the conversations they'd shared alone. Coming here with him hadn't provided the emotional distance she'd expected, only expanded the ways she felt drawn to him.

Connected.

She twined around a couple pushing a baby stroller and closed back in beside David. His longer strides kept a slower pace to accommodate her shorter steps. Her arms swung by her sides, her hands empty and lonely.

He gripped her elbow to guide her as a teen on Rollerblades sped past. The warmth of his fingers lingered long after he dropped his hand away. This evening spent with David and the children had been everything she could have wanted and feared.

Too perfect.

How simple it would be to slide an arm around his waist, tuck her hand in his back pocket. Too easy.

Sophie looked away and stared up through the webbing of steel bonding the Ferris wheel. Her life seemed just as convoluted as the workings of the carnival ride.

David tossed his trash into a metal can. "Do you want to ride? We can make the kids get on, too."

"I don't do carnival rides."

His eyebrows lifted in surprise. "You're afraid?"

"Hey, I was top of my class in survival training," she answered defensively. "I wear the uniform. I've pulled my time in a war zone overseas. I would rather not add any extra risks to my life, thank you very much."

"Isn't life all one big chance? We control what we can."

Pulling her gaze away from the ride, she shivered. Her husband had said much the same thing too many times to count. "It doesn't have to be all about the thrill of cheating death."

His jaw clenched, his skin pulling tauter across his prominent cheekbones. "I don't do my job for some sick adrenaline rush."

"I know that. But it's still such a part of who you are, being a part of the test world, taking just as many risks here as you do over there." Her throat closed, and she swallowed. "Even on a simple day like today, you're on alert. You keep your back to a wall most of the time. You scan the crowd as if looking for trouble."

"Not looking *for* trouble. Watching *out* for it." No humor shone in his eyes. "There's a difference."

Her father hadn't sought danger as Lowell had, but the end result had been the same. She didn't see the need to tell David, since it would only spoil the night. "Just forget about it. I'm being argumentative. Chalk it up to the lawyer side of me taking over, but I've got that reined back in again. Let's not ruin a really wonderful evening."

Nothing left to say, she turned away from the Ferris wheel and looked back at the log ride where the kids were piling into one of the cars. While the children set off on their ride, Sophie struggled to think of some benign topic for conversation to reclaim the ease they'd felt minutes earlier.

David cleared his throat. "Are we back to juvenile arm punching to avoid admitting how much we want each other?"

His words stunned her silent—for a second.

"I think that constitutes a major break in the unwritten rule to keep things light."

"By all means, keep me straight on the rules. That's your job."

Damn. There she went again, taking out her stress on him, fighting to cover up how much she wanted to jump his bones. He didn't deserve her anger after all he'd done for her family.

She tapped a gentle punch against his arm, her fist comically small and unthreatening despite her kick-ass training. "Sorry for picking a fight. We're not sitting in some war room with me spouting the laws of armed conflict from the Geneva convention. Although I have to think things would be simpler between us if we had a rule book."

Sophie unfurled her fingers and trailed a path down to his wrist. The feel of him grew more familiar with each touch. She lost track of how long they stood there, just staring at each other.

David linked his hand with hers. "I'm not going to make any move you don't want."

"What I want and what's smart don't always match."

He stepped closer. "Then I guess we're in the same boat."

Her body flamed to life, aching to explore the feel of

skin-on-skin contact with him. Would he bring that intensity and generosity into the bedroom? Into making love?

"Hey, Mom, David!" Brice shouted, racing toward them. "That was fun. Can we go again? And how about you get on the log ride with us this time? Please. Don't be a chicken."

Each child grabbed a parent's hand and tugged them to the towering wooden structure, water sluicing over the sides.

"Dad, come on!"

"Hurry before the line gets longer."

Sophie allowed her son to lead her, needing a breather from David. His shadow lengthened on the pavement ahead of her, bobbing and merging with hers. How easy it would be to blend hers with his. But then wouldn't she lose her own defining shape?

She'd been so sure on the dock earlier that she was ready to embrace life again. To stop being afraid.

The challenge was here—not just some amusement-park ride—but the real thing. She could have an affair with David that might even turn into more if she dared.

And right now, she felt like she could dare just about anything.

EIGHT

Bang!

David watched Sophie down tin duck after duck, impressed as hell. She'd been damn near on fire since she'd surprised them all by climbing into the log ride.

Although there wasn't much more he could do than watch, since she was so competent with the gun, she definitely didn't need instruction from him. So here he stood, burning with the urge to step up behind her, wrap his arms around her, and enjoy her bottom wriggled up tight against him.

"Yes." She pumped her fist as she won—again.

Her smile, her grit, reached out to him and his eyes held hers, about as much as they could risk out here with the kids around. But he wanted more from her, and he was sensing a green light from her.

The more he thought about it, the more it made sense. They could pursue this attraction without letting the kids know what was going on. Everyone would be safe.

And safety on all levels had to be his primary concern.

He'd worked every angle he could today, placing calls, then stuck waiting around for answers while he whacked golf balls and tortured himself with more tempting family time.

The mechanic's report had been inconclusive. It appeared the accident had been caused by a blowout. There hadn't been any foreign bodies puncturing the tire. His best guess had been low air. Which even though Sophie said she kept her car maintained, low air could happen at any time.

Or someone could *make* it happen and leave no trail leading back to the person responsible.

Frustration fired through him. A call to the new commander asking him to pull strings and get some extra manpower looking into all these accidents hadn't netted him jack shit in the way of help. Since their previous commander, Colonel Rex Scanlon, had transferred, the unit had been, for all intents and purposes, rudderless. Each test ran on its own, with no cohesive leader. David hadn't been able to decide if the new commander was spineless, lazy, or just so terrified of having anything going wrong on his watch that he did nothing.

Caleb had become distant as well. The enthusiasm that had made the young captain such an asset to the dark ops test world had been squashed. Even if he beat this rap, chances were Caleb would be so tentative in the cockpit he wouldn't be effective.

The thought stopped David up short.

Hadn't he become like that in his personal life? Letting the failure with Leslie hold him back from risking anything else? He'd told himself he was keeping relationships uncomplicated for Haley Rose's sake . . .

Now he wasn't so sure.

For the moment, he couldn't do anything more about the trial. But when it came to Sophie? He could follow this attraction, see where it led, be sure he was going into the affair with his eyes open and expectations in check.

He skimmed the back of his fingers down Sophie's arm. "Time to choose your prize."

A wry smile played with her lips. "I'm having trouble deciding what I want."

"You seem like a woman who knows her own mind." He ached to close the inches between them.

A shower of crushed ice sprayed them.

"Oops." Haley Rose clutched her empty cup, her eyes wide with overplayed innocence. "Sorry, Dad. Sorry, Sophie."

David brushed the ice chips from his shorts. "Don't worry, runt. Accidents happen."

"Hey, lady," the duck-shoot vendor bellowed, chomping her chewing gum. "Are you gonna pick something or not?" Chomp, chomp. "You can have one from this row or two from that."

"Why don't we just let Brice and Haley Rose choose again?" Sophie dabbed the wet spots on her cotton top, only just dried from their dousing on the log ride.

He grabbed her shoulders and turned her back to the dangling prizes. "They both already have a prize, since you've kicked this game's ass. Come on, Sophie. Be a kid for a minute. If you don't decide on something, I'm going to get the five-foot alligator and put it in your office."

Brice reached, stretching up on his toes to get a long stuffed toy snake. "Cool."

Sophie stopped Brice's arm midway and turned to David. "You've convinced me."

She paced along the stall, taking her time, gently touching different dangling stuffed animals, a spotted dog, a long-necked flamingo. As she analyzed her choices, David wondered if she ever made impulsive decisions. Not likely, given her legal-eagle mind.

Sophie lingered in front of a plush brown bear, and he thought she'd made her logical choice. Suddenly, the smile that never failed to drive him to his knees melted over her face.

"That one." She pointed to a two-foot-tall pink kangaroo. "I want that one."

All three of the vendor's golden nose rings glinted in the booth's flashing lights as she unhooked the neon toy. Sophie had surprised him again, but he wasn't going to argue. She'd probably settled because she couldn't make up her mind, and they needed to go home.

Sophie stroked a finger over the tufted head of the tiny joey tucked in its mother's pouch.

Seeing the gesture sucker punched him breathless. He understood why she'd chosen it. The mama with her baby.

This woman wasn't an affair type.

David felt like someone had doused him with a cup of ice.

Brice stepped closer to him and mumbled softly, "My dad bought her a golden elephant necklace once after he went on safari."

Sophie looked away, blanching.

David shook his head. "Come on, kids. Time to load up and head home."

He cut a path straight for the concession stand, where he slapped down a ten for cotton candy, scooped up his change, and searched for the nearest exit. Brice and Haley Rose bolted ahead, bags of cotton candy sailing like kites from their hands as they left the park.

Instinctively, he scanned the thinning crowd in the dark lot. Small clusters of bathing-suit-clad tourists wandered in and out of the endless stretch of T-shirt shops. A handful of familiar faces from the base. Nelson, the old subcontractor with a chip on his shoulder, strolled past now like a jovial Santa with his wife and grandkids, arms loaded with prizes. Even one of his fellow testers, Vince Deluca, sat at a tattoo booth with his wife, both too far away to call out. He would have to remember to ask the hotshot pilot what ink he'd added to his tat collection.

Normal loitering. Enough to keep him alert, but nothing out of the ordinary. The kids' school would undoubtedly be happy with the profits from this packed event.

David offered Sophie a bag of cotton candy. "Want some?"

"Thanks." She reached inside, dodging the blue to pinch off a piece of purple.

Spun sugar had never looked so good. Although a cheap bag of cotton candy was a far cry from a solid gold elephant necklace.

Yes, he wanted to sleep with her, even if she didn't seem like the affair type, but this wasn't exactly the right place to make his move. He needed a distraction. He mulled a question that had been burning in his mind since the courtroom. "How did you get your Bronze Star?"

Her mouth stopped working mid-bite, then she swallowed slowly. "I was deployed to Iraq five years ago. I was in a convoy. A roadside bomb went off, leaving a big hole that cut us off from the rest. An ambush ensued like clockwork."

All too well he could see the mayhem, smell the acrid gunfire and fear.

"We were all wearing full battle rattle for protection, but the others in the truck were injured. I held off our attackers until the rest of the convoy could swing back around with help."

She said it so simply, so unemotionally, but in reality, the heat of battle was anything but calm. Sure, a person had to be focused, but the mayhem? The death? He knew better than to ever reach out and pat her back, because that would connect the moment to too many bottled feelings. This wasn't the place to let them free.

A sigh rattled through her, her eyes becoming clear again. She hugged her stuffed kangaroo closer. "I wonder where I should put this."

The kangaroo or the memories? Sometimes moments just had to be segmented off because there was really no way to reconcile them.

There was a lot more to this woman than a sharp mind and a hot body.

He nodded to the toy in her arms, opting to assume she meant the prize, not the past. "Not exactly a golden elephant."

"It's better."

"Leslie would have rather had a golden elephant."

"I wanted another baby. I got an elephant instead." Sophie gasped, cursed, then filled her mouth with more cotton candy. "I didn't mean to say that."

For some reason he didn't want to analyze, he needed to know why she preferred a cheap, stuffed marsupial to that exotic necklace. So he ate cotton candy and waited.

She shook her hair back from her face, her smile at odds with her melancholy eyes. "I didn't want a football team or anything. Just one or two more children. It's lonely growing up an only child. Don't you think?"

"I wouldn't know. I always had Madison." Keep the answers simple. Give her time. What would he do with the information she divulged? He was a man who couldn't maintain a relationship with his own parents, much less his wife.

"Lowell put off having more until I gave up asking. Doesn't sound much like a model marriage, huh?" Sophie looked up at David, her eyes glittering like dew-kissed daisies again. "The toughest part was that I really loved him. He loved me, too. But neither of us got what we planned on from each other."

He wasn't surprised she'd loved her husband, since he couldn't imagine Sophie marrying someone if she didn't love him. That didn't mean he enjoyed hearing the words spoken. "What did you plan on?"

"Times like today." She sighed, futility weighting each word. "This wouldn't have been exciting enough for Lowell. He needed real roller coasters."

David tried to remember all the reasons he couldn't have her, why they would only hurt each other. Instead, he thought of a woman with tears in her eyes as she brushed her fingers over a little 'roo.

Without giving himself time to change his mind, he draped an arm over her shoulders. She didn't object, so he pulled her head to rest against his chest as they walked.

Sophie clutched the kangaroo and baby joey closer. She slid her other arm around his waist and tucked her hand in his back pocket.

She rested her head on his shoulder. "This is just a break. We still have to work."

"I know." Right now it felt like they were totally in sync. He wished that day to day he could have a lawyer like her working with them rather than the one who it seemed worked against them.

"Where do we go from here with the case?"

And with the two of them?

Her unspoken question hung in the air. Since they were in the middle of a park full of people and their kids were around, he settled for the more literal question.

"We have to return to where it all started. First thing tomorrow, we need to take another look at Ricky Vasquez's house."

That still left them with another long night under the same roof.

* * *

Slider steered his Bayliner ski boat closer to Madison's dock, about fifty yards out, close enough to check out the house without worrying about being identified in the dark. Lights blinked on a half dozen other craft partying on the night waters. He'd scouted this spot well earlier today. He could watch to his heart's content in complete anonymity.

And even if someone recognized him, there was nothing wrong with him being here. He would just claim he'd been coming by on a whim. There might be some surprise, but no one would doubt him or question his attraction to Madison. She was a sensual woman, without question, but the high-maintenance sort. Great for an affair, too much trouble for the long haul.

Sophie, however? That woman would hold a man's interest for a long, long time.

Floodlights clicked on, illuminating the Palmiere lawn a second before a side door opened. Slider tugged his baseball cap lower on his head, boat deck rolling lightly under his feet with the slap of wake from other crafts. Sophie stepped into view, David Berg just behind her. His palm was planted possessively on the small of her back as they made their way toward the dock. The sound of their voices carried on the wind, their words not distinguishable yet. Not surprising, given the way they ducked their heads close together, if it was flirtatious talk. Probably vanilla stuff, nothing with any real grit to it.

Sure, he liked a little kink in his sex, nothing way out there, just some light bondage. Thoughts of gagging and tying up Sophie Campbell made him rock hard. Yeah, he would enjoy introducing her to the pleasures that could be found in real power plays.

These days, *he* controlled his world. His old man would be proud of the way he didn't take shit off anyone anymore.

No one would humiliate him ever again.

Adjusting the idle on the engine, he powered up to edge closer to the dock, then cut back. He reached for a fishing rod and cast into the water, just for show while he watched.

He couldn't afford for the truth to come to light or the charges would be far worse than negligence. His ass would be nailed to the wall. He'd been taking kickbacks from subcontractor Keith Nelson for over a year, once he'd realized what the guy was up to. Nelson thought his gut instincts were infallible. So what did it matter if he skipped a few test runs to shave expenses? As long as he could supply the lowest bid, he could keep offering his "invaluable" services to the test world.

Shit.

Just went to show, the old axiom about getting what you paid for was true. Nelson swore his "adjustments" had never been a problem before the gun turret malfunction. All that mattered now was getting through the trial without their deal coming to light—without Sophie following the paper trail right back to him.

He cranked the reel, bringing in the line and casting again as Berg and Sophie reached the end of the dock. They clicked on the dock lights. They sat on deck chairs, side by side. Their voices carried louder, clearer across the water.

"We'll fly out after breakfast," Berg said.

Slider's ears perked up. He reeled slowly, listening.

Sophie stretched out her legs in front of her. "What'll we tell the kids?"

"The truth. We'll tell them that we're working."

She tipped her face up to Berg. "And what are we doing now, David? Where are *we* going?"

"Where do you want *us* to go?" He stroked her jaw.

"I would think that's obvious." She thrust her fingers in Berg's hair, guiding his head down to hers.

From the way she threw herself into the kiss, Slider wondered if he might have to reevaluate Sophie Campbell as purely vanilla. How her nails clawed Berg's back. The way she wriggled closer, demanding more.

A noise sounded from the house, a door slamming, and then the two brats came running down the wide stairs leading from the house to the lawn. The couple on the dock broke away sharply as a jumble of kid voices carried on the wind.

"Watch movie with . . ."

". . . made a huge bowl of popcorn . . ."

"With lots of butter."

"Please!"

Berg and Sophie stood, laughing softly and murmuring something about no time alone tonight, maybe tomorrow . . .

Tomorrow. When they were set to fly over the accident site. From the sound of it, they were seriously working together on finding a definitive answer.

Things had been so much easier when they'd been adversaries. He really hated this for both of them.

It would be a real loss to the air force if both of them died.

★ ★ ★

Sunday morning, Sophie finished loading the last of the breakfast dishes after the pancakes Nanny made for everyone—which translated into a lot of pancakes, topped with bananas and fat strawberries.

Even in this large home, they were all under one another's feet twenty-four/seven. She and David hadn't been able to sneak even a moment alone to kiss, much less take things further.

Within a couple of hours, she would be alone with David on a plane, checking out Ricky Vasquez's house—not where he lived now, but where he'd been injured.

She'd visited the accident site twice in the course of putting her case together. She knew what the Vasquez house looked like from the ground—the gaping holes torn into the living room where the six-year-old boy had fallen asleep on the sofa. But she'd never thought to ask to see the accident from the air, the bird's-eye view, the way Caleb Tate and his crew would have seen it that awful day.

In an airplane.

David had arranged to rent a private plane at a remote airport for all Sunday afternoon. He'd told her before he had a private pilot's license. She just hadn't thought about going up with him.

David had said the flight could give them both fresh insights, retracing the day. They would leave as soon as his friend arrived to watch over Madison, Nanny, and the kids.

Thank goodness David had made plans for the kids to stay safely behind so she didn't have to explain why there was no way in hell she would let her son go up in a small craft. The trauma, the memories, would be too much for Brice after the past year. His nightmares had only stopped a couple of months ago.

She wasn't sure when hers would end.

Madison sealed away the leftover strawberries in a container. "You didn't have to load the dishes."

"You've opened your home to use for the weekend. It's the least I can do."

Her hostess focused on the seal with extra concentration. "You and David had work to accomplish and a safe place to stash the kids. He's my brother."

"I'm sure we're just being overly careful, but I have to confess the car wreck on Friday rattled me, too."

"This case you're working on, the one with Captain Tate, how do you work together when you're on opposite sides?" She leaned back against the granite countertop. "Are you thinking he's innocent after all?"

Was she considering that now? Allowing her feelings for David to influence her? She didn't think so. If anything, she felt that David was coming over to her side.

What would it do to him when the evidence came through that someone he'd trusted had messed up . . . had quite possibly lied about it? "David and I are both just concerned with finding the truth so no one else gets hurt."

"There must be so much classified stuff you can't even discuss."

"There is."

"And all your paperwork here, it's just . . . minor stuff."

Where was Madison going with this? "We've done some brainstorming, reviewing of old records."

"Today, you'll be able to look more in depth, though, at work."

Sophie turned to Madison, something in the woman's voice niggling at her. Something off. She studied the woman's blue eyes, so like David's, searching for the hidden meaning. But for some reason, her lawyerly skills weren't as easy to tap into around this family. "It's always easier to work without the kids around."

"Of course." Madison shoved away. "I'll take good care of them, spoil them rotten with lots of junk food so they're completely wired when you get back."

Sophie hooked arms with David's sister, trying to ease the tension in the air. "You are an original."

"I'll take that as a compliment."

"I meant it as one."

David filled the doorway, looking so damn hot in a pair of camo pants and a plain T-shirt. "My buddy Chuck just called. He and his fiancée are only five minutes away.

So we can leave soon." He looked at Madison. "Mind if we use your car? Chuck's fiancée is a whiz with vintage cars like mine. She's itching to look over the Scout before they move, and I'm sure not arguing with a free tune-up. If my sister can help me out with a spare set of wheels . . ."

"Sure." Madison reached into her Hermès handbag, fished out the key fob needed to unlock her car, and tossed it to her brother. "Make sure you speed, or it's a waste of a good ride."

David snatched the key ring in midair. "My bad-girl sister to the end."

Madison shrugged, her smile brittle. "Life's boring otherwise."

Boring sounded good to Sophie right about now.

David palmed her back and led her from the house. The hot possession of his hand at her waist made her wish all their problems—the case, the crazy world—would fade away so she could enjoy this time away with him. In a regular world, they would go out to eat, walk along the lake, duck into his place or even a hotel for a long, long night together.

Instead, they were working on the damn case, and in an airplane no less.

Nerves tap-danced in her stomach. Lowell had loved to fly, too, and he'd been reckless as hell, which cost him his life. The first flight she'd taken for work after he'd died had been difficult to say the least. But she was in the air force. It was unrealistic to expect she could stay grounded.

Although, honest to God, she wouldn't have minded a Valium. Or a stiff drink. Something to calm her fried nerves.

Like all-night sex until tensed muscles melted?

Outside the garage, David punched in the security code and the door rumbled upward, revealing a sleek silver Jaguar—his sister's car. He opened the passenger side for her, like this actually was a date. "Climb in."

"But your friend isn't here yet."

"No worries. We'll wait around."

She slid into the front seat and sank into pure luxury. She caressed the butter-soft leather that had never seen a spilt sippy cup or a smooshed Gummi bear. "It's generous of your friend Chuck and his fiancée to hang out with the children and Nanny today."

"They're actually about to move to Texas next month, so Chuck took some time off before he starts his new job with the air force OSI. Jolynn's got some accounting job lined up."

"Then they must be busy with moving plans."

"Chuck and Jolynn are good people. They want to help Caleb. And they know I would do the same for them in a heartbeat." David started the engine, the finely tuned machine purring to life with a sensual power. "Besides, Jolynn had been itching to get her hands on my Scout for months. She's quite the mechanic in spite of her spike heels and love of jewelry."

A female vintage-car mechanic?

Now *that* was surprising, given what she'd seen of the woman when she sat with her husband one day in the court galley. Jolynn was a woman with a slim, sleek elegance that rivaled Madison's. Sophie smoothed her hands over her old jeans and double tank tops, reminding herself David's eyes lingered unmistakably on her curves.

Sophie gave herself a mental head thunk. When had

she become so shallow? But without question, they were both fast on their way to taking things to the next level. It was only a matter of finding the right time.

No more ifs or maybes. A slow simmer started in the pit of her stomach as she let the reality settle inside her. More than anything, she wanted to plunge down that roller coaster and trust that the safety bar would protect her.

She wanted a completely uninhibited night of sex with David.

★ ★ ★

Flying was almost as good as sex.

David gripped the yoke of the Cessna C-172, single propeller but powerful, sleek for a smaller ride. The clear sky spread out in front of him like satin sheets with pillowy clouds. The rush, the power, the total freedom pumped him full of adrenaline.

Had Caleb Tate felt the same way? Had he allowed the rush of the flight, of testing a new gear, to distract him enough to blow a hole into a civilian's house, nearly killing a child?

The rush of the flight faded. The tan stretch of desert stretched below them, housing developments behind them. The Vasquezes' old home was on a family farm rather than a subdivision, their land near a testing range. The Vasquezes had bought the place to give their children room to play and ride their horses.

"Sophie, we'll be over the Vasquez house in about five minutes."

When she didn't answer, he shot a quick look at her strapped in beside him. Her fingers were twisted in her lap, white-knuckled.

"You okay?" he asked. He hadn't considered she might get airsick.

She nodded tightly. "I'm fine. I've flown since Lowell died, and it's easier each time, but I'm not sure if I'll ever climb into a plane without thinking about how he died."

Shit. He hadn't even considered that angle, which made him an idiot. He wanted to haul her into his arms—but then he always wanted that. "We can turn back now. Just say the word."

"No, really. I want to do this. Anything I'm feeling is nothing compared to what Ricky Vasquez has been through." She swept her hair back from her face, so damn beautiful with the sky as a backdrop, she took his breath away. "Just talk to me, okay, David? Silence leaves me too much time to think."

"Fair enough." He pulled his eyes off her and back on the job of flying. He scanned the control panel, altimeter, fuel gauge, instinctively registering readings. "What would you like to talk about?

"You asked me about my Bronze Star. Tell me about your Distinguished Flying Cross."

"You already know the details." He increased his airspeed five knots.

"What makes you say that?" Her voice mingled with the hum of engines and nearly imperceptible rush of air over the craft, a sexy symphony to his ears.

"You cross-examined me on the witness stand and you're a damn good lawyer. Which means you did your research on me." He fed more fuel to the engine. "The write-up is in my file."

"I only know the facts, a simple paragraph with bare-bones details. There's always more to it than that."

And how right she was.

For him, there was always more. Secret missions had to leave out details by pure nature of the job. Anyone who worked dark ops tests or special operations had to check their ego at the door, because there would be no accolades in the news, no parties. Just him and his buds, toasting one another silently with a beer at the end of the day.

And that was enough for him, knowing the job made a difference. "I was the fire control officer in an AC-130. I was tasked to hold off Taliban fighters that were after some pinned-down SEAL team."

All of which was in the write-up.

"I heard you stayed in the fight well past daylight, into the night, at serious personal risk."

The night had been pitch black, with only antiaircraft fire lighting up the sky and ping, ping, pinging off the side of the plane, punching holes through metal. The AC-130 had stayed in the air, circling while he took aim, as he would continue to do until he won or they downed him. Quitting wasn't an option. Quitting meant those ambushed SEALs would have died.

"I stayed as long as I was needed, until a helo could drop in pararescuemen to pull out the SEAL team."

"You must have had to make each shot count for the ammo to last long enough."

"It was . . . tight." More than tight. If the battle had gone on another fifteen minutes, he would have been bone dry, out of ammo and options. "That new modification to the gun turret would have made that day a helluva lot easier for all our guys on the ground that day."

And for his crew in the air.

"If it works properly."

He didn't bother answering.

"David, can you deny that this case is personal for you?"

"Fine, yeah, this project has become a personal mission for me on a lot of levels. The 'gadgets' I test save soldiers' lives. The sooner a conflict ends, the more souls are saved on both sides. So when some lawyer tries to tie our hands and shut us down, sure, I get irritable."

He adjusted the fuel feed again, scanning the horizon for the Vasquez place.

"Well," he said, "anything to say to that?"

She shook her head. "Nope."

"This should be personal for you, too, Sophie; your job can't always be so . . . cool."

"Are you calling *me* cold?"

"Whoa, hold on, don't go putting words in my mouth there, Counselor."

He'd thought of her as coolly in control—before he'd gotten to know her. Before he'd felt the heat of her body against his, the passion in her response. There was so much more fire in his ice princess than he ever could have guessed.

Hell yes, she would be *his*. No more shadowboxing around the subject. The time had come to bring the attraction out in the open, to address it—to act on it.

He glanced down at the control panel to gather his words, the whole seduction gig was so far in his past. There hadn't been time for anyone else since his divorce, and the last year of his marriage had been an armed standoff at best.

This attraction to Sophie was so tenacious and special, he wasn't sure there were words. If his hands had been free, he could have shown her.

His hand twitched to adjust the fuel.

Again?

His brain went on alert, his eyes locking on the gas gauge. Was it his imagination or was the indicator moving visibly? Faster. Until there was no denying what he saw. Fuel was draining from the aircraft.

Training assumed command over thoughts of the woman beside him in danger.

"Sophie, we have a problem with the airplane."

NINE

★ ───

"What do you mean, 'problem'?" Sophie struggled to push the words past panic. Her fingers dug into the seat, her ears roaring with the mingling sounds of the engine and her heart.

"We have a fuel leak," David said calmly. "We need to land as soon as possible."

Sunlight streaked through the windscreen from the wide-open sky. It was a long, long way down to the stark desert below. Although the plane sounded fine, a leak didn't mean a crash. She needed to stop imagining the worst just because of Lowell.

She swallowed down the fear and dug deep for the warrior calm drilled into her. "Okay, so we don't see Ricky's house today. Of course we should go straight back to the airport."

"Sophie, it's more pressing than that." His voice stayed as steady as his hands on the yoke. "We're not going to make it to the airport."

She scanned the horizon, empty except for desert and more desert. "Is there another landing strip nearby?"

"We have to land here, now."

She looked down again, searching for some sign of civilization. No houses, just scrub, cacti, and Joshua trees. Her stomach lurched up to her throat. "We're going to crash."

"No," he said so confidently she almost believed him. "We're going to have a controlled emergency landing in that dry lake bed ahead."

She scrounged up her analytical lawyer side and studied the large, flat, circular patch that looked like an alien spacecraft had once landed there. Intellectually, she understood that plenty of planes landed on dry lake beds deliberately.

But this landing was not on purpose, and the leak could have horrific consequences. "How bad is the fuel situation?"

"At best, we've got three minutes left," he said as evenly as discussing how much milk remained in the fridge. "Make sure you're securely fastened. I need to call in our emergency to the control tower so they can send out someone to pick us up."

To pick up their remains?

She couldn't afford to freak out. The last thing David needed was a distraction. She would hold up her end, wouldn't let him—or herself—down.

Reviewing crash protocol from her survival-school days, she checked her seat belt again, going through the motions by rote, the way training should kick in. And through it all, she reminded herself to breathe. Just breathe.

Dimly, she registered him calling in to the control tower, his voice steady and calm. "Center, this is Cessna five-three-zero-zero declaring an emergency. Have a fuel leak and will be setting down on Delamar Dry Lake. Over."

After just those few words, he went silent, intently focused on the barren desert stretching ahead.

★ ★ ★

Bile burned the back of her throat. She'd stood down Taliban insurgents, ducked through incoming fire to run from tent to tent and write wills for soldiers. But something had happened to her since Lowell's fatal accident. She'd lost her edge, her nerve, her ability to distance herself from the situation and trust her professional instincts.

One breath at a time, she willed herself to focus. She couldn't surrender to the panic-inducing images of Lowell's crash, the mangled remains of the plane and his body battered beyond recognition. Fear for Brice, of leaving him orphaned, mushroomed through her as the plane dove closer and closer to the dry lake bed. Her son would not attend another parent's funeral, damn it.

The engine sputtered. Her heart echoed the staccato skip. "David?"

He didn't answer, his hands steady on the yoke and controls, adjusting the trim.

The engine stopped.

The single propeller on the nose slowed.

Her eyes shot to David, his lean body tensed and focused in camo and a cotton T-shirt. The world was painfully silent as, wings level, they glided downward. She grew light-headed in spite of each measured breath. Her heartbeat grew louder and louder in her ears, the eerie hush filled only with the sound of her gasping for air.

Lower, lower, only a few . . . more . . . seconds until . . .

The landing gear kissed the ground in a perfect landing.

She blinked fast, looking around as they cruised down the lake bed, dust poofing around them. As fast as the crisis started, it was over. The Cessna slowed, finally stopping.

David whipped his seat belt off. "Deplane. Now."

His barked order snapped her out of her fog. She needed to get the hell out of this leaking aircraft. She whipped her belt off and popped open the side hatch. Reaching for her purse at the last second, she leapt to the dry, dusty earth.

Her knees folded and she hit the ground. Sand and rocks tore at her palms.

David grasped her shoulders. "Run! We need to make sure the plane isn't going to blow."

Blow up? It was like a sadistic repeat of her car accident, merging with the horror of Lowell's death. She pushed herself to her feet again, stumbling away from the plane. David's footsteps beat a reassuring pace behind her. She knew he could go faster without her dragging him down, so she pushed herself harder and faster until he grabbed her by the elbow.

"Sophie . . . Sophie! Stop!"

She spun around to face him and slammed into his chest.

"You're okay, Sophie. We're okay." His breath ruffled through her hair, along her every ravaged nerve. "We'll just sit tight and wait for a state trooper to come pick us up. An hour from now, we will laugh about how we hauled ass across the desert for nothing."

"Don't! Do *not* trivialize this." She shrugged off his touch, inching back.

David hugged her again, securing her against his chest. He radiated steamy heat, pure power.

Sophie pushed his arms down and turned away. She wouldn't let herself drown in the molten silvery blue allure of his eyes.

"Sophie, I know you're upset right now." David gripped her shoulders with tender hands and spun her to face him. "Hell, I'm shaky myself."

"Upset? Upset!" Defiantly, she stared straight into his beautiful eyes. "I'm furious."

He held up his hands. "I understand. An accident like this is scary stuff. It's not unusual to be emotional afterward, and I apologize for putting you in harm's way."

How like David to assume he could save everyone, that through the strength of his will he could battle even mortality. Damn him for looking so strong, his broad chest inviting her to crawl into the circle of his arms and cry out her rage at an unfair world. His befuddled expression was almost comical, almost.

"You stupid, egotistical *man*, I'm mad at myself!"

"Sophie, I'm not following you," he said, reaching for her elbow. Her flinch stopped him cold. David held up both hands defensively. "Maybe it's best if we don't talk right now. We need to sit tight and wait for the state trooper."

A wave of nausea choked her. Her purse slipped from her slack fingers, thudding on the ground. It wasn't like she stood a chance at having cell phone reception out here anyway. She grabbed her knees.

"Sophie . . ." He massaged the back of her neck. "Hang in there. You're okay. Look around you, we're okay."

Straightening slowly, she glared at David. The heat

from his body fueled her wrath, one fire feeding another. "Excuse me, Major, for not being one hundred percent logical right now, but the way I see it, I'm entitled to my little breakdown, and I'm not asking you to do a thing about it."

"Not logical? You're the most logical woman I've ever met." The power of him crowded her. "You can reason yourself through a fifteen-minute decision on whether to have a grilled cheese sandwich for lunch. So take a deep breath and let's think through this clearly."

"I'm thinking clearly for the first time since I let my hormones grab hold of me in the courtroom."

"And what did you figure out, Counselor?"

"You love your job. If you didn't have the military, you'd find something else to give you the same jolt." Words flowed from her, resentment jumbling them one on top of the other. She had to make him understand before he could twist her back to his way of thinking. "I'm not denying what you do is honorable. I give you credit for channeling that macho need for a thrill into something that serves a purpose. But how is your daughter going to feel when she doesn't have a father anymore?"

Sophie held up a hand to forestall David's answer. "No need to worry, though. You've already lined up Madison as her surrogate mother. Just like Lowell knew he could play and I would take care of the home fires. Just like my father knew Nanny would pick up the slack with me. Have your children and then leave them for someone else to bring them up while you head off on your next crusade."

Even scowling he looked so damn sexy it angered her all the more that she could be attracted to him *now* of all times. She would have thought him completely unconcerned except for the betraying tic in the corner of his eyes, eyes usually creased with amusement. "Don't confuse me with your bastard dead husband."

She remembered the day in the courtroom when they had jockeyed for control. Stakes had seemed so high as she fought for her case, for financial independence, to stem a wayward attraction tangling her concentration.

The moment faded into the larger void waiting to absorb her. This man tempted more than her body. "The interesting part is that I don't think it takes much heroism to play your games. Either you win or you die."

Rage at David and at life in general sapped her, leaving her light-headed as she gasped through the pain. Did he even understand the line between courageous and reckless? "Don't you have some great joke you'd like to crack right now?"

"No." The gentle comforter had long departed. David stood silent, his lean body one fluid line of tension. "I'm just waiting for you to finish. Come on, Sophie. Why else am I no different than Lowell Campbell?"

The mere mention of her husband drove her the rest of the way. "You never have to face the backlash of your actions. You leave that part to the women, the stuff that requires more gut courage than you'll ever know. We're the ones who pick up the pieces of lives blasted to bits by your latest reckless endeavor. Step in front of a bullet. Smack a bridge. Honorable or not, the end result is the same. The woman explains to her children why they don't have a father."

Even though a portion of her brain whispered how she wasn't being entirely fair. Haley Rose's mother had bailed. David had lost his stepson . . . But the power of her emotions, frustrations, and fears just steamrolled over her logic.

Her eyes fluttered closed. She chewed the corner of her mouth, grounding herself in the mundane pain to avoid facing the larger ache as she pushed David away.

"But hey, kids, he was so *brave*." Her eyes snapped open. "Well, I've got a news bulletin for you, Major. Dying is easy. Being left behind, that's the tough job."

Sophie stared at the dynamic, fearless man in front of her and knew she would give almost anything to feel his arms around her again.

Anything except risk a repeat of the past year.

"So don't preach to me about keeping my head clear." She punctuated each point with a step closer. "Don't explain to me about being strong."

The roaring in her ears faded and the world around her grew as silent as the moment when the Cessna's engine had stopped.

All her senses fine-tuned to hyperaware. Her fingers gripped the warm cotton of his shirt stretched along the breadth of his shoulders. The scent of him, like crisp air and musk, saturated the air and chased away the acrid stench of fear. And she couldn't deny it. Her body burned for him.

His pupils dilated with an answering arousal.

An answering excitement stirred inside her, spreading, heating, sending a bolt of moist desire gathering between her legs. She'd wanted him, ached to have him fill her since that crazy moment in the courtroom, but the desire was nothing compared to this greedy hunger gnawing at her.

Yes, the adrenaline dump in the aftermath was always the most powerful, and the feelings coursing through her were multiplied by the crash. She knew this.

And still she bracketed his face with her hands and guided his mouth to hers.

★ ★ ★

David froze in shock.

For all of two heartbeats, and then to hell with restraint.

He palmed the back of Sophie's head, sealing his mouth to hers more firmly. Her mood changes were giving him whiplash, but then he was anything but steady right now himself.

The soft, sweet sweep of her tongue against his sent a bolt of undiluted need straight to his groin. Inhibitions peeled away out here in the vast expanse of desert nothingness, surrounded by more nothingness. Emotions flooded him with all the tension of the crash landing, the fear for Sophie, the restraint in holding himself in check in the crisis.

Awareness flowed between them, more tempting than a simple grope. Her verbal blast had shocked him more than the broken gauge. He wouldn't defend himself. Apparently there wasn't anything he could say that she wanted to hear.

Her curves molded to him, the lush softness of her breasts pressed to his chest, the give of her hips fitting into the cradle of his. They'd kissed before, but this was a whole different sort of coming together.

Unvarnished. Raw. Lust. Fueled by the life-and-death moment in the air.

She gripped his shoulders, her fingernails digging through cotton to push half-moons into his flesh. The power of her need fed his. His hands tangled in her hair, swept over her back and down to cup her bottom, lifting her, bringing her closer. Her legs slid up and around his waist, spreading her wide and hot against him.

"Sophie," he groaned against her mouth. "I want to be buried inside you right now, but this place is far from a bed and any of the romantic niceties you deserve."

Her arms went around his neck, her legs holding strong. "What I want, what I *deserve*, is to quit fighting this attraction. I need you here and now."

"God, Sophie." He pressed his face into the curve of her neck, drawing in the jasmine perfume of her shampoo. "You're killing me here."

Her legs slid down and she angled her face to look at him. "But you don't really want this."

He combed his fingers through her hair. "Wrong. I want you, make no mistake, but is this really the time or the place?"

"This is exactly the right time and place."

There was no missing the fiery conviction in her voice and eyes.

Still, he pressed, "You have to know that's adrenaline talking."

"What's so wrong with that as long as I'm a hundred percent sure this is what I want? And believe me, I want you. Here. Now. Quit trying to protect me all the time and just *be* with me."

The driving urge to keep her safe encompassed more than one level. "That's easier said than done. Hell, Sophie, I don't have protection."

A smile curved her kissed-plump lips. "I do."

She leaned to scoop her purse from the ground and yanked it open. She unzipped a hidden pouch and pulled out—thank God—four condoms, neatly folded.

"Ambitious woman."

"How long do you think we have before the state trooper arrives?"

He looked at his watch and the midafternoon sun over the deserted stretch of sand. "An hour, but we'll hear him coming long before he gets here."

She pressed the condoms into his hand and folded his fingers over them. "Then the question is, Do you want to have sex, here and now? No niceties, just you and I together . . ."

His free hand covered her breast.

Her mouth snapped shut, and her eyes fluttered closed. Her head fell back as she arched her spine, fitting her more firmly into his palm. He stroked and explored, and wondered where the hell control had gone. But then everything was a power struggle with Sophie.

Gripping his wrists, she moved his hands lower to her hips. Then let go. With deliberate precision, she peeled her doubled tank tops over her head in a sweep that left him stunned all over again. His mouth dried up, his eyes locked on her as she stood in her jeans and bra, tumbleweed rolling past her feet.

God, she was magnificent.

She reached behind her back to unfasten her ivory bra, bold and winning the hell out of this power play, and he was happy to lose. She flung aside the scrap of lace. The sun streamed over her, glinting off her golden hair, showcasing the tan lines around her breasts. Her dusky nipples were tight and calling to him. He tucked the condoms into his back pocket and devoted his complete attention to caressing, stroking, tempting her as much as she tempted him.

He filled his hands with her creamy softness, dipping

to taste her. He laved his tongue around the budding desire, flicking and pressing her to the roof of his mouth. Her husky "yes" stoked the flames hotter and higher inside him.

She tugged at his camo pants, slipping the button fly free so slowly his erection throbbed. Then—finally—her small cool hand slid inside his boxers. She stroked the length of him, then up again, her thumb gliding over the glistening tip of him.

The need to come all over her hand almost overtook him.

Her fist glided, her thumb sliding over the damp tip and slickening her hold. Too easily he could be a damn selfish bastard and let this play out right now. He was that close to the edge.

Before he lost it totally, he eased her hand from his pants and kissed her wrist, right over her speeding pulse. He nipped his way up his sun goddess's arm and back to her breasts, distracting her while he unfastened her jeans. But she wasn't a passive follower. She wriggled her jeans down and off—which shimmied her nipples against his mouth in a tantalizing brush that sent sparks exploding behind his eyes.

He slid his finger between her legs, exploring the slickness, reveling in how ready she was for him.

She bit his ear lightly, the rasp of her teeth catching just enough to sting without injuring. "Enough foreplay. I want it all. I want you, inside me," she demanded. "Now."

And he was more than willing to follow her order.

He yanked off his T-shirt and draped it on the ground. He lowered her onto his makeshift blanket, kneeling over her. Sand and pebbles dug through his pants, anchoring him in the stark reality of coming together out here in the elements. Her hair fanned on the desert floor. She drew her knees up, her feet planted, and for the moment he let himself just look at her, uninhibited, offering herself to him.

Her eyes held his, intense and full of passion. Something darker lurked in her expression, but hell, the feelings inside him weren't pretty, either. He pulled the condoms from his back pocket and tore one free. Her steamy gaze followed his hands as he sheathed himself.

She lifted an arm, linking her fingers with his and tugging him down until the sand grated along his elbows. He covered her, and her legs slid fluidly around him. Bringing him closer. Positioning him exactly where he wanted to be most.

He should go slower, for her, but Sophie's heels urged him to thrust deep and fully. Her damp heat clasped around him. Snapping the last restraints on his control. This joining was edgy . . .

Inevitable.

The sun beat down on his back, the wind rasping sand over them in a way they were going to feel later. Yet still she rolled her hips against him, her heels digging into his ass, urging him closer.

Deeper.

Faster.

Encouraging him like her breathy gasps that she was *close, so close*. Sweat slicked his skin and hers, melding them flesh to flesh. A flush spread over her chest, broadcasting her own rising pleasure.

She arched hard off the desert floor, her cries flung out. No need for quiet or careful holding back. Her release clamped around him, taking him, holding him, then sending him over the edge after her in pulsing wave after wave. Her nails scored his back, her body bowing in aftershocks.

Panting in the aftermath, he rolled off her, scooping her into his arms and shifting to sit on his shirt. As he cradled her against his chest, he couldn't hide from the truth. This out-of-control encounter wasn't just a by-product of adrenaline.

He was falling hard and fast for Sophie.

TEN

★ —————————————————————————————

What the hell had just happened to her?

Silently, Sophie eased herself from David's arms, needing some distance, and given they were in the middle of the desert, there was space to spare. Her nerves were every bit as sensitive as her well-loved flesh. While she felt the intensity of his gaze, thank goodness he seemed to understand she wasn't in any way ready to talk.

Or maybe he was just as shaken as she was.

She shook out her clothes. Still, perspiration glued specks of sand to her skin with a reminder of what they'd shared here. Never had she lost control of herself that way—not in an argument and certainly never during sex. She didn't consider herself inhibited, but she was the silk, candles, and romantic music sort.

Being with David here had been . . . intense. More than a little scary.

Out of the corner of her eyes, she watched him. David fastened his pants and whipped the sand from his T-shirt before tugging it over his head. The front was dotted with sweat—from him or her?

Or both of them.

Finally, she couldn't avoid his full-on gaze any longer. So she stared back, the wind whipping over her. He reached, and she braced herself for the power of their connection. His hand landed on her shoulder, a simple touch, yet more moving than a full-out stroke from anyone else.

She wished she could reach out as well, but even with her clothes on again, she felt bare and vulnerable.

Squeezing once, David's hand fell away. "It's safe to say the plane's not going to blow up. I'm going to take a look around while we wait for the state trooper."

"Good idea." She nodded, finding a smile and hoping he could understand her silence came from how much their first time together moved her.

And what a crazy time to think of her first date with Lowell.

She'd been twenty, he'd been thirty-two, which had seemed so very worldly to her then. He'd gone all out with a five-star restaurant, paid the lounge singer extra to serenade her, even bought exotic flowers. She still had one of the blooms pressed in an album.

It seemed a little cliché now that she looked back. A lot of glitz and not much substance, especially as time wore on. But it had seemed so wonderful in the beginning.

Which made her question what she was feeling now.

Her gaze tracked over to David at the plane. He'd already opened the engine compartment and now he lay flat on his back underneath the belly of the craft. As a military systems tester, he would have a more in-depth knowledge of an airplane's mechanics than the average aviator.

Of course nothing about David was average.

He tucked back out from under the plane and rolled to his feet. "Sophie, come here."

She wasn't ready to face him yet, but hiding seemed juvenile and would give too much credence to how rattled she was. So she braced her shoulders and walked to him.

"What's wrong?" She closed the distance between them, sand in her shoe scratching her heel.

"You need to see this." Frowning, he rubbed the back of his neck.

"See what?" she said just as the sound of an approaching truck rumbled in the distance.

David flattened his hand to the side of the Cessna, a scowl stamped deeply into his face. "There's a hole in the fuel tank and it doesn't look accidental."

* * *

Three hours later, David climbed the stairs to his sister's house. Sophie made tracks a step ahead.

They'd given their statement to the state trooper and showed him the hole in the fuel tank that looked deliberate. They'd questioned her on her cases, certain she must be the target, especially since she was involved in the high-profile Vasquez case. Investigators were on it, and Sophie had alerted the Office of Special Investigations on base to let them know someone had made an attempt on her life.

Prints would be lifted from the plane. Video camera footage from the airport would be watched. Hopefully answers would come soon. But not soon enough for his peace of mind. It was like Sophie was a sitting duck—a break-in, a car accident, a plane crash, all within the span of less than a week.

It was impossible to discount as coincidence. Someone

was after her. Most disturbing, how did that person know where they'd been going today?

One thing was clear, this threat was not going away. She needed round-the-clock protection, and her son and grandmother should leave town.

Not that she'd elaborated on her plans. She wasn't speaking much at all.

"Sophie." He pressed a hand to the door, stopping her. "We have to talk about what happened in the desert."

She looked up, her eyes wary. "Now?"

"About what happened with the plane," he clarified. "We should come up with a plan before we speak with the kids."

"I know. I've been thinking since we left the station." She rubbed her arms.

She was radiating a freaked-out, stand-back vibe he couldn't miss. With grueling certainty, he realized he'd launched himself into a situation that made his relationship with Leslie look like a picnic.

"What did you decide?"

"I'm going to send Brice and Nanny to visit some relatives back in Los Angeles. I have to stay here because of the Vasquez case."

He stepped closer without touching. "You have to know I can't just walk away from you."

"What happened between us today . . ."

He touched her lips. "I don't think now's such a great time to talk about that. Let's take care of your son first. I'm going to send Haley Rose to stay with her mom. I'll feel better if I didn't have to worry about her being caught in any cross fire."

Her eyes went wide and a little wild. "Oh God, David, I should just go."

"We'll talk once the kids are settled." He opened the door, certain if he gave her the chance to argue, she would be out in a heartbeat. Voices from the kids playing video games echoed, the sounds of family and home.

He was fascinated by the woman in the desert, her passion and fire. He also wanted to be with the laughing, laid-back Sophie from the amusement park.

Except now, she'd closed up. He'd seen warriors shut down in the heat of battle, and he could understand her need to numb herself until she had her child safe.

But he'd also seen people shut down permanently after one too many traumas. He wouldn't have minded a little of that numbing for himself right now.

Caged energy rumbled around inside him looking for an outlet. Watching her walk away, he would have to be dead not to want her.

Dead. She could have died in the plane crash, the car accident, the break-in. Someone was seriously gunning for her. Clearly she must have been targeted because of something in her job. But what? David rested his forehead against the door frame and willed his heart to slow.

Bracelets chimed, alerting him of his sister's approach a second before Madison touched his shoulder. "You're later than I expected."

"Sorry about that." He turned to face her. "Insane day."

"I'm not griping." She leaned back against the entry-hall wall, a monogrammed hand towel in her fist. "I was worried. Is everything all right?"

David straightened, shrugging through the kink in his neck. "Fuel leak on the airplane. The landing was hairy, but we're okay. By the time help arrived and we got back in cell phone range, I figured I was close to home anyway. It would be better to talk face-to-face."

Madison tipped her head to the side, a frown wrinkling her brow. "David, I'm glad you're both safe. I'll tell Nanny to put the pork chops back in the fridge. We'll order pizza."

"Good idea." The reality of what could have happened wouldn't release him. He sagged back against the wall and let the weight of the day show through for the first time. "The fuel leak wasn't an accident. Someone tampered with the plane and probably her car, too. Combined with the break-in, it's too much. Her son and grandmother need to leave."

"Oh my God, David." She pressed the hand towel to her chest. "I don't know what to say."

"There's nothing to say." He kept his voice low, although the video game in the next room was so loud the kids wouldn't hear a freight train. "I can't just leave her out there alone. She doesn't have anyone to turn to. So I'm going to watch out for her."

"Of course you are."

The sounds of his daughter's laughter in the next room tugged at him, making him wish they could all just leave and live on a deserted island. "I think Haley Rose should leave, too."

"You know I'll look out for her while you work. I feel guilty that I can't do more . . ." She squeezed his hand, her eyes full of . . . tears?

"Thanks, Madison, but I won't be able to think straight if she's anywhere near here. I'll be too distracted. I need to get her away from here."

"Where?"

Frustration twisted inside him. "Leslie can step up and be there for her daughter for a week."

"Sounds like you've got everything planned out." She

hooked an arm with him. "But who's going to take care of you? You can't run on adrenaline forever, in spite of what you think."

Her words struck deep. "Sophie says I'm an adrenaline junkie."

"An airplane crash will upset a person, especially one who lost her husband in a crash. She probably just needed to vent." She hugged his arm closer. "Hey, consider yourself complimented she pegged you as a safe target."

"Yeah, great." David nudged Madison's toe with his. "You didn't answer me. Was she right?"

Madison shrugged. "Does it really matter?"

For once, David envied Madison's float-through-life attitude. How strange that their father's overbearing upbringing could have sent the two siblings to such opposite ends of the spectrum: Madison with no focus and David with too much. Too bad they couldn't find a way to meet in the middle.

He let go of his sister's arm. "I should call Leslie."

"Good luck." Madison's smile faltered, her eyes still shiny with tears.

"Hey." David searched her face. "Is something wrong?"

"You've got your hands full now." She shook her head. "I'm okay."

"You've saved my ass since my divorce. I don't take that for granted. If you need something, I'm here for you, too."

"Maybe we could talk later tonight?"

"We can talk now." He stepped closer.

Madison fidgeted with her bracelets. "Later would be better. I need to feed everyone . . ."

"How much prep goes into delivery pizza?" His attempt at a joke fell flat, but it wasn't a particularly funny day.

"I want to make sure when we talk, we're not interrupted."

Fair enough. He had to agree with her on that. He didn't want the children to be frightened—cautious, but not traumatized. "All right. Later tonight."

He needed to shower and change . . . But first, he stopped in the open doorway of Sophie's room. She stood by her suitcase, pulling out a change of clothes. The pink kangaroo seemed to taunt David from its perch on the pillows.

A surge of protectiveness for all of them rolled over him like a rogue wave. And he knew full well if she saw what was in his eyes right now, she would only run further away. So he backed into the hall, reaching for his cell phone to call Leslie.

He didn't know if Sophie could even open herself up enough to let him into her life, into her heart. But whether she wanted to admit it or not, she needed him.

* * *

Freshly showered, Sophie slid Brice's shorts out of the drawer and stacked them in the small roll bag to go with Nanny to stay with relatives in Los Angeles—where she'd grown up before she'd come to Vegas for college and met Lowell.

God, he was all over her thoughts today.

Lowell hadn't wanted her to go into the military, but she'd already committed to an ROTC scholarship to pay for college. She hadn't wanted to be a burden on her grandparents when they'd already done so much, bringing her up after her father had died.

He'd even moved with her when she'd been stationed away from Vegas, vowing it was okay. He could start a casino in North Dakota on a reservation when she'd been stationed at Minot Air Force Base. He'd made frequent trips back to Vegas, keeping a condo, but she had to give him credit. Then, finally, the assignment had come around here and they'd been able to move home to Vegas permanently.

This was supposed to be the time they would settle down, give Brice roots. But if anything, domesticity made Lowell even itchier. She wondered now if those breaks from family life when he'd commuted back to Vegas had enabled him to sustain their marriage in a way he couldn't once they were together every day. Even when she'd deployed to the Middle East, Nanny had once again stepped in as the primary caregiver. Not Lowell.

Brice shuffled into the room, backpack slung over his shoulder and bulging with the cords of his video-game system.

She offered him a comforting smile. "You're just going to stay in California for a week. Nanny's looking forward to seeing her brother and showing you off. I'll make sure you have all your schoolwork so you don't fall behind."

"Great . . ." He rolled his eyes, hefting his backpack more securely.

"I'm sorry I can't go with you." Her heart ached over letting him out of her sight for even a second.

"You have to work. I know that." He sat on the edge of the bed.

Her hands shook as she refolded one of the shirts, then pressed it to her stomach so her son wouldn't see her nerves. "What if I take some time off when you get back? You can choose what you want to do."

"Sure, whatever."

She sat next to him and wished he would let her just

hold him until he wasn't scared anymore. "I wish it didn't have to be this way, but I need to focus on finishing up this case."

"Don't lie to me, Mom." His chin tipped, jutting just like . . . David's? "I'm not a kid anymore. I know something's wrong."

"You *are* still a kid, Brice, and that's okay." She smoothed back his blond hair. "But you're right that I should be honest with you. I'm a lawyer, and sometimes that means people get mad because I have to hold them accountable."

"This is one of those times?"

"I think so, yes." And she wished she had more choices for a safer life for her child, but she had to play the hand she'd been dealt the best she could. "I can't let them scare me off, though. If I don't find the truth, who knows how many other people could be hurt?"

"What if they kill you?"

She hauled her not-so-little boy to her chest and held him anyway. He held back for a second, then wrapped his arms around her and held on tightly. "I wish I could promise you nothing bad would ever happen to us again. But I can swear I will be very, very careful."

"Dad wasn't careful, was he?" He looked up with wide eyes full of too much wisdom for his age.

"No, son, he wasn't." Thinking about her charming but reckless husband hurt, but for the first time her son was opening up. "That doesn't mean he *wanted* to leave us."

"Whatever." He shrugged, picking at the cord hanging from his backpack. "When I go, are you staying to be with Major Berg?"

Ah, so that's where this was coming from. He'd picked up on her feelings for David, which forced the issue of reconciling feelings about Lowell. She could identify with that.

She chose her words carefully since she didn't know where things would go between them now. Their encounter in the desert had been explosive, but there was more to a relationship, something she'd learned all too well from her marriage to Lowell. "Major Berg works here, and I work here. We're friends and he's helping me with my case."

"But we're here, at his house."

"Actually, we're at his sister's house," she said evasively. What had happened to her world where she had so few friends to call on in an emergency? When she was married, all her friends had been from Lowell's world, and after he'd died, those friends had fallen away.

She'd let them.

"If he's your friend, how come I've never heard about him?" Brice pinned her with steady brown eyes and for once, he reminded her of herself. "I may only be nine, but that doesn't mean I'm stupid."

Forget letting Brice feel mature. She hugged him. The answer to his question, though, would have to wait, especially since she wasn't so sure she knew, either. "I'm proud of how mature you are for your age. But, sweetie, I'm the adult and you're the kid. I promise when there's something you need to know, I'll tell you. Okay?"

Scrubbing a wrist over suspiciously bright eyes, he nodded before an impish grin spread across his face. "Does this mean I can have a new video game?"

"We'll see." She kissed his cheek, so relieved when he allowed her the motherly indulgence. "Kiddo, I love you so much."

"Love you, too, Mom." He hugged her back, squeezing

hard for all of three precious seconds. Brice leapt to his feet and grabbed his ball cap.

She rubbed her arms. "Let's get packed so you and Nanny can hit the road."

Turning away so he wouldn't see her sentimental tears, she lifted out the stack of Brice's sleep shirts. Lowell's shirts. A blast of sunshine across the front promised "Fun in the Sun" in Acapulco. She hadn't gone with Lowell because of a big case. Lowell had flown with friends anyway.

"Hey, Mom?"

She glanced over her shoulder. "What, sweetie?"

"You can leave those shirts out." He twisted his ball cap backward. "I'll just sleep in my shorts like David does."

She held the T-shirts Brice had refused to let go for nearly twelve months, shirts his father had worn. Just as she'd suspected, her son was ready to move forward. Something she hadn't completely figured out for herself yet. "Are you sure?"

Brice studied the top of his gym shoes. "It's not that I don't remember my dad. I do, you know. The way he took me to air shows and out on Jet Skis. He wasn't so great at helping with homework like you are, but he tried with other stuff. Trying counts, right? We had fun."

She smoothed a hand along the worn cottony softness. Her own father lived in her memory, but somewhere along the line, she'd only remembered the sadness, not the happy times. She'd forgotten about the way her dad took her for ice cream on Saturdays, and sure it hadn't been every Saturday—he'd been gone a lot—but as Brice had said, trying counted for something.

How strange to think of him at this particular moment.

She'd been so caught up in her grief for Lowell, she hadn't thought about how losing her own dad could have played into her feelings.

It was too much to think through now. "Yes, it does matter. And he loved you."

"Maybe I can stop wearing the T-shirts now, because I'm not scared anymore that I'll forget him."

Her world quieted. She would never forget her father, either, but when would she be able to forgive him for leaving? One risk too many and he'd died, just like Lowell. Certainly not as selfishly as Lowell, but the betrayal had felt as potent in her young mind.

Did she cloak herself in anger like her son had worn the shirts, to ensure she wouldn't forget? Had that been the true focus of her tirade earlier? Push David away with anger before he had a chance to hurt her?

Brice zipped the small roll bag and tugged it off the bed. The handle gripped in both hands, he dragged it to the living room. She followed, her feet slowing.

David sat on the sofa, Haley Rose on the floor in front of him as he brushed her hair. Strange how she'd just assumed Madison braided Haley Rose's hair every day. She'd never once considered David might take on the job himself.

The little girl smiled, her blue eyes bright with excitement. "I'm going to my mom's. She said it was okay and we would watch movies together and eat popcorn with tons of butter."

Sophie's heart squeezed for Haley Rose. "That's great, sweetie."

What kind of woman had David chosen to spend his life with?

"Sophie, know what else?" Haley Rose wiggled, but

somehow David never lost a strand of hair. "She has a really neat new condo in Denver with a media room and an indoor pool."

David grasped the three clumps of hair between his fingers and layered one over the other. Slowly, large hands that held a gun wove together a symmetrical plait.

What was he thinking right now? She'd shouted some awful things at him, a total lack of control she regretted. Lowell would have walked out. Her father would have just stood there quietly, knowing he would leave soon. Gramps would have hollered back at Nanny. David didn't leave or shout. He'd got quiet.

Haley Rose waved a pale blue ribbon over her shoulder. "Here ya go, Dad. This matches best, don't ya think?"

David didn't look up from Haley Rose's braid, his hands moving at an even pace.

Sophie answered for him. "Perfect choice."

With the braid clutched in one hand and the hair band twined around his other, David hooked the ribbon on his finger. He caught the end of the ribbon between his teeth to free his hands while he finished.

Sophie stared at the blue strip trailing down either side of David's chin. The ribbon looked so incongruous between his teeth, contrasting with the ruggedly masculine face.

Regardless of all the logical parts of her brain reminding her of her vow to stay single, keep men at arm's length, her heart softened.

ELEVEN

★─────────────────────────

David gave the blue ribbon a solid tug, knotting the bow at the end of Haley Rose's braid. As his daughter leapt to her feet, he slumped back on the sofa. Sophie was right in one thing. He was abdicating his responsibility as a parent to the nearest female.

Part of him rebelled at the thought of letting his daughter out of his sight. But he also knew Sophie and those in her life would be at risk until he found the people responsible for these attacks. Which meant he needed to make sure his daughter was far away from him.

Hopefully he would have answers soon. This latest accident only added more confirmation that she was under attack because of a case. Caleb's case.

Which raised the stakes all the more for David.

And what about Sophie? Legally, she wasn't able to leave town. How could he convince her she needed to stay with him? He was putting a lot on the line for her.

If she dug her heels so deep in the sand they disappeared, it wouldn't matter. He was going to win this one.

He couldn't deny the need to stay with her went far beyond just protecting a neighbor or a friend, or even a regular girlfriend. Sure, he'd thought about trying a low-commitment relationship with her, but things were different now. Being with her in the desert meant something to him.

And he wanted to see where that could take them.

Haley Rose turned around fast, tugging her braid forward to check out the bow. Smiling, she flipped it back in place and planted a kiss on his cheek. "Thanks, Dad."

"No problem, runt." He patted her shoulder and looked at Sophie with her son. "Ready to pick up the rest of your things from your house?"

One look at her eyes sucker punched him. Unshed tears hovered, waiting for a blink to set them free. She held a stack of T-shirts clutched to her breasts. From across the room, David made out the logo on one of those damned nightshirts her son wore to bed.

Lowell Campbell's old clothes. The man she admitted to loving in spite of all *their* differences.

He didn't even bother dodging the second sucker punch.

Why couldn't he have met her first, while she still knew how to trust? While he was still stupid enough to believe in forever . . .

The ringing phone broke into his thoughts. Before David could stop her, Haley Rose plowed toward the hall to answer.

Brice shuffled across the room toward David, hands buried in his pockets. When Sophie decided to drop out of his life, she would take her son along, just as Leslie had robbed him of seeing Hunter again.

Damn it all, he'd known better than to wade into these waters. "Did you get everything packed?"

"Yes, sir." Brice swiped a wrist across his nose and leaned forward, close enough to whisper, "Watch out for my mom, okay?"

David tugged the bill of Brice's ball cap. "Will do, pal. I promise."

"Thanks, Major." Trust shone in brown eyes so like Sophie's.

Sophie cleared her throat. "Uh, David?"

"Yeah?"

She nodded toward the hall toward his daughter. Pale and dry-eyed, Haley Rose wavered in the entryway. The blue ribbon dangled from her hand.

"Dad, Mom wants to talk to you. She says something came up."

* * *

Coming home should have felt better than this.

Sophie stood outside her house, chilled in spite of the summer night. Of course, that could have more to do with watching her child leave than the breeze blowing in off the lake. David's friend Chuck Tanaka was driving her grandmother, Brice, and Haley Rose to Los Angeles to stay with Nanny's brother.

Taillights faded down the dark street. If only she could will away the three-hour wait to hear they had arrived safely in L.A.

If only Haley Rose's mother had come through for her.

Sophie pressed her palm against the ache in her heart.

She could still feel the tentative farewell hug from David's daughter, the two tears that had burned her arm. She wanted to make a Leslie Berg voodoo doll and turn the woman into a pincushion.

David had gone to great lengths to explain away Leslie's behavior for Haley Rose, how her mother loved her in her own way. She was just going through a tough time. That Leslie wanted to be a good mom and was working hard to get her life together.

Bottom line, the woman hadn't felt capable of dealing with her daughter in such a traumatic situation. But that didn't erase the pain reflected in a young girl's eyes as she realized her mother couldn't be there for her.

Through the whole careful explanation that no one really bought into, David's jaw had tensed. Tendons strained along his neck, a tic twitching at the corner of one eye. When had she become so adept at reading his body language? The sense of familiarity unsettled her.

At least Haley Rose had a father with more strength than ten people.

Realization burned along her skin. All those accusations she'd hurled at him in the desert were groundless. David was a strong father who'd stepped up where Leslie hadn't. He wasn't like Lowell.

David leaned against the outdoor banister, outdoor light streaming down over him. Nestled in the shoulder harness, his gun glinted in the moonbeams. He wove his daughter's discarded blue ribbon around his fingers.

Sophie jabbed another mental pin into the Leslie Berg voodoo doll. A very sharp pin.

And yes, she was feeling possessive about a man who wasn't hers. He deserved better than this.

David rubbed the ribbon while staring out over the murky night water. "Leslie was the one to file for divorce, not me."

Sophie willed herself to be still and just listen. The lawyer in her knew that silence often worked far better than questions.

"I would have stuck it out with my wife, even though I didn't love her anymore. I wanted my kid to have a regular family. I didn't want to lose my stepson, Hunter. I knew if we split, I wouldn't be able to bring up my daughter, not the way I wanted to. And I would have no legal rights to Hunter. So I stuck it out, and she left me anyway. Hunter's father insisted on a clean break."

With each hoarse word he shared, she could sense the gritty wind wearing away his walls.

He handled the hair tie with such care, contrasting to his other hand clenched against the banister. "I hired the best lawyer I could find, even went to my old man for help. I didn't want some fancy settlement. I just wanted to see my kid and find some way to stay in contact with Hunter." He half smiled. "I guess you don't need me to tell you how high divorce rates are for military families."

She knew he didn't expect an answer. What could she say?

They did have one thing in common. She and David were survivors. Maybe they came out of the fray worn and defensive, but they were still standing.

"I thought I would have to fight for every other week-end and alternating holidays with Haley Rose." He glanced at her, his grin darker, if possible. "Joke was on me. Leslie decided she wasn't ready for motherhood at all, and Haley Rose would be better off with me. Hunter would go with his biological dad."

His pain reached to her. Being a survivor didn't make a person numb. Sometimes there were no words to offer, no way to comfort.

"Hunter used to sneak calls to me every three or four weeks. I would remind him his father would still see the number on the cell phone bill and that he shouldn't lie to his dad. But it was so damn good to hear his voice, to know he's okay. He hasn't phoned in two months."

"You lost a lot in your divorce. Too much, and I'm so sorry. None of this sounds fair to any of you."

"I guess I should feel lucky Leslie didn't fight me on custody for Haley Rose. But all I could think was this beautiful, quirky, brilliant kid—the most miraculous thing I've ever seen—would always know her mother didn't want her."

The ribbon fluttered from his hand. There were so many ways to abandon people. Maybe she'd been better off not knowing her mother, a woman who wasn't equipped to raise her daughter, either. Had her father felt any of the betrayal that seemed to haunt David?

He pushed away from the banister and strode toward his car. Stopping beside the passenger door, he waited. She didn't speak or move, mostly because she ached for him. Leslie hadn't come through for him, and now neither had she. He carried so many burdens on those broad shoulders of his.

Who did David have to comfort him? Something almost maternal flared within her, a need to hold him. And how twisted was that?

"David . . ." She took a step toward him.

His eyes spoke a pain his lips didn't acknowledge. *Life*

hurts. "We can stay here to wait for the call that the kids have arrived safely, but I have to be honest. I'm not sleeping with you under *his* roof."

His clenched fist proclaimed, *I don't want to be alone right now.* "So do we stay here? Or do we go to my place at Madison's guesthouse where I'll make love to you until both of us can't think about anything else?"

His fingers, losing color with the ribbon twisted so tightly, declared, *I need you.*

It wasn't the most eloquent proposition she'd ever heard, especially with his voice so matter-of-fact. But she didn't need the flowery words dripping with emotion.

Right now, that pale blue ribbon told her all she needed to know about David Berg. She turned away from her house and walked to David's Scout.

* * *

Madison sipped Vitaminwater while monitoring her driveway and ignoring the ringing phone. She had avoided three calls from Caleb in the past hour since David and Sophie had gone back to her house to gather the last of Brice's things for his trip to Los Angeles. She needed to talk with her brother. She couldn't delay any longer telling him about her affair with Caleb.

The thought that she may have been played by Caleb so he could gain closer access to David's private files on the case left her mortified—and furious. But as much as she wanted to hide, something was seriously wrong. David deserved to hate her forever because she hadn't told him everything last night. If she had, he might not have been in that plane crash.

She couldn't bear the thought that her brother and Sophie could have died because she'd been too embarrassed to confess she'd been taken in by a man again. She was a mature, experienced woman in her forties. She should have more self-confidence than this, damn it.

Her cell phone rang and rang. And what had possessed her to choose a song from *Top Gun* as the special ringtone for Caleb's calls?

Headlights cut through the late night toward her home, two lights like David's classic car, not a single motorcycle headlamp. Her stomach knotted. David's Scout pulled into the driveway, past her home, toward the guesthouse in back.

Before she could lose her nerve, she sprinted across the house and through the French doors, out onto the balcony. Her brother was already halfway into his home, his hand planted on Sophie's back.

"David, can we talk now?"

He froze mid-step, his head swinging around. "Later, Madison."

His voice was wearier than she could ever remember hearing.

"I'd rather not wait."

Sophie stepped around him. "Did you hear from the kids?"

"Not yet. I would have let you know that straight-away."

David clasped Sophie's shoulder, his head tipped up to Madison. "Then turn on your security system and go to sleep."

They looked so perfect together, she couldn't dodge the stab of jealousy. What a petty, selfish feeling after all that her brother had been through. He deserved happiness. But damn it, so did she, and right now she wanted more than anything to believe in Caleb.

Hating herself, she took the coward's way out, as she always had, and ducked back into her home.

* * *

Stepping inside David's place, Sophie wondered how fast the hours would pass until she heard the kids were safely settled. She desperately needed a distraction.

So much had changed in a day. Had it only been this morning that they'd all eaten pancakes with strawberries? That she'd crash-landed?

Then made love in the middle the desert?

She rubbed her arms and looked around, soaking in the layout of the guesthouse. Like soaking in *David*.

Restlessly, he moved through the compact living area with a denim sectional sofa, tossing newspapers in the trash. The place was far neater than she would have expected, just some clutter stacked by the sofa and on the kitchen table.

She stood adrift in the middle of the living room and looked around the kitchen cubicle. If nothing else, their refrigerators were similar, a parent's refrigerator littered with papers anchored by magnets. Her heart squeezed as she thought of the picture Ricky had drawn of his accident. Somehow thoughts of him had gotten lost in the hell of this day, and that wasn't fair.

Abandoning his cleaning, he opened the refrigerator and pulled a bottle of water from the back. "Want one?"

"No thanks."

"Sophie, it's okay to sit. Just because I want you doesn't mean I'm going to pounce on you."

Relieved—sort of—she sank onto the sofa. The back of the couch rubbed against the cut on her head. While the wound had closed after the courthouse incident, it still felt tender to the touch, rather like her heart. She ignored the pain and smoothed the hem of her sundress over her knees.

"It's late, Sophie. If you want to sleep, I'll wake you up when the kids call." The bottle hissed as he unscrewed the top.

How could he just stand there and talk so dispassionately to her after propositioning her a few minutes earlier back at her house? Then his eyes steamed with unmistakable heat as he looked at her over the top of the bottle. Goose bumps raised along her arms in spite of other worries.

Something simmered in him. Something dark, a little dangerous. Part of her wanted to just take the oblivion she could find in his arms. Another part of her needed him to make the first move this time.

He set the bottle on the counter and swiped his wrist over his mouth. David crossed the kitchen in three strides, kneeling inches in front of her.

Sleepy-lidded eyes stared down at her as he braced both hands on either side of her on the sofa. If she leaned even a hint either way, they would touch. Her every nerve ending would ignite.

"David?"

"Until today, for over a year I've resisted the urge to take you to bed, uncover every inch of you, and show you just how good we can be together." He seduced her without a single caress, using his low, husky tones instead.

Over a year?

That gave her pause—and excited her. But then when had anything with David been clear-cut or simple?

Making love—she corrected herself—*sex* with this man wouldn't be simple, wouldn't be uncomplicated.

A no-strings relationship was simpler. The emotional baggage they'd accumulated in the past hours complicated everything.

He's wanted her for over a year.

His words still sent a ripple of excitement through her. A year and a half ago. She'd pushed the memory of their first meeting to a far niche in her mind.

She had gone to his squadron to question an airman with a DUI. David had been in a briefing room as she stood in the hall trying to decide which way to go. He'd tipped back in his chair and their eyes locked.

He'd straightened, his chair squeaking a long, slow call. Then he'd smiled, a confident grin with sleepy bedroom eyes. *Can I help you?*

She'd always been faithful to Lowell, knew she always would be, but in that one weak moment, she yearned. Lowell had resented her job, which tied her more firmly to the home life she loved. He'd loved to fly, travel, wander, and continued to do so until they drifted further apart in their final year together.

So for a moment, she'd allowed herself to yearn.

Sophie had returned David's gaze, and unwittingly, or maybe in subconscious defense, she'd twisted her wedding rings. The light in David's eyes had dimmed. She still remembered the sense of loss over something so brief but exciting all the same.

"Sophie," his thumbs stroked along her thighs, "being with you today was even more fan-fucking-tastic than I could have dreamed, and believe me, I dreamed about you. A lot. Vivid dreams of undressing you, tasting you, being inside you. Maybe that doesn't sound romantic, but you've gotta know you rock the ground under my feet."

Her hands slid to cover his. "Actually, heartfelt, impromptu words can be more romantic than scripted, flowery speeches."

"Good thing, since I'm not a flowery sort of guy."

"But you're honest. That means . . . everything to me."

His hands slid from under hers, down her thighs, over her calves. "I can honestly say you turn me inside out the way no woman has before."

He stroked her ankles, lifted one foot, and pressed his thumbs into the arch.

Her breath hitched. "I don't know that I can do this, not while I'm waiting to hear from the kids."

"Does this feel good?" He massages her heel, then rolled her foot.

Groaning, she sank deeper into the sofa. "Yes, of course it does. I just don't want you to think this is automatically leading to more than sex because of what happened after the crash."

He rubbed her calf with restrained strength. "I don't take anything for granted with you. This isn't about sex. It's about making you feel better, relax, and maybe even for a few minutes forget about all those worries we can't do a damn thing about." He paused at her knee, dipping his head just shy of kissing the crook. "Okay by you?"

"Yeah," she said, her breath husky and so transparent, she couldn't even lie to herself. "Make me forget."

His lips grazed the inside of her knee, and she'd had no idea how sensitive that spot could be. He took his time, his body wedging between her legs. She parted for him without hesitation, the ache inside her desperate for release, even a physical one.

Inch by torturous inch, he nudged her hem up, following with warm kisses and nips. Closer. Closer still. Until her dress bunched around her waist and the soft denim against her skin reminded her of the sensuous rub of his jeans when he'd taken her in the desert. Tingles flushed upward, all the way to the roots of her hair.

She wriggled nearer, needing firmer pressure at the core of her. He grasped her hips and held her in place while his mouth touched her everywhere just shy of making contact where she wanted him most. Her head pushed back into the sofa, releasing his scent lingering on the fabric. The scent of his soap, aftershave, and something uniquely him. She reached to grip his hair, urging him closer, to the place that ached for his touch. His kiss. The stroke of his tongue.

His smile stroked her stomach just before he gripped her panties in his teeth and tugged them down. She arched off the sofa to help him sweep the pink satin bikini down and off. Cool air swept over her a second before . . .

The warmth of his breath brushed the core of her. She couldn't stop her moan or keep her knees from falling farther apart to give him complete access. Her fingers tangled in his close-cropped hair restlessly, then finally— thank goodness—finally, his mouth closed over her. Kissing and sucking, nipping and licking, he worked the nubbin of nerves impossibly tighter, needier.

And for minutes or however long—she lost track just letting the delicious sensations roll over her—she did forget everything but the feel of David's fingers digging into her hips. The rasp of his late-day beard against the inside of her thighs. The sensation of his mouth taking her as completely as if he'd been thrusting inside her again.

Memories of their abandon in the desert sent a hot rush of bliss pumping in her veins until she flew apart. The power of her orgasm slammed through her, the force taking her by surprise. She bit her lip until she tasted blood. But David kept drawing on her oversensitive nerves, sending her higher again until her cries of another release filled the wide-open room every bit as completely as David filled her life.

Wilting in the aftermath, she relaxed into the sofa. He eased from her slowly, pressing a kiss to the inside of her thigh, then her hip bone. He wiped his face on the hem of her dress.

Smoothly, he scooped her up and into his lap as he settled on the sofa. He smoothed her dress back over her legs, even though her panties still lay somewhere on the tile floor. She didn't speak—didn't think she could have yet—and thank goodness he stayed silent, too.

He'd done exactly what he'd promised in making her forget for a while. But even David Berg couldn't keep the outside world at bay forever.

TWELVE

★───────────────────────────────

Court had been torturously long today.

Sophie smacked her briefcase on the wooden counsel table, frustrated over how the verdict could go either way if something big didn't happen soon. She wanted definitive answers in her work.

And yes, in personal life, too.

She slapped the files inside, one after the other, then pitched her pen on top. She was tired, cranky, and desperately in need of David.

After their encounter on the sofa, they'd made love again in his king-size bed. Once the phone had rung with a call from Nanny that the kids were safe and sound in Los Angeles, Sophie had curled up next to David and slept.

Deeply.

So much so, she'd overslept and almost been late for court. There'd been little time to talk this morning, just enough to toss on clothes and put her makeup on in the car while David drove. They had agreed on one thing.

The time had come to visit with Ricky's family tonight, to review their statements and those of the cousin who'd been babysitting him the night of the accident.

A hand landed on her shoulder, and she jolted. Looking back, she found her boss. Her husband's old friend. Here in the courtroom, though, he was definitely her boss.

Lieutenant Colonel Geoffrey Vaughn leaned on the edge of the table. "Hang in there. This case will be over before you know it, and life can return to normal."

"I'm fine, Colonel. Just a little tired."

"Sophie," he lowered his voice, "seriously, off the record, how are you?"

"I appreciate your concern, and I know Lowell would, too, but I am truly all right. I'm doing what needs to be done to get through this," she said, hoping he would go so she could just leave and rest her head on David's shoulder.

"As long as you and Brice are okay." He spun a loose pencil on the table. "Did your flyboy friend find any leads?"

"He's digging around today into earlier test data on the new gun turret system. And we're going to speak with the Vasquez family tonight. I want to review the cousin's statement."

"The cousin who was watching the boy the night of the shooting accident. Right? Any particular reason you're consorting with the enemy officially?"

"This is a military proceeding. Our job is to find out the truth, not win for the sake of winning." She glanced at her watch. "I'm supposed to meet David, so I really need to go."

"Come on." Geoffrey gripped her elbow and led her toward the door. "I'll walk you out."

"Thanks. Actually, I would appreciate that." She shrugged off the unease prickling along her neck.

Was there some hidden danger lurking in the courtroom?

Or was that simply paranoia after all that had happened in the past few days? She hated not knowing who to trust.

Her gaze skated to Caleb as he talked with his lawyers across the aisle. Could he truly be capable of trying to kill her? It was one thing to accept he could be guilty of dereliction of duty. Granted, that moment caused horrible damage. But it was a stretch to tie negligence to the type of person who would deliberately try to murder her, and David, too, given the evidence of the Cessna's compromised fuel tank.

Could the fresh-faced blond captain be that desperate?

The uneasy sensation of being watched returned. Sophie resisted the urge to check behind her and picked up her pace, her heels clicking against the floor.

When she passed a jean-clad man in the back row, he slid from his seat. The man had observed the trial all day, but she'd thought he was just a friend of Tate's. Blatantly, the guy in jeans followed them, his every footstep reverberating in her mind. Sophie tucked closer to Geoffrey.

She wanted David.

Sophie searched for his reassuring presence. Once through the double doors, she scanned the hallway until she located him lounging against the wall just beyond the metal detector. She walked faster.

She knew the minute he saw her. Straightening, he gave her his lazy-lidded smile, almost like the first time she'd seen him. His smile stirred inside her, like a jolt of warm and rich coffee.

The young man passed her, and Sophie sagged with relief.

Until he stopped by David, looking too leanly handsome in his green flight suit and boots.

"Hey there, Major."

David clapped the guy on the back. "Thanks, Smooth. I owe you."

Sophie gripped her briefcase tighter. "You two know each other?"

David gestured to the guy. "Sophie, this is a friend from the squadron, Master Sergeant Mason Randolph."

Damn, of course. Now she remembered him, but seeing him in civilian clothes rather than a flight suit had thrown her.

Randolph smiled. "You can call me Smooth, ma'am."

"Were you here to support Captain Tate?" Although Tate's supporters usually showed up in uniform and shot daggerlike glares her way.

The sergeant shifted from foot to foot. There was no mistaking his uncomfortable body language. "I'll leave that for Ice here to explain."

Ice . . . David . . . She'd almost forgotten his "cool under pressure" call sign. She didn't like being kept in the dark.

But she didn't want Geoffrey witnessing the tension. "Colonel," she said, using his title to give herself distance as much as to adhere to protocol on base, "thank you for everything. I'll e-mail you an update if we uncover anything new."

Geoffrey walked backward for a couple steps before turning away.

David palmed her between the shoulder blades, his touch familiar. Stirring.

Distracting.

He steered her toward his Scout. She really did need to start looking for a new car of her own, since hers had been totaled in the accident.

But first things first. "Did you send Smooth to play watchdog over me today?"

His boots thudded a steady pace beside her along the walkway. "I only asked him this morning. He was on leave, stopped by to shoot the breeze."

"You could have called or texted." She measured her words to keep from snapping. "I was freaked out here, thinking I was being followed by whoever's trying to kill me."

She reached for the car door.

He flattened a hand on the door, barring her. His broad shoulders blocked out the late-day sun, the long zipper of his green flight suit calling to her fingers to tug it down, down, down.

The air hummed over the place he'd almost touched. "I'm sorry, Sophie. I didn't think of that."

While she appreciated his apology, she knew he would probably do the same thing again. Not purposefully but purely by instinct. His instincts made him stellar at his job—edgy and consistently right. But it also made him a tough man to have an equal relationship with.

A relationship? There that word came again, the thought, the knowledge that the connection between them was getting deep and complicated.

Her heart raced faster. "Thank you for worrying about me."

"Do you want to hear what I found out today?"

An olive branch? She clutched it. "Absolutely, Major."

"How about a Coke for the road, Counselor?" David's

appreciative smile eased the bundle of tension, unraveling it into sparks dancing through her. When his gaze flickered over her legs, David cleared his throat. "It's about a half hour to the Vasquez place. We can talk on the way and give the kids a call on the cell phone."

Her boss's censorious look from earlier tugged at her as firmly as the wind whipping across the parking lot. Damn it, she could work with David without jeopardizing the case. They were working together for truth, not personal agendas. He'd proved himself nothing but trustworthy.

And if she kept telling herself that enough times, hopefully she could quiet the sense that she was making a mistake.

*　*　*

Envy chewed at David.

He stared at the middle-class suburban home and drooled like a kid with his nose pressed against a candy store window. The Vasquezes had moved here after their home had been hit. They'd given up their dream of owning a place with land and horses to move back into a neighborhood. Ricky said he felt safer with houses around him. So they'd rented this place.

A folded stroller rested beside the front door of the single-story, ranch-style house. The minivan and sedan in front of the garage shouted *family*.

He'd dreamed of this kind of life, so long ago he'd almost forgotten its draw. But he simply couldn't imagine getting married again and going through another breakup. Although he had to admit, celibacy had been damn uncomfortable the past year.

Sophie pointed toward the driveway. "Pull in behind

the van. Dr. Vasquez has to leave after supper to teach a night class."

David whipped the Scout behind the parked mama-mobile. Sophie unbuckled her seat belt and grabbed her briefcase off the backseat. "He's taken on the extra class load to help with bills. They need the additional money to tide them over until everything settles out with insurance . . . and who . . ."

"Who else to sue?"

She shrugged.

Guilt replaced envy. How could he have been jealous of the Vasquezes when he had the one thing they would trade all for? A healthy child.

David struggled to stifle images from the day of the accident. Sophie set him on edge, making his memories tougher to suppress. With a will of their own, thoughts of the six-year-old's accident unfolded anyway, one of those haunting images that would stay behind his eyelids even in sleep.

Aided by years of practice, David tucked the horror away with hundreds of others he would never forget.

David leapt from the car and circled to Sophie's side. "Let's get to it. We're already running late as it is." They hadn't even had time to change after work.

She swung her feet out. Gripping the door for balance, she slowly stretched one leg to the ground. Every inch toward the pavement tugged her skirt up, exposing more skin, offering a distraction he welcomed right now. Just when he thought he might have to arrest her for indecent exposure, she landed beside him.

Ricky Vasquez pushed through the front door "Hi, Major Campbell."

The child's face creased with a lopsided grin that

almost managed to hide each wince as he powered forward on his crutches.

Sophie's eyes radiated determination, and his eyes dropped to the Bronze Star on her uniform. Ricky had a fierce protector in this woman, a determined guardian of his rights. Without question, it wasn't about the money for her.

She gave Ricky one of those smiles David coveted, the same smile she gave Brice, the same smile she had given Haley Rose when they'd hugged good-bye.

Ah hell. He was in big trouble.

Ricky worked his way down the step awkwardly with his crutches, followed by his parents. David couldn't help but think of that horrifying flash in time when Ricky would have been hit—something adult combat vets had trouble coping with.

While it would have helped piece together what happened if Ricky remembered more. But still . . . Thank God the boy had no memory of actually being hit. Sophie relied on witness testimony to build her case.

Did the boy have nightmares anyway? He must.

Too often, they returned at night.

He knew that firsthand. Only a strong woman could live with a man haunted by such tenacious ghosts. Leslie had vowed it was too much. But Sophie? She'd even faced the same hell when she got her Bronze Star. Had her husband been any kind of comfort to her?

A couple should be partners.

David looked at the yard, stroller, and porch with husband and wife arm in arm. Envy returned.

With a startling flash, he realized he still wanted this life, not just for his daughter but for himself. He wanted to hook his arm around the shoulders of a woman who could love him without reserve, who wouldn't try to change him and would simply accept him as the man he needed to be.

He wanted the woman to be Sophie.

* * *

Sophie twirled her tongue around the *helado frito*. Fried ice cream. Ecstasy. Or as close as she could get since waking up today. Her gaze slid to David longingly.

But she couldn't lose sight of why she was here. The supper had been designed to put the cousin at ease for the questioning . . . except Juan wasn't around.

Setting her spoon on the saucer, Sophie turned to Angela Vasquez. "We need to go over your nephew Juan's deposition before I put him on the stand."

"He should be here soon," Angela said, sitting at one end of the lengthy dining room table, her husband at the head bouncing a baby girl on his knee. "Juan had a date. Not much longer before your son will be dating, *hmmm*?"

"Too soon. I'm not quite ready for that parental hurdle." She glanced at the silent hottie beside her. Strangely silent. Since they'd pulled up in the driveway behind the minivan, David had been staring at her with the most pensive expression. "What about you, David?"

"Excuse me?" His spoon clanked against the dish in front of him.

Sophie resisted the urge to check the mirror. "Just commenting that I doubt you're ready for Haley Rose to start dating."

That caught his attention. "Nuns don't date."

Dr. Vasquez and David shared a sympathetic chuckle, which was cut short by the front door slamming. The noise reverberated, startling the baby until her bottom lip quivered while she seemed to be deciding whether or not to cry.

Dr. Vasquez frowned. "That should be Juan now."

Footsteps echoed in the hall until Juan entered with his arm encircling the shoulders of a teenage girl wearing a purple dress one string shy of indecent.

Something about her looked familiar. Sophie struggled to remember. The girl's three nose rings glinted in the light from the chandelier, and Sophie recognized the girl from the duck-shoot booth at the school fund-raiser night at the amusement park. Memories of cotton candy, pink kangaroos, and kisses swept over her.

Angela patted Juan's shoulder. "You remember Major Campbell, don't you? She talked to you when Ricky was injured."

The teen went still, then strolled to a chair, his baggy jeans slipping low on his hips. "Hello, Major Campbell," Juan said, nodding to her before leaning in to kiss his aunt's cheek. "Hope you don't mind, *Tia* Angela, but I brought Hannah with me."

Hannah? The girl with three nose rings was named Hannah? Of course, Hannah didn't have body piercing jewelry and magenta hair when her mama had named her.

Hannah dropped into a seat beside Juan. The duo looked like they would prefer a weeklong block of advanced algebra to answering her questions.

Sophie pulled an easy smile, one that guaranteed to soothe any antsy witness. "You probably don't remember me, Hannah. We were at the amusement park this weekend. I won that crazy-big pink kangaroo at the duck-shoot booth."

"Oh, yeah." A weak grin, more of a grimace, fluttered over Hannah's face. "You had a couple of kids with you."

Conversation wilted like the leftover salad in the serving bowl. Dr. Vasquez stared at Hannah with ill-disguised disapproval. David focused on Dr. Vasquez bouncing his daughter on his knee.

That must be the reason for David's bad mood. He must be preoccupied worrying about Haley Rose. She sympathized since her heart ached for the day she could safely bring her son home. Being a parent, knowing how to keep a child safe, was the toughest job. Entrusting her child to others was beyond frightening.

Her mind hitched back on the thought of Juan as a babysitter. Even though the kid wore baggy pants, he was a straight A student.

Angela circled to the teenage couple with two dishes of ice cream, placing one in front of her nephew's girlfriend.

Ricky slurped drippy spoonfuls. "Hannah helped babysit me the night of the accident. They played smoochy face while I watched cartoons." He gagged dramatically before scooping up more ice cream.

Hannah was there the night of the accident? No one had mentioned that before. And from the surprised look on Angela's face, she hadn't known, either. The original statement read that she and her husband had gone to a movie, taking the baby with them, leaving Ricky with Juan.

Sophie eased forward in her chair.

Follow the thread.

Unsure where it might lead, she didn't want to put David in an awkward position based on what he might hear. She also hoped Juan might be more forthcoming without a looming guy in the room.

"Hey, Ricky, would you mind showing Major Berg

your video-game system while I talk to your cousin? Major Berg is a real pro at high-tech toys, but I bet you can beat him. David, maybe you could take the baby along, too?"

Hannah jumped to her feet, her smile glistening as brightly as her gold-plated nose rings. "I'll take the baby."

David's eyes widened with ill-disguised horror at the mention of entrusting the baby to Hannah. Dr. Vasquez looked none too pleased, either.

Sophie rested a hand on the girl's arm. "If you don't mind, Hannah, I'd like you to stay. Since you were here, maybe you can help me with a few things."

"Uh, sure." Hannah resumed her seat with all the enthusiasm of a student facing finals.

Sophie moved her hand from Hannah's arm to David's. "David, do you mind?"

David looked from Hannah to Juan. "No problem, Counselor."

He scooped the gurgling baby from Dr. Vasquez and tucked her in the corner of his arm. The chubby little girl studied him with wide eyes. Her bottom lip quivered. Her eyes swam with big fat baby tears. David stroked the back of his fingers over her cheek until she turned her head and latched on to his knuckle.

David grinned.

Sophie melted.

He cradled the baby while he leaned forward to snag the bottle from the edge of the table. "Ricky, come show me all those video-game moves you've been bragging about."

Ricky eased to his feet. Sophie couldn't help but notice the wince of pain, the slow pace so different from the healthy gallop she took for granted in her son.

Someone would pay for what had happened, damn it.

Even if that implicated David?

She didn't have a choice.

Juan fidgeted in his chair. "I've been thinking about everything, and I, uh, was wondering, do I really have to testify?"

His aunt leaned forward to touch his arm. "Of course you do. No cold feet, Juan. We need you."

"Will they even believe what I say about that night?" The teen stared at the top of his shoes.

"Why shouldn't they?"

"What if the jury just thinks I'm another illegal?"

Sophie blinked back her surprise. Anger rumbled deep inside her.

Angela's eye glinted with anger she quickly covered, keeping her face smoothly controlled in front of her nephew. "But you are not. You were born in the States, just like Ricky. My brother and I came here legally. Your uncle's family has been here for nearly a century."

Sophie reassured Angela with a touch to the arm. "I promise that won't be an issue. I'll do my best to protect you on the stand. We'll trot out those great grades of yours and your volunteer work up at the animal shelter. You need to tell the truth about what you saw for your cousin."

Hannah looked overly complacent since Sophie's attention had focused elsewhere. Time to play her hunch, all the while she prayed her instincts stunk.

"But you two weren't watching Ricky that night, were you, Juan? You didn't see the impact because you weren't in the room."

Guilt flared on both teenage faces.

Damn.

The foundation under her already borderline case crumbled. "Where were you, Juan?"

Juan looked at his aunt, his brow furrowed with fear. "I'm so sorry, Aunt Angela. Ricky fell asleep on the couch watching cartoons, and if he woke up, we didn't want him to see us, uh, making out. So we went to another room. I'm really sorry," he repeated, his words tumbling faster over themselves. "I heard all the noise and found out Ricky was hurt."

His voice choked off. He dropped his head into his hands.

Angela shifted to sit beside him. "If you'd been sitting there with him, it wouldn't have changed the outcome."

Juan looked up, his eyes tortured. "But if we'd made him go to bed, we would have been on the sofa. We should have been the ones hurt."

The teenager scrubbed his wrist over his tear-filled eyes, and his aunt hauled him in close.

Her heart hurt for the boy, even as frustration stirred. Coming here hadn't given her anything new to work with. No doubt, Tate's lawyer would use this to discredit anything coming from Ricky's family. And in the ensuing mayhem, the truth would be buried even deeper.

Although had she been any better in sending David from the room so she would hear everything first in hopes of strengthening her case and to hell with the consequences for him or Caleb? She'd been so busy immersing herself in work to push back her feelings over Lowell's death that she'd only thought about winning, not realizing the grief was still there, perhaps even clouding her judgment. But the best way to win justice for Ricky was by finding the truth, so he could pursue his quest for justice. Not that any amount of money would make up for what he'd lost, but at least things would be eased for him and for his family.

Had she buried other feelings because they were too frightening to face? She'd never considered herself a coward. She was a uniformed warrior, for heaven's sake.

A warrior who wasn't afraid of a gun but was terrified of getting her heart broken again.

Damn straight she'd been hiding from her feelings for David for a very long time. She was attracted to him, intrigued by him, drawn to him. She'd been so busy demanding David to live up to her expectations, she hadn't given a thought to being the kind of woman he deserved.

There wasn't anything more she could do for Ricky tonight. But she could meet David halfway, be an equal partner in this affair they'd started. No more hiding behind her fears.

She was all in.

★ ★ ★

David downshifted the Scout as he turned into his driveway, wind and music whipping through the open-air ride.

The streetlamps over the highway flashed by.

The family life at the Vasquez home still left him feeling raw. And then for Sophie to shuttle him off while she questioned the teenagers? She was blocking him out on all levels. Sure, she'd briefed him afterward, but he wasn't sure that was enough for him. Ever since that day when he'd been on the witness stand, she'd been throwing barriers up between them, keeping him from getting too close.

"David?" When he didn't answer, she tipped her head to look into his eyes. "Are you all right?"

"Yeah, why?" He shut off the engine, night sounds swelling around them.

"You're quiet."

"Just have a lot on my mind." He reached into the back for the grocery bag. Sophie had insisted they stop on the way home to restock his refrigerator. He stayed a step ahead of Sophie on his way up the steps.

Just to be on the safe side, David eased his gun from the holster and unlocked the door. He stepped to the side, shielding her. Aided by a tap of his toe, the door creaked open. After a quick sweep of the living area, he motioned her inside.

She entered the guesthouse. "What a day."

David leaned forward, his cheek just beside hers. "Hold tight while I make sure we didn't have any 'visitors.'"

"Did I get booted out of the military today and some-one forgot to tell me?"

She had a point. But damn it, he couldn't stem the protective urges. "Fine, look along with me."

In sync, they swept the apartment, his daughter's room and his bedroom. No signs of anyone or anything dis-turbed. One look at his daughter's ribbons tangled up in a bowl threatened to knock his knees out from under him.

He forced himself to turn away and return to the living room. He placed his 9 mm on the counter by the grocery sack. "All clear."

Sophie prowled restlessly, browsing his music collec-tion and popping in a CD. New Orleans jazz pumped through the air. She met him in the kitchen.

He followed her, pulling groceries from the sack and trying to decide how to confront her about the way she'd handled questioning Juan.

Groceries?

He double-checked the contents, paying attention now in a way he obviously hadn't at the supermarket.

David reached into the sack. "Do you think you got enough ice cream?"

He tucked the third carton into the freezer.

She slid in front of him, holding a fourth container—rocky road—the fire in her eyes so hot it could have melted the whole batch. "I wasn't sure what flavor I would want after we have sex."

Thirteen

The blast from the freezer frosted over his face. Music filled the silence since David couldn't manage to put two words together.

Slowly, he shut the freezer, pivoting on his heels. The woman lounging against the wall bore no traces of the reserved counselor. Her sultry eyes, dark and smoky with passion, called to him, promising him things he'd barely dared dream.

He tilted his head to the side. "Did you just say what I think you said?"

She opened her briefcase and pulled out a small paper sack. "We used my stash of condoms, and you haven't offered any of your own." She sent the bag sailing through the air until it thudded against his stomach as he caught it.

Paper crackled as he opened the bag and discovered . . . a box of three dozen. His eyebrow lifted.

"You're ambitious." His breathing double-timed. "I'll take that as a yes to sleeping together."

"Smart man." Her husky voice floated across the room as she draped her uniform jacket over the back of a dining room chair. Then she freed one button at a time down her starched blue shirt.

She parted the fabric one flick at a time until her bare midriff showed through the shirt hanging open and loose. Full breasts swelled above her creamy satin bra. He itched to dip his hand inside, then his face, because tasting her beat everything else.

She unzipped her skirt.

He closed the last five feet between them. Their time together would show her how right they were for each other. He could convince her. He had to.

Her skirt hit the floor, pooling around her feet. David forgot how to think, reason, or convince. She kicked it free, her shoes following, each landing with a thump as she flung them loose.

Sophie's shirt flowed over her curves, exposing those tan lines bordering every forbidden inch. He intended to take his time with her. Tucking a hand under the billowing silk, he filled his hand with the tantalizing swell. She gripped his wrist just before he touched the satiny flesh he burned to stroke.

Slowly, she lowered his arm back to his side. "I want to touch *you* this time."

"You can touch me all you want." He lifted a hand to her face so he could kiss her deep and long, without thoughts of stopping because they were wrong for each other.

She grabbed his wrists again and pulled back. Smiling, she shook her head, pinning his arms to his sides. "I mean I do the touching. Just me."

He considered simply leaning forward and sealing

their bodies together. He could win her over quickly. But the passion in her eyes urged him to reconsider. Her smile widened as her fingers lightly scored a path over his hands. He relinquished control, his body hardening in response.

She skimmed higher. Cotton muted her caress as she skimmed over his wrist, up his arm, the near contact torturing him. Her hands played along his shoulders while she pressed a kiss to the patch of skin at the base of his neck. A need too long denied wrenched through him.

Sophie took her time sliding down his flight-suit zipper, one torturous link at a time. Her knuckles grazed down his chest, lower, lower still, gently down the fly of his boxers. Five more seconds and he would trade his bed for the floor and sink inside her.

His flight suit open now, she swept it down his shoulders until it bunched around his waist, and then she tugged his T-shirt over his head. Gusts of air over each inch of exposed skin raked across his already ragged senses.

Finally, she flattened her cool palms to his chest. "*Hmmm*. Very nice."

He needed to touch her, had to soon, but pride demanded he see just how far she would go. She angled forward until her scantily covered breasts brushed him as she yanked the cuffs free. Muscles in his arms twitched, his hands manacled to his sides by her unspoken mandate.

She reclined against the wall, smiling a siren's call.

"Sophie," he groaned. "You're killing me here."

"*Shhh*." One finger rested against his lips, rubbing back and forth.

Sophie was right. They shouldn't talk and risk losing what they both wanted, needed, to finish.

David trapped her finger between his teeth. Blood pounded through him, roaring in his ears, then lower.

He nibbled across to the tender palm of her hand, over her scented wrist. Her smile faltered, her brown eyes darkening as her pupils widened.

All the while, his hands stayed by his sides. He thought of a hundred other places he planned to place his mouth. His body throbbed, and he hadn't even touched her.

Yet.

With a brief caress against his jaw, she pulled free. Sophie skimmed a feathery light stroke down the side of his face, over his shoulder, and down his arm until her hand rested over his. Her fingers laced with his, guiding him toward her.

If she stopped, he would seriously lose it.

She didn't stop.

Her hand curved his around her satin-covered breast. The feel of her was so familiar, yet every sensation held an extra edge of awareness.

Sophie held him against the generous softness straining into his palm, tantalizing him with firmer pressure. Less steady this time, she lifted his other hand to her bare midriff and moved it over the softest skin he'd ever felt, a texture he could never forget.

Her eyes fluttered closed, then opened, staring straight at him. She slid his hand lower, urging his hand lower still, until he cupped her.

David groaned deep in his throat.

The clouds of dazed passion in her eyes shifted. Her bravado seemed to seep from her. He didn't wait for her lead this time. His fingers slid inside the white satin panties and stroked, caressed, coaxed her into moving against him.

Her hands fell to her sides. His stayed. Sagging against the door, she sighed.

His mouth crashed down over hers, and she opened to him without hesitation. He anchored her to the wall, his hands trapped between them as he dipped into the damp core of her. She arched against him as their tongues battled for dominance, entry, satisfaction.

"Sophie," he growled against her lips between hungry, moist kisses. "Let's move this to the other room, preferably one with a bed."

"What if I want to stay right here?"

"I guess I'll have to accommodate you." He hooked his hands along her thighs and lifted. "Or convince you to see things my way."

Squealing, she wrapped her legs around his waist and locked her arms around his neck. "You're going to throw out your back, and that would be so tragic for both of us."

"Not a chance. I've got you, and there's no way in hell I'm letting you go."

He walked them both toward his room, kissing her the whole way. His hands slid to cup the curve of her bottom. His erection throbbed harder between them, and the jasmine scent of her filling his senses only made him harder.

She had to know this chemistry was rare. Special. And something he intended to explore further starting now. He carried her down the hall, past the wall packed with family photos his sister had reprinted in black and white to give Haley Rose a sense of home when they'd moved in.

But he didn't want to think of his sister or his daughter right now.

He lowered Sophie to his king-size bed. She sprinkled kisses across his chest.

Her lips traveled over him, tasting as her tongue flicked across his nipple, drawing it painfully tight. Did she have to embody his every fantasy? He didn't stand a chance.

David tore into the box of condoms.

His flight suit still around his waist, Sophie slid her hand into his boxers and freed his erection. In imitation of her earlier move, he curved her hand around him. She slowly stroked along his throbbing length. His control slipped away once again. He reached for a packet from the opened box and sheathed himself.

Any hope of finesse went out the window. He tore her panties off and stretched over her, his feet still on the floor. She wrapped her legs around his waist, urging him forward. He entered her in a hard, fast lunge.

They clung to each other for balance in a world suddenly tilting out of control. Then she rocked her hips. He sealed his lips to hers, not sure whose moan floated free between deep, gasping kisses. Their bodies found a matching rhythm.

She sighed his name over his mouth, along his jaw, against his neck. Her arms convulsed around him. Already he could feel her breath flow over his skin faster, heavier, hotter.

Her satiny heat gripped him, tightening in spasms of pleasure until his legs gave out and he pressed her deeper into the mattress. His next thrust wrenched a cry of release from her. She pulsed around him in throbbing caresses that knocked him the rest of the way over the edge with his final stroke.

Waves of pleasure crashed over him, shifting the ground beneath his feet. And shit, he hadn't even gotten his flight suit or boots the rest of the way off. Still joined, he pushed them both farther onto the bed until he blanketed her fully, finally. Her renewed cries heated over his already flaming body.

Shuddering in the aftermath, he buried his face in her hair until, slowly, reason filtered back into his passion-fogged brain.

Damn straight, he wanted Sophie, the kids, the front porch, the whole deal. She had to see she was wrong about risking a relationship again. She was wrong about him being a risk taker in his job. He was careful, damn it, because that meant he could live to fight another day.

And right now, he intended to fight for her, to be a part of her life, no more walls between them. No more holding back. He loved her, damn it, and she wanted no-strings sex. He should be happy. A hot woman wanted an affair.

He just had to convince her they could have it all.

* * *

Sprawled beside David on his king-size bed, Sophie indulged in a full-length, tabby-cat stretch. His heartbeat thudded rapidly beneath her ear, slowing with each breath. His hands glided over her body without pausing, as if compensating for the day of distance. Staying at his place, in the guesthouse behind Madison's, it felt like an island away from the rest of the world. She needed that right now, just losing herself in being with him.

Dim light flickered across their bodies with each swish of the ceiling fan. Her fingers wouldn't still, smoothing over his hair, across his temples, then along his top lip. Yes, she needed to store memories.

He smiled, eyes closed. Lightly, she retraced a path

over the bristly skin above his mouth. "What happened to your mustache?"

His unshaven face scraped against the pad of her finger. Trembling with renewed longing, she remembered the rasp of his cheek against her tender flesh after they had moved from the door to his bed.

The door.

Thank goodness David's eyes were still closed so he couldn't see the heat stinging her cheeks more than any scratch of a five o'clock shadow.

She'd enjoyed sex with Lowell, but never as the initiator. Of course, she hadn't minded the moments when David had taken the lead, either, but the give-and-take was new and exciting to her, so different from anything she'd experienced.

"Huh?" David's voice rumbled low under her ear pressed to his chest.

"Your mustache. The day you testified in court, I couldn't help but notice you'd shaved it." The awakening he'd begun in the courtroom, he'd finished that evening. White cotton sheets were twisted around their damp bodies. Pillows dotted the floor after being tossed aside in a frantic need to clear the bed.

"Haley Rose slammed the bathroom door into my elbow while I was shaving. Took a chunk out of my mustache." His chuckle vibrated beneath her. "I'm lucky she didn't cut off my lip."

Sophie stroked the pad of her thumb over his wonderfully perfect mouth. She couldn't regret the courtroom awakening, not when it had resulted in her time with David.

Scooting up his chest, she brushed her breasts against him, a dual-edged sword as his swirls of hair scraped against her already sensitive nipples. She kissed the bare spot above his lip, then focused her undivided attention on his mouth, her kiss deepening with renewed fervor.

She nestled on top of him, enjoying the rare chance to study his face without him watching her. "Are you going to grow it back?"

He shrugged, his hands moving in time with even breaths.

If he did, would she lay beside him and stroke her fingers across it? Or would they resume exchanging greetings as they crossed paths on base?

She didn't want to think about the future or the risks and complications of an actual relationship. She wanted to enjoy this amazing pocket of time with David.

Except time kept right on ticking.

His touch no longer comforted. She rolled away and swung her feet to the floor.

His eyes snapped open. "Where do you think you're going, Counselor?"

"Time to get back to work, Major. I always bring things home from the office. Have a problem with that?" She padded across the carpet.

"I don't think I'm really being asked."

The sheet gathered low around David's waist as he reached for her. She almost succumbed to the temptation to crawl back into bed with him.

Almost.

Gusts from the fan and air conditioner rippled over her, reminding her of the warmth she'd pushed away. She felt so exposed to him physically and emotionally.

After a self-conscious walk to her suitcase, Sophie shrugged on a cotton pajama-shorts set and scraped her hair back from her face.

David watched her from the bed, his bare chest and legs honed with whipcord strength. A tic in the corner of his eye belied his air of lazy nonchalance. "The mustache was my proverbial nose ring."

"What?" Talking with David could be dangerous, as she'd found out that night at Madison's. Sex, even making love, was easier than whispered revelations.

"Kids like Hannah pierce their noses to shock adults, prove they can be different from their parents." He nodded toward the hall, to a framed black-and-white photo on the wall of him and Haley Rose. "My father wanted a clean-shaven attorney for a son. I grew a mustache."

Apparently taken in the early days of his career before he'd become a major, David wore a uniform as he cradled a chubby toddler. Haley Rose's pigtails sported matching blue ribbons.

"And you joined the air force. What about your mother? What did she want for her son?"

"She wanted peace at any price."

At the expense of her children's happiness and emotional well-being? Obviously David had made different choices for himself as a parent. He was a great father.

Her breath hitched on achy emotions. Sophie looked away from the picture. The combined impact of the ribbons and uniform choked her, the picture too like one of herself and her father tucked in the back of a drawer.

"I didn't join right away." David combed his fingers through his hair, still mussed from their lovemaking. "I grew a mustache the summer before law school, as some sort of symbol that I wasn't completely knuckling under to what my old man wanted."

She blinked to clear her mind of the past, certain she must have misheard David. "Law school?"

He glanced at her quickly before looking away, his eyes taking on a distant look.

"In spite of my hell-raising high school years and partying while I did the semipro golf circuit, I managed to get college grades good enough to squeak into law school. I had to go. Berg men only play golf to make business contacts on the course."

An image of him hitting golf balls along the shore came to mind, how natural he'd looked, how at ease. How sad that his father couldn't celebrate David's successes and strengths. It sounded to her like the old man had been too busy trying to bring up a clone. And with these peeks into his past, she wondered what he was trying to relay. She'd found he shrouded his own needs so often, she had to dig through his words to find the hidden meaning. So she sank to the edge of the bed and listened.

"All the areas of gray you lawyers deal with—I hated it. Nothing is right or wrong, everything has mitigating circumstances." He scratched the back of his neck. "If halfway through a case I discovered a client was guilty, I wouldn't be able to defend him. No way would I be able to take the oath."

She didn't see it quite that way, but arguing would stop him from talking. "How deep into law school did you get before you changed your mind?"

"I made it through the first year before I realized I was living my father's dream, trying to make up for all the grief I caused him while I was a teenager. I dropped out. Dad about had a coronary." His familiar humor shone through, but with a darker edge. "Mother and Leslie weren't too pleased with my revised career plan, either. But the colonel's mentorship stuck, and here I am."

"You love your job."

"I am my job."

Sophie let loose a sigh she hadn't realized she'd been holding. Although she had difficulty reconciling how Leslie had treated Haley Rose, Sophie began to see the edges of gray as well. The woman in the picture was so young. Dark smudges of weariness marked the pale skin under her eyes. Just as she and Lowell hadn't found what they were looking for in their marriage, neither had David and Leslie.

"Sophie, I understand you've lost a lot the past year. I'm not saying your fears aren't important. But I'm not Lowell Campbell. I'm careful. Yes, I get a thrill out of my job, but I have my priorities in order." He gripped Sophie's shoulders, his silvery blue eyes intense. "The job can't offer anywhere near the rush I'll get from walking my daughter down the aisle someday."

She winced, more from his words than his insistent touch. Gramps had walked her down the aisle, because her father had been fifteen years in the grave.

David lifted her hand, holding it in his. "With the upcoming promotion to lieutenant colonel, I'll be riding a desk most of the time. Think about it, Sophie. Before you turn away, use that reasonable legal mind of yours and think about it."

Think about it? Think about what? "David, what exactly are you saying?"

"I'm saying you and I should give a real relationship a try. Yeah, I know we've known each other for a year and a half at work, but we should try to know each other outside of base. Date. Hell, maybe even more. I haven't made any secret about being wary after my divorce. Still, I gotta confess there's a part of me that wants to have it all again someday. The white picket fence, family, you know . . . a life together."

"Marriage?" Even thinking the word scared her to her toes.

He kissed her wrist. "Hell, forget I said anything and give me a chance to take you out on a real date with flowers and music."

Except he'd already hinted at more when she was only just coming to terms with the idea of an affair. And even though the possibility of all those old dreams filled her with wishful longing, she wasn't the girl she'd once been. The woman she was now was wounded, wary, and hell yes, too afraid to risk having her world shattered again.

His eyes narrowed, and he set her hand down. "What's wrong?"

She shot to her feet, overwhelmed. Her teeth chattered as if she was going into shock, for God's sake. "David, I can't deal with this right now."

"Sophie." He reached for her. "Come on, let's forget about talking and just make love until we're too tired to walk."

If she fell into his arms . . . "I have to plan a strategy for tomorrow. That's tough enough to do when I'm worried about our children."

Our children.

Her heart leapt from her throat straight into her mouth. She ran. Not caring if she appeared cowardly, she pushed past him and dashed straight for the ice cream in the freezer.

* * *

That hadn't gone remotely like he'd wanted.

David rolled from the bed and to his feet. He hadn't

planned on proposing to Sophie so fast, it just seemed like the moment called for it. Was it so wrong to want her in his life forever?

He yanked on a pair of cargo shorts and shrugged into a T-shirt. If he went back out there, things would just be awkward between them. And damn it, her look of horror at the mere mention of the word *marriage* stung. More than a little.

Some space would be welcome to get his perspective back. His sister had been pestering him all day to talk, and she really deserved better than to be blown off because he'd turned into a sap over Sophie.

He jammed his feet into deck shoes, without socks, and made tracks back into the living room. Sophie stood at the kitchen counter, scooping pistachio ice cream into a bowl. He wanted to walk up behind her, wrap his arms around her, and nuzzle aside her hair to kiss her neck. But the way she refused even to look at him said far more than any words.

"Sophie, I'm going over to Madison's. I won't be long. Keep your gun and cell phone in reach. The security system is fully armed. I'll have my eyes on this place the whole time." Still she didn't speak, which torqued him off. He didn't deserve the cold shoulder. He pulled his 9 mm from his gear bag and strapped it to his ankle. "Does that work for you?"

It was one thing to ignore him talking but another to blow off a direct question.

Sophie turned, her eyes guarded as she leaned against the counter. "I'm qualified to enter a combat zone on my own. I'm sure I'll be fine here while you check on your sister."

He didn't bother correcting her assumption that he

was only looking after Madison's safety. The less said right now, the better, because angry words were brewing in his gut.

Double-checking the security system, he locked the door after him and shifted his attention to his sister's place. The night was quiet, only a couple of boats on the water. Not much road traffic, either, just the rumble of a motorcycle shutting off a house or two down.

Madison's stucco mansion was lit up like a Christmas tree, just as he'd asked her. Floodlights illuminated every inch of the yard and the two-story home. Although she should learn to pull her curtains on all those walls of windows. The whole world could see her doing her yoga workout in the great room.

He started across the lawn.

And so did someone else.

A man sprinted from the yard next door. Lights streamed over him, but with his face turned away, there wasn't much to go by. Male. Tall. Athletic. Blond.

David leaned down to draw his 9 mm out of his holster, sidestepping behind a stone statue to evaluate. His whole body hummed with tension. No one would get past him to Sophie. Back flat against the oversize lion, he monitored the lawn. His mind barely registered the rough concrete.

The guy would have to go by him to get to Sophie. David would tackle the bastard on his ass before he could blink. David's grip tightened on the gun, his muscles tensing for action.

Except the intruder pivoted toward the main house, not the guest quarters where David lived, where Sophie was now.

The man was headed directly for Madison's steps.

David launched forward like a bullet out of a gun. His legs ate the space between himself and the man in seven heartbeats. Launching, he caught the man by the shoulders and slammed him to the gritty Nevada earth. The intruder bucked under him, thrashing and twisting with more strength and dexterity than David was expecting.

But then that's why he'd brought a gun. Just in case.

He pressed the 9 mm to the bastard's head. "So much as breathe and I'm shooting."

The guy underneath him stopped moving. "Major Berg?"

Now David felt like someone had slammed him in the gut, because he knew that voice. He knew this man.

He rolled the intruder to his back, confirming his guess. "Caleb Tate? What the fuck are you doing breaking into my sister's house?"

FOURTEEN

Madison flew down the steps barefoot toward her brother—who had his fist twisted in Caleb's shirt. "David, stop." Dread swelled through her, along with a feeling of inevitability. What she'd had with Caleb had been too good to last. "It's okay, David. Caleb's here for me."

Or at least she hoped he was.

More than that, she wished she'd talked to her brother before now. Her attempts to reach him, to make him listen, had been weak at best because she'd desperately hoped to be wrong about her lover using her. Floodlights cast harsh light over the angry tendons standing out in both men's necks.

Pushing away from Caleb, David stood, but he didn't stand down. The ugly black gun stayed firmly in her brother's hand. "What's Caleb doing here heading up the stairs to see *you*? At this hour?"

Caleb stood, dusting off his cargo shorts. "I can speak for myself. I've been dating your sister."

"Dating?" The look of pure shock on David's face was almost insulting.

She shouldered between them and pushed her brother's gun hand down. "Let's go inside and talk like reasonable adults. I would prefer the neighbors not hear everything."

Without giving them a chance to argue, she started toward the stairs again, too aware of the caress of Caleb's eyes over her in her workout clothes. But was it an act or for real? Damn it, she hated the insecurities whispering through her.

She opened her door and let them keep right on following her. Rolling up her yoga mat, she hugged it to her chest like a barrier and sat in a chair, giving herself space.

Her brother didn't even bother sitting.

"Talk, Madison," David barked.

Caleb stepped forward, chest puffed. "That's no way to speak to her."

"Really, kid?" David lifted an eyebrow. "You're going to lecture me about my sister? What are you really? Her boyfriend? Because if you were, I think I would have heard about it by now. The same with dates. I would know. Nobody sneaks around with my sister."

"I'm with Madison." He stopped talking, his jaw jutting.

She couldn't help but be touched how he didn't point fingers at her for insisting they keep their relationship secret. Maybe he was as honest as she hoped.

She set her yoga mat on the ground. "David, it's my fault you didn't know, that nobody knew. I didn't want to tell anyone yet." Ever? "I didn't want people whispering about," God, this part hurt to say, "how pathetic I looked sleeping with someone so much younger than I am."

"Sleeping together?" Wincing, David scratched the back of his head.

Caleb crossed to her chair, lifted her hand, and held firm. "Madison, babe, you know better than that. I'm damn lucky to be with you."

David smiled tightly. "Then you should have been shouting from the rooftops how lucky you are to breathe the same air as my sister."

God, she loved her brother, and she had so royally messed this up. None of it was their fault, but she didn't know how to make this right.

Her lover braced her shoulders. "I know how lucky I am. And I also know I'm not in any position to be with anybody right now, not with the trial still hanging over my head. I didn't want people thinking bad things about *her* because she was with *me*. I want to clear my name first."

David's head tipped to the side. "How long has this been going on?"

Standing, Madison stepped between them again. "Hello? I'm here, so don't ignore me, please. Do you hear me saying anything about what you and Sophie have going on together? Or where she's sleeping tonight? Nope." She jabbed her brother in the chest with her pointer finger, then looked over at Caleb. "In fact, Caleb, I think you should go. Let me talk to my brother."

"Madison, I'm not going to confirm everything he's thinking about me by walking out now." He turned to David. "We started seeing each other two months ago."

Anger radiated off David. "You started an affair with my sister while you were in the middle of a trial that could send you to jail for two years. That in and of itself isn't all that cool in my book. But what I really want to know is why the hell you didn't tell me. Were you hiding something? Because God help you if you were using my sister to get some kind of inside track on any additional information I have on the crash investigation." "Wow, Major," Caleb said dryly, "nice to know you've been blowing smoke about believing in my innocence. But then I should have guessed as much if you've been spending time with the lawyer determined to send me away for two years."

Suspicion snapped in David's eyes. "Do you have another reason for being here?"

"You insult Madison by even hinting at something like that." Mouth tight, he turned to her. "Do you believe that, too? That I'm here to somehow sway the case or find out information?"

She hesitated for a second too long.

"Shit," Caleb hissed. "I'm an idiot for thinking you actually wanted *me*. I should have known better when you refused to tell anyone. Consider your embarrassing, inconvenient affair over."

Sadness and betrayal twisted inside her, along with a sense of inevitability. She'd known there was no way their affair could last. She just hadn't expected it to hurt this much.

Turning away, Caleb left through the kitchen, like he knew the way through her house. Which he did. He paused, though, at her refrigerator. His face paled as he touched the edge of the picture held up by a magnet. That sad photo drawn by the boy who'd been hurt. Sophie had put it there as a reminder, saying she'd promised the boy she would.

And that she'd promised his parents justice.

Caleb slammed the door on his way out.

Madison winced. Her brother cupped her shoulders and she flinched again.

"Surprise, surprise," she said, "I've made a mess of things again. I'm sorry if I've compromised the case in any way by letting him in here when Sophie's notes were lying around." Tears burned her eyes. Over hurting her brother, right? Not because Caleb had just walked out of her life. "I'm sorry for not saying something sooner."

He hauled her to his chest. "You tried to talk to me, and I didn't listen. I owe you the apology."

How like David to shoulder the blame for everything. She angled back, thumbing away her tears. "I didn't try very hard, and I'm so sorry about that, too. You're the only person I haven't alienated. We sure don't have much of a track record in relationships, do we?"

"Apparently not." His wry smile didn't reach his eyes. "Are you okay?"

"No, but I will be." She patted his face. "I really would just like to be alone. Go back to Sophie, baby brother. It would give me hope if one of us could figure out how to make a relationship work."

He didn't move at first, studying her with those intense eyes until finally he must have realized there really wasn't anything he could do for her. Nobody could. Her brother walked away, pausing by the refrigerator. He took the picture from under the magnet. "Be sure to arm the security system."

And he was gone.

Her big, beautiful house echoed around her, empty, secured, like a damn fortress. Too bad they didn't issue that kind of protection for the heart.

* * *

Sitting cross-legged on the floor, Sophie stirred her melting pistachio ice cream. She stuck the spoon in her mouth and sucked it clean while flipping a page in the file resting on the coffee table.

Her eyes focused on the names and numbers detailed as she fidgeted against the itchy carpet irritating her legs. Of course the carpet was the cause, not the man she longed to wrap herself around for hours on end.

David sat on the edge of the sofa, a hand's reach in front of her and too enticing in just cargo shorts and a T-shirt. Resting his elbows on his knees, he cradled his bowl in one hand. He jabbed at his chocolate mocha swirl. The picture Ricky had drawn lay on the coffee table where David had placed it when he'd come back from checking on his sister. He'd seemed pensive, but when she'd asked him if something was wrong, he just shook his head. He'd said he needed to think through some things.

Guilt still stabbed her over the way she'd handled his impromptu proposal. They were both walking on eggshells now. She missed the way they'd been before—open, at ease.

She popped the spoon free and concentrated on the maintenance records of the AC-130, instead of on the muscular calves a stroke away. Sophie shuffled her papers—printouts, test data, and government contracts—unveiling David's bare feet visible through the glass tabletop.

Mesmerized, she watched him scratch his toes over the top of one foot. Why did that seem so intimate?

She shook off the sentimental notion and traced along the edge of Ricky's drawing. "I wish we could call Brice and Haley Rose again, but they've got to be asleep by now."

"You spoke with them three times today."

"I'd call again. I won't apologize for worrying."

David propped his feet on the edge of the table. "You're a good mother."

"I had a great role model." If only she could be half as patient as Nanny.

"You've never mentioned your mother before."

Accustomed to thinking of Nanny as her mother figure, Sophie hadn't considered his misunderstanding her remark. He'd divulged a part of himself and apparently wanted something in return.

She decided it might be wise to share a piece of herself with him after all. Maybe then he could understand her better, not think as poorly of her when she couldn't come through for him. The subject of her mother offered a safe confidence to exchange since it no longer hurt her. "I've never met my mother."

David paused, eyes narrowing for a flash before he scooped another dripping spoonful of ice cream.

"My dad and his girlfriend—I've never thought of her as my mother—let things go a little too far in the backseat of a car. You can guess the rest. She hid the pregnancy from her folks until it was too late for an abortion. Lucky for me, huh?"

David didn't smile.

"Her parents made arrangements with an adoption agency." Sophie wrinkled her nose with a grin. "Then Nanny got wind of things."

That earned a chuckle from David.

"I see you understand my Nanny quite well. While Dad finished school, we lived with Nanny and Gramps. Even after Dad finished the Academy, we never bothered moving out."

"Your dad was an Air Force Academy grad?"

Sophie's spoon stopped in midair. Slowly, she brought it to her mouth and ate. How did he manage to lead her into saying more than she wanted? Lowell had always pushed for answers. David seemed to have an artist's touch for letting her talk herself into a corner.

The ice cream melted on her tongue. "Just like you, David, he was a great aviator with a wonderful sense of honor and justice." She set her bowl aside and stared at the strong man in front of her. For once her ice cream offered little comfort. "There were no shades of gray in his world. He put on his flight suit every day and fought the bad guys. I respected him, just like I respect you."

The next part never got easier. Forcing the words, she hoped to somehow prove to David, as well as to herself, that she wasn't like Leslie. She had powerful reasons for pushing David away.

"He died, David. He died in combat; his fighter jet held back enemy fire while they sent in a rescue team to get pinned-down soldiers." Her mind filled with images of her father on that mission, so close to the same mission that had earned David his Distinguished Flying Cross. "Then he got shot down. He died in the crash. I know what my father did was honorable, but I was still so mad at him for leaving."

While the ache would never go away, surprisingly, the anger eased with being acknowledged. Sharing with David helped. "You and Haley Rose, well, it's difficult to watch you two sometimes."

She tossed her napkin on top of the remaining ice cream, her appetite long gone. "My teenage years were rocky. It's no big secret that I married Lowell as a father-figure substitute—without the risky uniform. Who would have thought he had dangerous hobbies like flying under bridges?"

Dangerous and deadly.

"Now do you understand?" She needed his understanding, his forgiveness. "Yes, I know you're different from Lowell. But I'm not a risk taker, and you're one great big sexy risk. I tell myself I don't want Brice's life disrupted. The truth is, I can't go through watching another man die. I wish I could be strong enough to say none of it matters, but it does."

"You're turning me down before I can even propose officially."

"David, damn it, why do you have to rush this and push so hard?"

"For the very reason you just said. Life is fragile. There are no guarantees." He tapped the picture Ricky had drawn. "This tells us that all too well. Things can change in a flash. We can't afford to waste the present."

His words settled inside her so heavily, she wanted to scream in frustration. She knew that, damn it. She didn't need reminding. She'd definitely had enough talking for one night.

She swept aside her files and leaned across the coffee table. She grabbed David by the shirt and hauled him toward her for a full-on, no-holds-barred kiss.

His arms banded around her without hesitation, his mouth opening. The sweet taste of ice cream lingering on his bold tongue. When he swept her into his arms, she didn't bother protesting this time. She knew David wouldn't drop her, and he'd been very clear on how much he enjoyed her curves.

Living for the moment sounded like a damn fine idea right now.

*　*　*

David stood at the bedroom window, watching the sunrise and checking the lake for any suspicious boats. Sleep was hard to come by, even with a security system in place.

He glanced back at Sophie, still sleeping, curled up on her side, hugging a pillow. She looked tired, too tired, with an exhaustion that went beyond dark smudges under the eyes.

The furrows of worry across her brow hadn't quite smoothed in sleep. He didn't know how to take those burdens on for her. For a man of action, the lack of control frustrated him.

What had her father been like? Had the happier childhood memories been tainted by his death? His thumb rubbed at the creases in her forehead as if he could remove years of sorrow.

If something happened to him, would Haley Rose remember the good times? She already carried a sack full of anguish from her mother's neglect. What kind of adult would she grow into if she lost him, too?

While death on the job was an unspoken reality, he didn't dwell on it overmuch, couldn't afford to let it steal his concentration. Sophie's father could have been any number of men he'd worked with, friends he'd lost. Littered among other nightmares, he could hear the strains of funeral taps, the keening of bagpipes, the choked cries of families.

He could continue his determined path of persuasion and possibly earn Sophie's love. But would she be happy? Would he?

Yes, he wanted her, even loved her, but could he withstand another relationship where he wasn't accepted unreservedly in return? Could she watch him strap on his shoulder harness every day? He didn't know. For once, he settled for an area of gray, certain the answer would steal away the woman in his arms.

He traced an almost translucent stretch mark gracing her hip. She wore her motherhood with pride. His fingers splayed over her flat stomach, and he couldn't stop from thinking of his child growing there.

Too easily, he could imagine spending the rest of his life with her, not just as the mother of his children but a woman he could laugh with, talk to, enjoy listening to the same piece of music with. Even with the areas of gray, they enjoyed untwisting the tangled legal system. So much right, so much more than sex. Although sex with Sophie had been beyond his expectations, and his expectations had been pretty damned incredible.

Thoughts of her guiding hand stirred a response. A quick glance at the clock offered him the reassurance of another half hour until the alarm launched them into a day of uncertain outcome.

Once he took Sophie to base, he needed to backtrack and talk to his sister again, get more details on what happened between her and Caleb. He needed to tell Sophie about his sister's affair as soon as he had the facts straight.

But before either of them started what promised to be a rough day . . .

Curvaceous breasts begged his mouth to taste. The dip of her waist tempted him to caress. Sliding his arm under her shoulder, he palmed the back of her head to angle her mouth toward his for a wake-up call better than any alarm.

Seeing the smudges under her eyes and furrows lining her brow stopped him.

David nestled Sophie against his chest. He held her while she stole final minutes of sleep and another piece of his heart.

* * *

Nibbling kisses tugged at Sophie's lower lip.

"Time to wake up."

David's husky drawl slid over her with as much arousing power as his touch. His roughened hands smoothed over her brow, gently stroked over her closed eyes.

"*Uhmmm.*" She cuddled nearer, nudging her leg between his. Her throat raw from too little sleep, she opted for another moan of appreciation instead. She willed the world to stay outside for a few precious memories longer.

"Come on, lazybones." He nuzzled a kiss on top of her head.

Her eyes fluttered open. A perfect view of his stubborn chin, peppered with morning stubble, greeted her. His determination had some definite benefits.

She wiggled against him, pleased to discover he might be amenable to lingering in bed. "What's your hurry?"

"You've got court." He untangled her arms from around his neck. "I've got some details to track down at work."

"I'll put on my makeup in the car." Even with muscles still deliciously achy from their night of lovemaking, her body reacted to his.

"Court in an hour."

"David!" His words startled her fully awake. "Why did you let me sleep so late?" She kicked aside the covers

and bolted for the bathroom before she had too much
time to miss his strong arms.

Their frenzy of readying for work with only seconds
to spare added another level of intimacy, enticing her with
how right being with David felt. No time for modesty,
Sophie showered while he shaved. He dressed while she
dried her hair, nothing but a towel wrapped around her
body, a towel that slipped no less than three times with the
assistance of a lusty flyboy.

She raced through the living room, grabbing her files
from the coffee table and the floor. She straightened the
stack and tucked it in her briefcase, leaning at the last
second to grab the photo Ricky had drawn for her and
place it in as well. That burst of light, the flash, the last
thing he remembered before his memory blanked and the
shell hit his house . . . The picture would keep her focused
today.

Buttoning her uniform jacket, Sophie dashed across
the driveway as fast as her pencil-straight skirt would
allow. Her high heels caught in the hot, sticky asphalt,
nearly pitching her forward. She stopped by his car, juggling her makeup bag under one arm and tossing her briefcase on the backseat.

Sophie started to leap into the passenger side. David's
hands slid around her waist, his fingers spreading across
her stomach and circling a gentle massage. Resting his
cheek against the side of her head, he pressed his body
flush against her back. His breath ruffled through her
freshly washed hair.

"Sophie, I heard what you said to me about your dad,
your mother . . . your husband. I listened, and I understand. That doesn't mean I can stop myself from wanting

you or trying everything I know to make sure we risk more together."

He kissed her cheek, a tender stroke more moving than his most ardent plunder. She pivoted in his arms to face him, his clean-shaven, stubborn chin telling her all she needed to know. Just as he'd said, he would fight for her.

The mere thought fluttered in her stomach.

She brushed her knuckles over his chin. "Decisions are so easy for you, David. Clear-cut answers. How do you work through the gray areas so fast?"

"We all have our own pace." His tanned face creased into a smile. "I know from experience, when you commit to a decision, your determination is a force to be reckoned with."

His roguish grin chased away a few of the gray-tinged shadows. She turned away before she cried. Or caved.

Gently, he lifted her inside. "We both need to get to work."

She watched him circle the hood and settle behind the steering wheel. His whipcord vitality stirred her. "It's not that I don't want you."

"I know that." He pressed her against her seat, his mouth covering hers, hard and fast, stealing her breath, her will. With a wink, he pulled back and started the car. "You think too much."

Gunning the accelerator, David turned up the radio, ending conversation.

Sophie struggled to put on her makeup as they wove through traffic. He'd left the car top on to keep her hair in place for work. Somehow even the minor darkening shade mingling with the melancholy tunes from the CD player cast a pall over her mood.

She missed the sun on her face, the stinging breeze.

David had taught her how to enjoy the moment. The wind rippling over her during their night rides had been invigorating, tying them together with an elemental bond.

Parked outside the courthouse, Sophie grabbed her briefcase and jumped to the ground without waiting for David. She almost convinced herself she was running to court, not from him. When they moved proceedings from the courthouse to the accident site, she could dive into routine.

She heard David's longer strides closing the distance between them. He tugged her to a halt near the same spot where he'd tackled her when the gunshots sounded. Fear and longing had bound them then as well as now.

Gentle, calloused hands caressed either side of her face. David lowered his lips to hers, skimming, then deepening into a lazy kiss of a couple who has eased the edge of passion but know it will soon build again. Her briefcase slipped from her grasp and thudded to the sidewalk.

Sophie closed her fingers around his wrists, holding him in place while she surrendered to temptation. The decision seemed so much easier when he held her. The strength of his arms and his will infused her with the courage to push her boundaries a little further.

Then he backed away, nodding to the guard standing watch at the door. She just stood, swaying like someone dazed by a first kiss. She couldn't stop herself from watching him walk back to his Scout, taking in how damn hot he looked in his flight suit.

Damn straight, he had a fine backside and broad shoulders, along with a sharp mind that challenged her. Was she being stupid to put the brakes on letting their relationship move faster?

A hand tapped her on the shoulder. "Major Campbell, can I speak with you?"

She turned fast. Caleb Tate stood behind her, stepping back.

"Excuse me, ma'am. I hope you won't be angry with Madison."

Angry with Madison? Why in the world would she be mad at Berg's sister. Sophie struggled to sort through the captain's words. "I don't know what to think, other than to remind you we shouldn't be speaking without one of your attorneys present."

"This is my decision and has nothing to do with them. I know Major Berg is pissed off and suspicious, but I didn't start seeing Madison because of any ulterior motive. It just happened. And I never saw anything of yours and, God knows, Major Berg would never bring anything classified to the house."

Understanding swiped away the confusion. Understanding . . . and anger.

Tate had been seeing Madison all this time and David—damn him—hadn't said a word.

FIFTEEN

Frustrated as hell, David downshifted through the late afternoon traffic, the snarl of cars making the drive twice as long. Which also doubled the time for Sophie to give him the silent treatment.

Nearly an hour into the ride, he'd had it. Especially after the unproductive talk with his sister last night and an equally unproductive day at work arguing with the subcontractor Keith Nelson.

He couldn't do anything about his sister or the contractor. But here, in the car, he could dig to the root of the problem. "So, Soph, are you going to ignore me for the rest of the evening?"

Sunglasses shading her eyes, she looked up from the open file in her lap she'd been pretending to read. "Pardon?"

"What. Is. Wrong?"

"Nothing." She looked back at the file, her thumb fanning a corner of the papers.

"Something's obviously eating at you." He accelerated past a tourist driving at least ten miles per hour below the limit. "I was married long enough to know that when a woman says it's nothing, it's definitely something."

She peered over the top of her sunglasses. "I do *not* appreciate being compared to your ex-wife."

"Okay," he conceded, "that was a cheap shot, but at least you're finally talking."

"Talking? You finally want to talk?" Her voice rose with each word. "Fine. How about this for a conversation starter? Why didn't you tell me Madison and Tate are having an affair? That he's had free run of her house with my notes for trial lying around for him to see?"

Her anger sent him back in his seat. And he couldn't even deny her accusation. He wasn't sure exactly why he'd held back.

"I only found out last night." Which sounded lame even to his own ears now. He tapped the brake as traffic slowed to a crawl.

"It would have been nice to have a heads-up before I walked into court today. That information could have influenced how I targeted my cross-examinations."

"And why did you send me out of the room when you questioned Juan?" he snapped back, not realizing until now how much that had grated at him.

"Because I had a job to do."

"So do I, damn it." He thumped the steering wheel. Traffic came to a total standstill; just his damn luck today.

Digging into the file, she pulled out the photo Ricky had drawn and held it up inches away from his face. "And our job should be about this. Only this. Ricky may not remember getting hit, but he remembers the flash, that split second of horror that something was about to hit his house. It's up to us to figure out why that happened, even if it sends your sister's lover to jail. Even if it closes down your whole damn squadron."

The drawing held his eyes, homing in his complete focus as something shifted in his brain, pieces of information shadow dancing with each other. What had he and Sophie talked about last night? How this picture was a reminder of that moment Ricky's life changed in a flash.

David shut out the world and worked to grasp that elusive something his subconscious was trying to tell him about the childish picture. A house. A boy on the couch. A flash outside the window.

A house intact.

The flash *before* impact.

"David? Are you even listening to me?"

He held up his hand. "In a flash. Sophie, it's about the flash. We've got to get back to the squadron. I think I know exactly what happened the night Ricky Vasquez was injured."

* * *

Parked in front of a row of computer screens, Sophie watched footage of an AC-130 in flight, shooting its cannons, the target exploding. Again and again, the test footage rolled.

David had doubled back to the base, making record time since the traffic congestion was only for outgoing cars. He'd refused to tell her what he thought he'd figured out from Ricky's picture. Instead, David had driven her to his squadron. He'd ushered her through security, where she'd have to leave her purse and cell phone behind before entering a vaulted room full of computers.

Aviators and testers sat at different stations, some reviewing data, others monitoring night flight missions in progress.

Blocking out the buzz of activity around her, she pressed her hands to the table, shaking her head. "David, I don't know what I'm supposed to be seeing here."

Other than shooting up a bunch of old, deserted trailers set up as targets in the middle of the desert range.

He leaned over her shoulder, typing on the keyboard, tightening the focus on the next trailer about to be blown to smithereens. It sure appeared to her that the new gun turret modification worked just fine. Her frustration increased all the more with the musky scent of him so close and distracting.

Their argument still lurked on hold between them, neither of them touching. Instead, he seemed to be using the case as an excuse to avoid talking through why he hadn't been up front with her about Captain Tate's involvement with Madison.

"Sophie," he tapped the screen, "look closer. Watch the flash."

Fingers flying over the keyboard, he slowed the footage to a frame-by-frame playback.

"Okay, so a flash happens before the explosion. Is the shell blowing up prematurely?"

"No, that's the laser checking the target before the shot. The fire control officer has to trigger that laser before he fires."

"So Captain Tate would have made two mistakes?"

"Or maybe none at all." He shifted to sit at the computer next to her. That screen was filled with data rather than doomsday explosions. "Here's the log data for the flight in question. If you look here, it shows the laser was in the *Off* position even though Ricky remembers seeing the flash. There's no way Tate could have fired the laser. It must have malfunctioned and fired itself. And if the laser malfunctioned, then the gun could have as well."

A malfunction could explain everything, but it felt like too convenient an answer. "Why do you have data that shows the laser was off, but no data on whether or not his gun controls were in the *Off* position?"

"The plane had left the range, and data readout ends once the plane leaves the range. Except for the laser. We have to track how many hours the laser is used for maintenance purposes. The laser was off. This level of malfunction would also explain why the computers didn't register that there was still a round left."

"How did this contingency never come up before?" She leaned back in the chair, her eyes locked on the frozen image. The flash and intact target mirrored Ricky's drawing, the laser flash he would have seen before the impact.

"We were too focused on the data we had inside the range. This changes everything. If the laser fired on its own, then the gun could have as well. We can send the new turret system back to the subcontractor for review. With this data, he should be able to trace the malfunction in the programming, to tell us what went wrong. This could clear Tate—and keep this from happening again."

She rolled back the chair from the monitor, fast, energized by the possibility of a real break in the case. "This could also bring the contractor's work into question. We'll have to scrutinize his part of the testing process more closely." She looked up sharply at David. "I assume you don't have a problem with that?"

"None whatsoever. I only want the truth."

There was no missing the hint of anger—even disappointment—in his eyes. Her accusations about Tate had upset David, and he wasn't ready to forget.

Neither was she. And yes, she embraced the distraction of work to keep from dealing with her jumbled feelings for David. "I have to get back to my cell phone and call Geoffrey. We need to file for a continuance until we can sort this all out."

For the first time since this horrific trial started, she saw light at the end of the tunnel work-wise. She just prayed that flash of hope brought the answers she sought, and not a bigger explosion personally.

* * *

David paced outside Sophie's office building, cell phone pressed to his ear. He'd been hauling people out of bed for the past hour, setting the wheels in motion. Sophie had already notified her boss, and Lieutenant Colonel Vaughn was going to try and get a continuance for Tate's trial.

But they couldn't count on that. With only a week left, he needed answers from the contractor. Keith Nelson would no doubt require babysitting through the entire search through the data. The contractor had such a huge chip on his shoulder, owning up to a mistake on his side wasn't going to come easy.

Not to mention his company would then be open to a major lawsuit from Ricky's family.

And this still would bring backlash to the new squadron commander for not keeping closer tabs on the program rather than sending in David to tighten the reins *after* an accident.

Nelson's voice mail picked up.

David resisted the urge to pitch the cell phone into the bushes and instead dialed again.

Sophie was inside, gathering up all of Keith Nelson's contracts to scrutinize. If a mistake had been made, hopefully it was an honest error. But if Nelson had tried to pull something? Then God only knew what else he may have done. Sophie wasn't leaving anything to chance, and he appreciated her legal eye.

Between them, they had it covered.

They made a helluva team. He just wished she could see that.

Nelson's voice mail clicked on again.

Damn it, why wasn't Nelson picking up?

With BlackBerrys and cell phones, there was no such thing as "unreachable" in their work world.

He thumbed Nelson's home phone, even though he preferred to discuss this over their secured cells.

The phone rang three times before someone picked up. About damn time.

"Hello?" a woman's hesitant voice answered, sniffling, hoarse . . . As if she was crying?

"Sorry to bother you so late, ma'am. Could I speak to Keith Nelson? Tell him it's Major Berg calling with an emergency."

She gasped, hiccupping on a sob. "Major Berg? Keith can't come to the phone." Her breath hitched, as she started crying again. "He, he . . . shot himself. He's dead. My husband killed himself. The police are here and an ambulance, but he's gone . . . He's . . ."

David sagged down to sit on the top step. What the hell? He forced his stunned brain to go on autopilot and offer the woman condolences. "Ma'am, I am so very sorry for your loss."

"It's your fault," she cried bitterly into the phone. "He said in his note it's all your fault, that you were going to dig into all his old contracts and send him to jail . . ."

Her voice trailed off, keening in her grief. He heard someone talking soothingly to her in the background, then picking up the phone, "My mother can't speak to anyone now," a young man said into the receiver. "So leave her alone and talk to the police."

The line disconnected and the world went eerily quiet, much like the moment right after the crash landing. Everything had been life-and-death horrifying one second, then safe the next. *His old contracts?* Finally, they had a solid lead on who must have been threatening Sophie.

All signs indicated Keith Nelson was responsible for the malfunction that caused the AC-130's gun to misfire. Given his desperate act tonight, it stood to reason he'd been willing to do anything to hide his mistake. He'd certainly had the ability and access to tamper with the Cessna's fuel tank. He'd been stalking and attacking Sophie too . . . ? Keep her rattled, keep her from getting too close to the real answer of what happened?

Hell, they might never know his reasoning, and God, nobody wanted this sort of outcome. Furthermore, Keith's suicide would make it all the tougher to figure out if he'd had accomplices or underlings.

Exhaustion weighted down his shoulders. Adrenaline seeped from him after running full tilt for so long. Wearily, he pushed to his feet again. He needed to tell Sophie what had happened. The judge would have to halt the case now, until this mess could be sorted out. All AC-130s with the new gun turret system would be grounded.

There was nothing more he could do tonight.

* * *

Sophie downloaded file after file, contract after contract, while David checked in with others on his test team. She would be up all night reading—probably for days. She wasn't sure exactly what she was looking for in Keith Nelson's proposals. But it had been her experience that when someone skirted the rules in one place, that person usually blurred the lines in dozens of other ways as well.

Larger government contracts had dozens of attorneys review them. But the smaller subcontractor bids and agreements? Those often sailed through with only one set of legal eyes checking them over. Some had even been reviewed by her boss, although smaller bids usually went to the junior legal staff. It would be easier to try and slip things by one person, especially a newbie, and if they were noted by the reviewing lawyer, then the contractor could simply call it part of the negotiating process and make a line edit. She could get started now, then pass them along to Geoffrey to review as well.

At least if she was working nonstop, she could put off thinking about her fight with David. Now wasn't that just a mature attitude?

Her head fell to rest on her desk, and she squeezed her eyes closed tightly against the sting of tears. When had she turned into such a coward?

"Are you all right?"

The masculine voice pulled her upright sharply. Her boss stood in her office doorway, still wearing his uniform.

"Lieutenant Colonel Vaughn, I didn't know you were still here."

"It's after hours. You can call me Geoffrey." He leaned against the door frame. "Thanks for the heads-up on Keith Nelson. What a lucky break for Captain Tate."

"What a lucky break for the air force overall that we'll know what really happened." She rolled her chair back.

"Of course." He rubbed behind his neck. "What are you doing here so late? You should be out celebrating your victory with your new boyfriend. Or picking up your kid in California now that you're all safe again."

She wouldn't say she felt safe. Not yet. Not until she'd absolutely ruled out everyone in Nelson's office as a possible accomplice.

Shaking her head, she pulled the CD out of her computer. "No celebrating yet."

"Ah, come on. I'll bet your son's ready for more baseball by the beach. I'm happy to help him out. I was famous on campus in law school for my slider."

Distracted, she looked up. "Slider?"

"Slider. You know, a type of pitch . . . Wow, your boy really does need my help."

"Thanks, Geoffrey. I'll keep that in mind." She closed her briefcase. "But before I can have my family back together, I need to go over all the government contracts made with Nelson's company."

"Are you questioning the work of this office? Of *my* office?"

An uneasy sensation prickled up her spine, the same feeling she'd gotten right before her convoy had been ambushed in the Middle East. Standing, she grabbed her briefcase and started for the door. "I should go home now. David's waiting for me outside."

Geoffrey's hand shot out, blocking her path. "I'm afraid I can't let you leave. And since I've sealed off the front entrance, your boyfriend won't be getting through the front door until long after I've left from another exit."

Her boss pulled a gun from behind his back and pointed it directly at her chest, right above the rows of ribbons pinned to her uniform.

Confusion jockeyed with fear. What the hell was Geoffrey doing? And why was he so freaked out over the Nelson contracts?

Then, as she looked at the gun before staring up into his eyes, the truth exploded in her mind with the flashing clarity of a legal case solved.

Except there was no victory here. Just utter rage as she peered into the eyes of the man who'd been behind all the threats on her and those she loved most. She didn't know why, but she'd been betrayed and ambushed by one of her own, someone she should have been able to trust to have her back. And even worse, she'd been caught without a weapon, with nothing more than a briefcase for armor.

"Geoffrey, you've got to stop and think." She worked to keep her voice calm, but outtalking another lawyer was a dicey proposition at best. "I don't know what's going on here, or why, but this is crazy."

"Damn straight it's crazy." He held out a hand. "Now give me the CD you just burned from your computer and put in your briefcase."

The CD? With all of Nelson's contracts? The "why" became all too clear. She would bet her last dollar Geoffrey was the lone reviewing attorney on many, if not all, of Nelson's agreements with the government. The money to be made off those kinds of cover-ups could be huge.

"If Nelson wasn't such a fuckup, this wouldn't be happening." The gun pressed deeper into her flesh.

"Since you're obviously going to kill me, could you at least give me the satisfaction of knowing what I'm going to die for?" And please God, if she could keep him talking and bragging long enough, David would come looking for her, would sense something wrong with the sealed doors and find a way in.

If she hadn't put emotional walls between them, he would have been here with her now. And the thought of him being in harm's way, too, made her physically ill.

"Nelson knew about the computer malfunction with the gun turret, but he didn't want to soak up the cost of stopping the project." He pushed the barrel of the 9 mm harder against her, pushing her back one step and then another. "He hoped to fix the problem before it finished the test phase. Then the accident happened, and he was really scrambling to cover his tracks."

The back of her legs bumped her desk. "Cover your tracks, too, apparently."

"No need to get bitchy, Sophie, dear."

"And what should I be right now? Happy?"

He crowded her, walking her around the desk until she sank into her chair again.

"You should be nice, Sophie, because I'm in control of how badly your death will hurt. Since Nelson has already killed himself over this cluster-fuck, I figure why not go for two suicides? You were in this together, and rather than face the consequences, the dishonor, you killed yourself as well."

She barely bit off the gasp of horror. Could he actually pull that off? And, oh God, her son who'd only just come to grips with losing his father would think his mother did leave him. Full-blown panic threatened to mushroom through her brain, pushing out any chance of reasonable thought. She sucked in breath after breath, praying for the calm to listen, to outthink this monster she'd foolishly trusted.

She had to stay clearheaded, try to think of some way to leave David a clue so that even if she didn't make it, he would know she hadn't committed suicide. David would fight for her even if no one else believed she'd been murdered.

"I'll be so very sad as I tell everyone how distraught you've been since your husband died, how I wish I'd seen the signs." He knelt in front of her, his aftershave thick and cloying. "If only I'd realized you were so deeply in debt you've been taking kickbacks from Nelson. It will be a simple matter for me to adjust the name of just who read over and approved those contracts."

"Women don't commit suicide by shooting themselves." She searched for something, anything to say to delay him. "We don't like to leave a mess for others to clean up."

"That's why you're not going to shoot yourself. Faking a gunshot suicide is too tricky anyway, what with all the forensics on the directionality of blood splatter." He reached inside his jacket and pulled out a pouch of white powder. "You're going to overdose. Once you're pliant from the coke I'll send up your nose, then I'll shoot you up. A painless way to go. You should thank me."

"Not a chance. I'll fight you, kick, scratch. I'll claw your DNA so far under my nails, you'll never get it out."

He leaned in so close his fetid breath steamed over

her face. "Then I'll shoot you and hide your body so deep in the desert, once the wild animals are through gnawing on your bones, there won't be anything left to find."

★ ★ ★

For the first time in his career, David faced a crisis like a civilian instead of a man in uniform. Seeing the gun in Lieutenant Colonel Geoffrey Vaughn's hand rocked the ground under David's feet.

Getting the security guards to open the building had been tough—for about ten seconds. Then he'd spelled out just how many heads were going to roll if he woke up the wing commander to let him inside to meet up with his girlfriend.

They'd sent him in with their blessing, waiting outside and obviously not overly swayed by his concerns.

The sound of Vaughn's threats echoing softly down the hall had shaved ten years off his life. He'd considered going back out for the cops, but gauging by what Vaughn was saying, Sophie didn't have seconds to spare, and he couldn't risk his voice alerting the bastard. David had sent out SOS texts as fast as his fingers could fly over his phone.

At least she was still speaking, her beautiful voice a balm to the roaring rage threatening to consume him.

David swung into the room, offering himself up as a target instead. "Vaughn, it's over."

Vaughn shot to his feet and swung the gun right at his chest. "Don't move."

Sophie stared at him from across the room, terror lurking just below the surface. But she was alive and he would make damn sure she stayed that way. She inched away from Vaughn.

"Stop moving, Sophie," the lawyer hissed from beside her, "or I'll shoot your boyfriend."

David switched gears. The warrior within him assumed control. He eased forward a step, forcing himself to focus on Vaughn rather than surrendering to the desperate hunger to look at Sophie. To reassure himself she was alive and safe. "Consider what you're doing here. You are trapped with no way out."

"I'll shoot her." Vaughn's body shouted desperation. "Don't think I won't." He swung the gun back to her, against her forehead.

Any hope of control evaporated. David swallowed bile. He'd thrown up after missions. Never during. He wouldn't start now.

David scrambled for objectivity—but no luck finding it. His sight turned hazy red. Fear churned the barely banked rage back to life.

Sophie bit her lip, her eyes fluttering closed. David saw it all, her breathy gasps, her fast blinks, all her signs of how hard she was pushing down the panic, and he couldn't do a damned thing. Memories of those moments before the Cessna crash landing stabbed through him.

She'd asked him for time, just more time. A woman so afraid to trust again had offered him everything she had to give.

Vaughn's hand skimmed the underside of her breast. Sophie gasped, then the counselor facade slid into place. David gritted his teeth, unable to decide if the man was a moron or a genius.

Every buried nightmare from battle roared to the surface. David knew all too clearly what a desperate man would do.

Sure, there was a chance help could arrive in time to

storm the office and take out Vaughn. But a chance wasn't good enough for him.

Finally, Sophie's angry words after the airplane crash made sense to him. He couldn't imagine the hell of having to tell Brice his mother had died, that he hadn't protected her as he'd promised. It would be the worst thing David could imagine.

No. He changed his mind. Being left behind, living if Sophie died, was *beyond* imagining.

David stepped forward again, ready to offer himself in her place, not that he expected to be lucky enough for the bastard to take him up on the offer. Sophie's eyes widened, with no attempt at all to hide her fear now. He could see in her face that she knew what he intended to do.

She shook her head slightly. She mouthed, *No. Don't. Please.*

He shook his head as well, mouthing back, *I'm sorry.*

And then he launched forward, drawing Vaughn's attention and gun directly on him as he'd hoped.

Sophie shoved hard at Vaughn. David could see the desperation in her eyes, the near superhuman strength of how she fought Vaughn. Her foot hooked behind his leg in a picture-perfect move to down him.

Picture perfect, but too late.

The gun fired.

A bullet tore through his arm. Professional instincts drove him forward even as Sophie's screams filled the office.

Another bullet ripped into David's shoulder, pain detonating through his chest. Love for Sophie powered his feet the final steps.

SIXTEEN

Screaming, Sophie launched herself onto Geoffrey. Fury propelled her with a frenzy that smothered the grief for now. She tackled him backward into the bookshelves, legal tomes pummeling both of them. Her every cell focused on pounding the man who'd just shot David.

Even thinking his name made her shriek in rage again as she fought back. Fought dirty. Using Krav Maga and street fighting. No rules.

Only a fight to the end, to win.

She pressed her forearm to his windpipe, her other hand slamming his wrist against the edge of a bookshelf. When he tried to swing at her, she bit his arm until she tasted blood. Vaughn's roar filled the room and echoed the one inside her.

Hands grabbed her shoulders. She jerked reflexively, pressing harder on Geoffrey's throat. She wouldn't let him threaten David again. She refused to waste the window of opportunity David had gained with his blood. She wouldn't give this traitor another chance at him.

"Ma'am," an insistent voice—not Geoffrey's—penetrated the battle haze, "please hold still, ma'am. We'll take it from here."

Disjointed thoughts sparked through her mind. The security police . . . Somehow they'd arrived. David must have called them. But didn't wait. She rolled from Geoffrey and came face-to-face with David on the ground.

Blood soaked his arm. A fresh stain of red spurted from his chest over his name tag.

A woman screamed.

Sophie tried to shrug off the security police reaching for her. They should be dealing with the hysterical woman anyway. Somebody should shut her up.

David needed help. That's all that mattered.

The carpet burned her knees as she scrambled to him. Only then did she realize her jaw was moving. The screams were bubbling from within her. She barely registered the pair of cops dragging Geoffrey Vaughn out to the hall.

Hysteria took control. With frenetic strength, she struggled to her feet, fighting the arms that held her back.

"No! No, no, no, no," the moans ripped through her throat. "David!"

He didn't move. His unconscious body was sprawled on her office floor. A security cop leaned over him, shouting into his handheld radio.

"Man down! Man down!" he shouted, rattling off the address and order for an ambulance.

Sophie pitched forward to her knees. Her hands slapped the industrial carpet. She wouldn't lose another man. Sobs tearing through her, she grabbed David's hand, searching for his pulse. The thready throb against her fingertips reassured and terrified her all at once.

"David . . ." Sophie sat on her feet and held tight to his hand. "Don't you die on me, damn it. You've got to walk Haley Rose down the aisle one day. And you've got to wake up so I can tell you I love you and you can tell me back."

Apparently the security police saw the power of a loved one's presence—or they were too busy stemming the flow of blood—because they left her alone. She rested her ear against his chest, desperate for a sign of life. Her own gasping cries masked any whispers of sound. She held her breath, counting the beats of his heart.

One, then two, with the third she exhaled, listening to the steady thrum. A hand cradled the back of her head, fingers threading through her hair. Afraid to dare hope, Sophie closed her eyes. Tears seeped from her eyes into his already blood-soaked flight suit.

"Sophie." His voice rumbled low and weak.

Unable to talk through the tears choking her, she kissed his chest, cheek, and forehead.

"I'm sorry, Sophie. I'm so sorry." His dark lashes closed over blue eyes turned hazy gray with pain before he passed out again.

★ ★ ★

Madison had spent hours a day mediating but never had she prayed as hard as she did sitting beside her brother's hospital bed through the night, waiting for him to wake up. Midmorning sun streaked through the hospital window, casting a warm glow through the sterile room. An IV was strapped to his hand, oxygen tubes feeding extra air to his lungs. A monitor beep, beep, beeped reassurance of his steady heart.

Both doctors had told her David was lucky. Both bullets had passed clean through, so they'd only had to stitch him up, give him some blood, and pump him full of antibiotics. He should recover with rest and TLC.

Sophie had called her from the cop car, her voice overly calm as she'd explained what happened. She'd asked Madison to sit with David while Sophie gave her statement to the police on what happened.

Madison had forgotten to get shoes as she raced to the car in her yoga clothes.

Her brother could have died. Caleb had no part in the shooting and apparently wasn't involved in Ricky Vasquez's accident. But she didn't feel one bit like celebrating while her brother lay pale in a hospital bed.

The sound of him shifting, of the sheets rustling, drew her attention.

"Sophie?" David's voice came out hoarse, his eyes still unfocused and darting.

"*Uhm*, I'm your sister, you goof." Her laugh got choked off with tears of gratitude. "But yes, Sophie is fine. She's giving her statement now."

His eyes closed again briefly, his mouth moving in a labored swallow.

She reached for a Styrofoam cup of ice chips on the rolling table and passed it to him. "I'm not sure if you're allowed to drink or eat yet. But I can call the nurse."

He took the cup from her. "This is good." He shook a third of the contents into his mouth and sighed, swallowing easier this time. "Vaughn?"

"Under arrest." She gripped her brother's hand, careful of the IV. "I'm so sorry for not telling you about Caleb. My history with men is just so awful, I couldn't bring myself to acknowledge the possibility that . . ."

"That you might have feelings for the guy?"

She nodded tightly, her throat closing up until she reached for the cup of ice for herself.

"Madison, maybe you should tell him to his face." David pointed over her shoulder.

Her blood chilled, and it had nothing to do with the ice chips melting on her tongue. She looked behind her and . . . Oh God. Caleb stood in the doorway with two other guys in flight suits. *Her* Caleb—blond, so young and handsome, and focused totally on her. The shock on his face would have been funny, except putting her heart on the line felt anything but humorous.

David squeezed her hand. "Go talk. I've got plenty of company."

She kissed his cheek. "Love you, little brother."

"Love you back."

They may have had a domineering dad and a doormat mother who let him rule the roost, but she and David had always been able to count on each other. She should have remembered that. She wouldn't let insecurity ever make her forget again.

Turning back to Caleb, she gestured to the door, her borrowed hospital slippers anything but elegant. But then the appreciation in his eyes soothed any concerns. He palmed her back and she tossed her loose dark hair over her shoulders.

One of the other fliers, a bulky bald guy she thought they'd called Vapor, applauded softly. "Nice, Tater, nice."

The door swished closed behind them, and as much as she wanted to wrap herself around Caleb right now, she wanted a little privacy more.

Once they reached a small sitting area, she let her legs give way. He joined her on the industrial sofa.

"Madison, babe . . ."

She pressed her fingers to his mouth that had brought her so much pleasure. And yet seeing him smile pleased her even more.

After the way she'd insisted they keep their relationship quiet like it was something sordid, he deserved a little groveling on her part.

"I like you, Caleb, I mean I *really* like you. And in my book, that's a lot more important than attraction." Something she wished she'd figured out a long time ago instead of confusing lust for love. "Sex, well, that's the easy part. But the feelings, the emotions," she forced out the next word, the toughest of all, "the trust, those parts are more difficult for me."

He stroked her hair back from her face with broad hands. "Why is that? You're the most confident, mesmerizing woman I've ever met."

"And I'm a total loser at choosing men." She touched his chest carefully, tenderly, tracing that silly, endearing Tater call sign on his name tag. "You seemed too good to be true. So I waited for the other shoe to drop."

"What do you mean you're a loser at choosing guys?" His earnest green eyes stayed locked on her face.

Not her body. Had she missed other signs he was interested in more than sex? She hadn't given him the chance. "We haven't spent that much time talking, have we?"

A killer grin dug a dimple into his one cheek. "We tend to drop our clothes pretty fast, and then there's not a lot of talking."

"What if we had sex and talking?"

"What about a date, talking, then sex?" He rested his forehead against hers.

"I can do that," she whispered against his mouth. "I *want* to do that."

"Nice," Caleb smiled against her lips, "very nice."

★ ★ ★

Gaze focused straight ahead, Sophie watched the numbers flash by in the crowded elevator. Hospitals would never be her favorite place to visit, but she had more important things on her mind than fears that wanted to rob her of a future.

Finally, she was free, after hours spent repeating what had happened in her office. She'd given her statement to the security police, then the Air Force Office of Special Investigations, then the wing commander, who was justifiably freaked out over what one of his JAGs had been doing right under their noses.

She'd been brought updates on David's status through the night, but not in anywhere near the detail she'd wanted. Only that the bullets had passed clean through. No internal organs were affected. He'd been stitched up and was resting comfortably. Thank God they'd let her change out of her bloody uniform into an air force T-shirt and gym shorts from her gym bag.

There hadn't been time to talk with him before an ambulance had whisked him away, but at least she'd been able to phone Madison to be with him. A security cop had taken Geoffrey into custody. It would take more than one night to unravel all the damage he'd done.

Had she blown it with David when she'd fought with him earlier? How could she have judged him for being a risk taker when danger had lurked so near her? Life was full of risks. She might as well make her risk worthwhile, choosing David.

Finally, she'd learned to fight for what she wanted. She wanted David. With the combined strength of their determined wills, they could fight the odds of military relationships.

Sophie ignored the curious stare of the man beside her as he took in her bruised face and the bandage on her scratched-up arm. He cradled a plant in his hands, a balloon floating over it proclaiming, "It's a Boy." He raised an eyebrow.

Sophie shrugged. "Tough day at work."

Laughter felt so good. Another gift from David.

The elevator doors slid open.

Walking down the corridor, she reminded herself these days of fear were coming to a close. She was getting out of the air force, and David would be safer once he took the Pentagon job.

Knocking with two knuckles, she pushed open his door, familiar voices swelling out. David's friends from work— Smooth and Vapor. Her eyes skimmed them and went to David, pale but sitting up. His eyes held hers, and he extended a hand. She linked fingers without hesitation.

The duo exchanged looks and backed toward the door.

Smooth cleared his throat. "I think that's our cue to leave."

Vapor patted David's uninjured shoulder. "Congratulations, Commander."

The door swished closed after them.

Commander?

She pushed the question aside for the moment and just took in the sight of him, blessedly alive. She secured her hold on his hand. "I want to touch you, but I don't know where you're hurt."

"Anywhere on the right side's good." He tugged her closer.

She hovered by his bedside, all the things she'd wanted to say jumbling up in her mind. Because she was tired. Not because she was scared at this first test to her resolution to be strong, to make this relationship work.

"Commander?" The word fell out of her mouth. "As in commander of the test squadron?"

David watched her warily. "Interim commander. The new guy was already not working out, and now with this gun turret catastrophe on his watch . . . Yeah, the rumor is I'm being offered the position. For now."

Her blood rushed from her face straight to her toes. "Congratulations."

And she meant it. Truly.

What she had with David was special, not just their time with the kids, not only making love but laughing over a bowl of ice cream. They'd enjoyed challenging each other, bringing out the best in each other.

One enduring fact shone through. She loved Major David Berg, crusader, father, man. And nothing scared her more than not having him by her side for the rest of her life.

★ ★ ★

David held on to Sophie's hand and waited for her to say something, anything, to give him some sense of where they would go from here. His chest burned like hell, not to mention his arm flaming all the way down to his wrist, but he wasn't taking anything for granted until he had this out with her, until he figured out how to make sure she stayed by his side.

Forever.

Then Sophie smiled, that amazing one that never ceased to knot his stomach. Only this time, her look held a new element. Steely determination had replaced the glimmer of vulnerability.

He hoped that smile meant they were on the same side, because she looked ready to down a mountain lion.

Hope eased the sting in his side. "When I was lying on the floor in your office, I think I remember you saying a lot of things to me."

Her smile faltered, pain flashing through her eyes. "I did."

"Things like how much you love me."

"I do," she said simply, firmly.

Even knowing he didn't deserve it, he took it, every bit of love she would offer. David looked at Sophie and let his own wave of love fill him, no more fighting it. He would be the man she needed, the husband she deserved, and that was one tall order because she was one hell of a woman.

He had expected Sophie to do all the changing, accommodating. How could he demand she give to him what he wasn't willing to give in return? Such a premise didn't say much for his love. He intended to fix that.

David reached for her other hand, flinching at the tug to his stitches. Just as she had done with his hand at the condo, he wove his fingers with hers. He rested her palm over his heart and held it in place with his. "Good. Because I love you, too."

Her hand trembled, as did her smile. "I thought you might." She splayed her fingers over the place where his heart picked up speed at her touch. The machine hooked up to him beeped faster. "What are we going to do about it?"

"That's up to you, Sophie." Whatever it took, he would make sure she felt safe.

"No, that's where you're wrong, David." Her smile steadied. "This is something we figure out together."

Together. He loved the sound of that word. He loved *her*. "I swear I didn't know I was even in line for this job. I thought the Pentagon gig was a done deal." The mere mention of giving up that Pentagon test job and staying in the more dangerous test squadron made her wince. He'd been wrong to expect her to magically get over her past. "You've got to know I wouldn't lie to you."

"I know. If anything, you're honest to a fault." Sighing, she stroked a soothing hand over his hair. "Okay, I can give it a try, but I won't promise not to worry. I fell in love with the man you are, and you're stuck with me just as I am."

He'd told himself it didn't matter which she chose, but hearing her acceptance offered him a peace he'd never expected to find. Years of resentments rolled from his shoulders.

"You aren't listening to me, Sophie. I didn't expect the commander job. I didn't apply for it. I'm not going to take it."

"But you want it."

She knew him too well. He knew her as well and didn't want to hurt her again. "No lies. Yeah, I want it."

Her hand flinched under his, but her gaze never wavered. "Then take it."

Staring at the magnificent woman in front of him, he wasn't even tempted by the job. Her voice offering forever tipped the scales in their favor. "Do you remember what I said back at the condo when we were looking at family pictures?"

"About what?"

He thought of how beautiful she'd looked that night, all tousled from making love. Seeing her now, rumpled, scraped, and disheveled, she was equally as incredible. "I said I couldn't think of any thrill greater than watching my daughter get married. Remember?"

She nodded, her eyes moist with tears. "I think that was one of the things I may have yelled at you on the floor in my office."

"Well, I can think of one thing that rivals walking my daughter down the aisle. Watching you walk down the aisle toward me." He swiped away her spilling tears and vowed to make that dream come true. "Yeah, I want the job, but I want you more."

She lowered the bed rail and sat beside him. Her hip fit against his right side as if she'd been made for him. "I'm telling you that you can have both."

While he would have given anything to hear those words from her even a few hours earlier, he was glad for their delay. He might have stupidly taken her up on the offer and thrown away their chance at forever. Sophie deserved better from him.

"Sophie, thank you. Just hearing you say it . . ." He gripped her hand. "Thank you. But I'm not accepting it. You seemed to think the Pentagon job would be a workable compromise. So let's give it a try and see how it goes. If you can handle my staying in the air force, I'll do all I can to make it easier for you." Even breathing hurt, but he had to be certain she understood. "I promise you I won't do anything to risk what we have together."

"I know." She cupped his face with her hands, her hold firm. "Just as you are, I want you, Major Berg. Days in the park, pink kangaroos, bowls of ice cream, and our children."

He wanted to climb out of the hospital bed, drive her home, start on more children, sleep, then gather the two children they already had. They might very well have a minivan in their future after all.

"Sophie, when you cuddled that pink eyesore, I knew I didn't stand a chance." He slid a strand of her hair behind her ear and looked forward to repeating the action for years. "You aren't a golden elephant kind of lady. Why the big house? The whole image just doesn't fit the woman I've come to know."

Her eyes deepened to a melancholy brown, those dew-kissed daisies returning for a flash. "A child should feel safe—Ricky Vasquez, Brice, Haley Rose. I know what it's like to be young and scared. I thought if I kept the house and all the other trappings Lowell saddled me with, somehow I would be giving Brice security." She smiled, her whole body radiating peace. "Silly, huh? All I really need is to know you'll always love me."

What had he done to deserve her? The day she'd chewed him up in court had been the luckiest day of his life.

"You're making this too easy." He kissed her wrist. "I'm supposed to do something tough to win you."

"*Uhm*, hello? You took two bullets for me today." Her pulse raced under his mouth. "And what you're offering me now, to compromise, that isn't easy for everyone." Her eyes sparkled with a velvety chocolate look, no ghosts clouding them. "So, did I hear a proposal in there somewhere?"

"If you have to ask, then I didn't do it right." Using

his good arm, David pushed himself upright the rest of the way. He stared into the warm brown eyes that would greet him every morning for the rest of his life. "Sophie, will you marry me? Not because you're a good mother or because you turn me inside out with those sexy curves, but because I love you."

"David, I do love you, too."

"And?"

"Yes, I will marry you. Not because you're a great father or because you flip my stomach with your slow, sexy smiles, but because I love you."

Tucking her to his side, he sealed their vows with a kiss and knew the wedding was just a formality for them. Sophie was his. He was hers.

He thumbed the nurse's call button.

Sophie elbowed up. "Do you need pain medication?"

"Nope, you and I need to pick up our kids and go home."

EPILOGUE

TWO YEARS LATER

Sophie dropped her legal pad on the deck and clutched her knees as close to her as her second-trimester stomach would allow. Maternal pride filled her as she watched Brice and Haley Rose playing touch football with Aunt Madison and her fiancé Caleb. They'd come in from Nevada this week for Sophie's baby shower.

Haley Rose squealed as she jumped to catch the ball, stumbling back into the fence. Their yard here in a suburb outside D.C. wasn't as large as her Vegas place, and it wasn't waterfront.

But it was theirs. Paid for. Full of love that offered more security for their whole family than any fancy address.

Sophie stretched her legs the length of the deck recliner. The sun warmed her skin below the hem of her shorts. David's appreciative gaze warmed her more.

A year and a half of marriage hadn't dimmed their

passion—not even pregnancy had slowed them down. The longing, as well as their love, burned stronger while they worked together to build a future for themselves and their children.

David nodded toward the backyard. "They're good kids."

"Yes, they are."

She'd worried they might be jealous when she and David had announced her pregnancy. Instead, the baby seemed to give Haley Rose and Brice a blood kinship, cementing their relationship as brother and sister along with David and Sophie's roles as father and mother. Love, laughter, and even the occasional sibling battle blessed them with the richness of a normal life. Hunter's father had even eased up on his rules about visiting with his son, and they'd enjoyed some time with him, too.

Sophie inhaled the fresh breeze and watched the children tumble on the lawn. The child within her rolled as well. She rested a hand on her stomach.

David checked the ice-cream churn beside her, stirring. The scar on his arm peeked out from under the sleeve of his T-shirt.

Memories of his being shot still woke her at night, but she'd learned not to dwell on possible scenarios. Life carried risks for everyone. The Pentagon job gave them both a breather from deployments and the high-pressure test world. She knew he would go back to the squadron, all of his friends from the unit found their way back there eventually. But the past year had given her the chance to firm up her balance.

No one had been more surprised than her when she'd decided to stay in the air force. As she'd helped sort through the contract mess left behind by Vaughn and

Nelson, she'd realized she couldn't leave. She was called to serve in uniform, just like her dad.

She'd been so damn proud and happy the day Ricky Vasquez had received a hefty settlement from the company that had made the malfunctioning part. It wouldn't give him back what he'd lost, or change the past, but at least they had answers, closure.

Scooping ice cream into a bowl, David offered her a taste. "Give this a try."

Sophie swung her legs to the side and leaned forward. She closed her mouth around the spoon, sighing as the raspberry taste slid over her tongue. The baby leapt in response.

David caressed a hand over her stomach. "How do you feel?"

"Happy." She brushed her knuckles over the fresh sprinkling of silver at his temples.

The wind suit whistling sound preceded Nanny as she bustled onto the redwood patio. "Oh, that looks delicious. I could take care of passing out ice cream to the kids, Madison, and her fella, give you both a rest from entertaining. You two look like you could use a little, uh, *nap*."

David arched his arms and gave an exaggerated yawn. His eyes glittered with almost as much mischief as Nanny's. "Perfect. I'll just put the rest of the ice cream away." He leaned close to Sophie's ear. "Hurry, Counselor."

"Absolutely, Flyboy." Sophie looped an arm around her grandmother's shoulders for a hug. "Thanks, Nanny."

"Well, honey, your man does have one fine backside."

Sophie watched her lanky husband lope inside, the ice-cream churn tucked under his arm. Love, contentment, and more than a little anticipation shimmered through her. "Yeah, Nanny, he sure does."

Turn the page for a sneak peek at
another Dark Ops novel by Catherine Mann

PROTECTOR

Available now
from Berkley Sensation

"I've lost my edge, Colonel."

The admission burned its way up Captain Chuck Tanaka's throat, each word like acid on open wounds inside him. But he was an ace at embracing pain, and he'd be damned before he would endanger anyone else by taking the colonel up on his offer to put Chuck back in the action.

F-16s roared overhead, rattling the rafters in the gaping hangar. Colonel Rex Scanlon stood beside him as airmen prepped for deployment to the Middle East with immunizations, gas masks, duffel bags full of gear. Close to two hundred warm bodies going to war.

Including his crew. His old crew from the top secret test squadron.

Pilots Jimmy Gage and Vince Deluca lined up with loadmaster Mason Randolph standing in a long, long line for a gamma globulin immunization along with an assload full of other shots to prepare them for the diseases overseas. He remembered well how the huge needle left a lump that made for uncomfortable flying. Back when he'd been their navigator. Before his injuries grounded him for life.

These days he was the squadron mobility officer. He ensured all deploying personnel were up to date with training, shots, equipment.

In a nutshell? He rode a desk and pushed paper.

Musty gear and a low hum of chitchat filled the hangar. All familiar. Jimmy, Vince, and Mason shuffled forward, flight suits down around their ankles in boxer shorts while the doc shouted, "Next."

"Tanaka?" Scanlon leaned forward, staring him down from behind black-rimmed glasses. "I need you on this mission. You're the man. You have the skills."

Not the skills he wanted, not the job he wanted. Better just to exist.

Chuck took a folder from an overeager airman and signed off on the bottom of a form. One more ready to deploy. Around them, uniformed men and women carried large green deployment bags stuffed full of equipment picked up at numerous stations. Security cops were posted throughout, watching and talking into radios. Off to his left, a dozen more who'd completed drawing equipment sat on the floor fitting the ballistic plates into their body armor. Another group checked over their weapons, disassembling and putting them back together.

His fingers twitched with muscle memory from performing the same tasks countless times. In the past. Speed mattered, and he couldn't trust his hands or his feet any longer.

Chuck slapped the folder closed. "I figure I've given

my fair share to Uncle Sam. He won't mind if I sit out the rest of my commitment to the air force at my desk, rubber stamping paperwork."

Scanlon scrubbed his face, sighed hard, his eyes too full of the hell that went down when they'd both been in Turkey two years ago. "Without question, you've sacrificed more than your fair share for your country. But this op, this enemy, these people . . ." His jaw clenched, and the pity shifted to something harder. "This is our chance to even the score for what they did to you and those other servicemen they kidnapped."

Hunger. Mind games. Torture. Chuck's grip tightened on his clipboard.

Thankfully, his thoughts were broken by another airman thrusting a folder at him. He opened it and took a few minutes to calm himself by reading the checklist before signing at the bottom. He embraced routine and monotony through the days and sweated through the nights.

Chuck passed the folder back to the airman and waited until he stepped away before meeting the colonel's gaze dead on. "A very wise nun in the Hawaiian orphanage where I grew up always told me holding grudges is bad for the soul."

"In case you didn't notice, I'm not laughing."

Neither was Chuck these days. But he was getting by. Surviving one step at a time, as he recovered from the ass kicking he'd taken overseas at the hands of a sadistic bitch bent on prying secrets from servicemen, then selling the info to the highest terrorist bidder.

She hadn't gotten jack shit from him about the covert test missions he used to fly or the cutting-edge equipment he developed in the dark ops squadron. But he'd paid a heavy price for keeping those secrets.

"Pardon my bluntness, Colonel, but have you taken a look at me lately?" His eleven broken bones had healed as well as they ever would, and he was lucky to be on his feet again. Reconstructive surgery had taken care of most of the scars. External ones, anyway.

His ex-girlfriend claimed he was still an "emotional cripple." Whatever the hell that meant. "Sir, I know exactly what I'm worth these days, or rather how little. You're not fooling anyone here. Offering me a mission is the equivalent of a pity fuck. Sir."

Scanlon's thick eyebrow hitched upward through two shouts of "Next" before he pulled the clipboard from his hand and gave it to Chuck's assistant, a surprised master sergeant.

The colonel guided Chuck away from the bustle and behind some pallets loaded for the deployment. "Chuck, this mission could be the backbreaker for what some of the intel spooks think is a major attack here in the States. Our equipment, equipment you helped test, is the only way to exploit the one hole we have been able to find in their organization—"

"Not interested," he interrupted, desperate as hell to stop the colonel from taunting him with what he could not have anymore.

Scanlon continued as if he'd never been interrupted. "You'll go in undercover as a blackjack dealer on an Italian cruise ship next week. You won't be going in alone. I'll have your back, and David Berg will be running the surveillance equipment on board the *Fortuna*. Think about it. At worst you'll get some sun and great food. And at best, you'll bring down a terrorist cell."

Hunger for the chance to fight back gnawed at his gut. "You don't need me as the front man." Maybe . . . "Why not let me operate the gadgets? Nobody runs the packet analyzer and translator algorithms as well as I do. It's more art than science."

Shit, he was already envisioning himself there. "Forget I said that. I'm exactly where I should be—"

Pop! A gunshot blasted from the other side of the pallets. A chunk of wood splintered into the air.

Chuck jerked hard and fast, looking over his shoulder even as he knew it had to be some dumb ass who'd slipped a round in his weapon, then seriously screwed up with an unintentional discharge. He looked across the hangar—

And stared straight into the cold, emotionless eyes of a gunman who looked too damn much like one of their own firing wildly into the clusters of airmen.

So fast. Shouts and more pops. Bullets. From the gunman and the security cops, but no one could get a decent aim as the guy ran and bobbed. The gunman turned toward Chuck's old crew. Fired. Jimmy spun back as a round caught him in the shoulder. The gun tracked Jimmy for another—

Chuck drew his sidearm before he could think and centered on the uniformed gunman's chest. *Pop. Pop. Pop.* He squeezed off three shots, center of mass.

Everyone and everything in the hangar went unearthly still. The only sound was a haunting echo of Chuck's shots.

The gunman crumpled to the ground a second before the acrid scent of gunfire bit the air.

Chuck's fist clenched around the familiar weight of his 9 mm. The hangar seemed to freeze frame, imprinting itself in his brain. Cops with weapons drawn. Others with their fists wrapped around the butt of a gun. The unarmed huddled, hugging their heads protectively.

Slowly, sounds of sirens outside pierced his consciousness and snapped the frame back into motion. Security cops swarmed the downed gunman. His old crewmate, Jimmy, sat up, clutching his shoulder with blood pouring between his fingers while the rest of the crew checked him over. No one else had opened fire, but the edgy need to stay on guard seared the air as three other injured held on to a bleeding leg or arm. No one dead, though. Thank God.

Chuck scoured the hangar. Adrenaline coursed through him, his pulse pounding in his ears. The gun felt right in his hands. Taking out an enemy felt even better.

The colonel secured his unfired weapon back in the holster and stared at Chuck's smoking gun, now pointing upward. "Still think you've lost your edge, Tanaka? Because from where I'm standing, it appears you just stopped a massacre."

Chuck lowered his weapon slowly, the inevitable flooding his veins with each slug of his heart. "That same old nun also told me gloating is as dangerous as grudges."

"Fair enough, Captain. I take it then you'll be joining Berg and me at the morning briefing?"

He nodded once without taking his eyes off the unconscious gunman.

"Good, good." Scanlon righted his black-framed glasses. "Meanwhile, you may want to brush up on your blackjack skills."

Chuck thumbed the barrel of his weapon, an undeniable thirst filling him. The need to get back in the fight. The need to defend his comrades.

The need to avenge.

There were still a lot of blanks to be filled in, but then that's what briefs were for. He didn't need to hear any more well-executed persuasive arguments. He already knew.

He was going all in.

★ GENOA: CRUISE TERMINAL OF
   PONTE DEI MILLE

"Who wants eight the hard way?"

"I'll take that. Gimme twenty on eight."

"Come on, little Joe from Ko-ko-mo!"

Jolynn Taylor parted the pervasive smoke with her body, winding around slot machines and frenzied gamblers. Her eyes stung, and she tried to blame the moisture on the thick cigarette haze. She wanted to be as far away from this sleazy, sometimes dangerous world as she could get.

Why hadn't she just ignored the message and stayed in Dallas rather than racing all the way to Genoa, Italy? Security for intercontinental flights was hellish right now after that attack at the Nevada military base last week.

Sure, her father was recovering from a heart attack. But he employed plenty of people to care for him while he recuperated at a local rehab center and then in total luxury on one of his cruise ships. He was the one who chose to live overseas floating from port to port, Italy, Greece, Croatia . . .

She slipped between an aging Italian contessa playing the slots and a newlywed couple plastered together by the one-armed bandit chanting out their desire in French. The casino's nerve-tingling clamor contrasted in her mind with the quiet sterility of a sickroom . . . her father's sickroom, which she couldn't avoid much longer. Nothing short of hearing he was at death's door could have drawn her back into his seedy realm.

Bells chimed and lights flashed as she elbowed through the crowd in search of her cousin, Lucy, the director of operations. Once she dropped off her luggage and got the latest lowdown on her dad, she would drive over to his rehab center.

"Hello, love." A Brit with slicked-back brown hair held a pair of dice in one hand and palmed her leg with the other. "Be a dear and blow on my dice. A pretty bird like you could change my luck."

Jolynn offered him her best insipid drawl reserved for soused morons who put on fakey accents. "Wish I could help you out, sugar." She moved his hand firmly. "But I can't be giving anyone a house advantage."

She tapped her laminated security pass, resisting the urge to tell him to "sod off." Forging ahead, she passed a young couple walking from machine to machine, silver mining for loose coins.

The ship's lounge singer took the stage and started off her next set with a morose Italian ballad to some mooney-eyed guy, which only darkened Jolynn's already bottomed-out mood. She wanted no part of her father's world. Yet she missed him with an ache as annoying as the blister developing on her heel.

Jolynn shouldered through the press of overheated bodies until she escaped the circle of gaming tables into the hollow center designated for dealers and the pit boss. The open area provided a clearer, and calmer, vantage point from which to scour the area.

She pivoted, only to pitch forward. Her feet tangled with someone crouched near the blackjack table. Her arms pinwheeled before smacking the floor, halting her gangly tumble. Jolynn's body bridged the huddled individual's back. A man's back. Pressed against him, she could feel every whipcord muscle of his slim physique. His musky male scent pleasantly distracted her from the casino's smoky odor.

"Excuse me." She walked her fingers along the carpeted floor, inching up and using the man's broad back as her final boost. "I didn't see you down—"

"*Ooof.* Careful. That's my kidney."

His protest tickled her ears, his American accent bathing her in familiar sounds of home. Jolynn skimmed her hand over his spine to his shoulder, enjoying the sinuous trek a little too much. "So sorry. I was preoccupied and didn't look where I was going."

She grabbed the blackjack table for leverage as she stood. She shook her skirt in place with a little shimmy, not wanting to know how much she'd exposed during their impromptu game of Twister. "Did I inflict permanent damage?"

"Everything seems intact."

"Good." Jolynn looked down at the kneeling man staring back up with mesmerizing mocha dark eyes.

She'd never been much of a romantic, but his eyes seemed to glint with hidden depths . . . Okay, okay, light from the crystal chandelier may have added something to the dreamy effect. Even so, she couldn't look away.

He shook his sleek black hair into place again. His forearm rested on his bent knee, his other hand pressed to the floor. He had a broad forehead, a firm chin, and fine creases around exotic eyes, perhaps with a hint of Polynesian ancestry. He was a total package kind of guy, with a strong, handsome face. She judged him to be in his late twenties or early thirties.

He rose, finally stopping just at her level, around six feet in her heels. Perfect. In her father's world of burly men and overblown personalities, she found calming reassurance in the man's understated power.

Safe. Sexy, yet safe. "Are you sure you're all right? Your kidney, I mean."

"I've taken worse hits and survived," he said softly. "How about you?"

Better than three minutes ago. She welcomed the opportunity to think of something, anything other than where she was. "Just fine."

"Glad to hear it." He nodded slowly, his thick hair sliding over his brow.

Smiling, she backed away—and bumped into a waitress who shouldn't have even been in the pit area. A tray of drinks flew from the woman's hand and crashed to the floor. Jolynn winced.

Not even back in her family circle for a full day and already she'd reverted to her gangly teen moves. Years of cultivating a poise that rivaled her father's multitude of Greek and Roman goddess statues evaporated with a simple glance from this guy.

He grinned, creasing dimples in his cheeks. "Sorry to trip you up like that—again." He extended his hand, offering her the silver token gleaming in his palm. "I didn't mean to start such a ruckus just to retrieve this."

"No harm done." Jolynn accepted the token with an ironic smile.

"I'll be happy to pay for your dry cleaning."

"You don't have to do that." She would settle for another one of those distracting smiles instead.

"At least let me help you dry off." He grabbed a stack of cocktail napkins and reached out to blot her travel-weary suit jacket. His fist clenched just beside the damp fabric covering her breasts.

He passed the wadded clump to her. "You may, uh, want to take care of this yourself."

"Uh, thanks."

Fantasy gave way to reality as she refocused on the man in front of her. He wore the standard casino uniform of creased black pants, a loose white shirt, a red bow tie . . . and a name tag. *Charles Tomas: Blackjack Dealer.*

Her safe, beautiful man was a two-bit blackjack dealer. Of course he was. How could she have forgotten where she was?

Jolynn resurrected the vapid facade she used as a defense against the smarmy losers she attracted like flies to sticky paper. "See you around, sugar."

She watched his smile fade.

"Jolynn Taylor!"

The high-pitched squeal of her only cousin carried over the mayhem, breaking into any further temptation to daydream.

Long ago, when she'd learned the truth about her father's international mob connections, Jolynn had quit believing in fantasy princes. Trusting in fairy tales got people killed. She'd toughened up fast and didn't plan to change.

As soon as she helped her father settle in on his floating barge of iniquity, she'd be back on a plane to a normal life. By then, the nagging ache to reconnect with the old man would be soothed and all thoughts of dark-eyed princes would be left behind with the Mediterranean Sea.

* * *

Chuck Tanaka watched Jolynn hug the casino's director of operations, before the cousins commandeered stools at the bar.

When the leggy redhead had charged through the casino, he hadn't even needed to glance at her security pass to clue him in. He'd recognized Jolynn Taylor, knew her bio in the report he'd received on Josiah Taylor's operation. The past week had been spent packing his head full of information, preparing as the CIA brought in the NSA as well as the air force OSI and their special ops test unit.

Some of the briefing had been done in person, some by telecom, some anonymously. For their own protection, supposedly, but it sucked not knowing who all the players were.

For his own protection, they'd assured him. But then he already knew he couldn't only rely on his test squadron brothers.

Implementing their setup and cover stories had been easier than expected with the rest of the world preoccupied with the soldier who'd open fired on the deploying troops.

Thank God no one had been killed.

He brought his attention back to the moment. He was in the game again. A last-ditch effort to resurrect himself. Do or die.

Already he'd almost fumbled when the colonel had slipped the warning about Jolynn's unplanned arrival. Chuck had nearly botched calling the game when from across the room Colonel Scanlon had pointed her out by that British dude.

Chuck had known it must be important for Scanlon to break their established routine of exchanging info at designated times. The colonel had whispered the alert under the guise of asking for directions to the lounge to hear his Italian girlfriend sing. The warning that Josiah Taylor's daughter was due in for an obligatory sickbed visit had come just in time for him to toss himself in her path, literally. Not one of his smoother moves, but his klutz act had gotten the job done. Contact had been made.

Except she'd rocked his balance right back.

He monitored Jolynn and her cousin as they ordered drinks. He'd made the requisite attempts to cultivate a low-key relationship with the director of operations. But she was too wrapped up in her security guard fiancé to talk about anything other than wedding plans.

Chuck mentally reviewed the facts on file about Jolynn Taylor. Boarding school education. Six-figure accounting job in Dallas and dating life that made the social pages. The rumor mill churned with stories of Josiah's estranged daughter.

His systematic analysis faded as he remembered the press of her breasts against his chest. He'd almost forgotten to breathe. She'd come too damned close to finding his Beretta strapped in the ankle holster.

Across the room, her auburn hair gleamed like a warning light. Damn, he'd been too long without. His breakup was already six months old and that relationship had been, well, a mixed-up mess.

He was better served staying clear of female entanglements. Making contact was one thing. Letting attraction get the better of him was another. A mistake he'd made two years ago and it had cost him. Big-time.

Chuck turned his back on Jolynn Taylor and dealt the next hand. He wasn't done with her yet. Thanks to the surveillance device in the token he'd given her—which she'd so accommodatingly placed in her purse—he would be reviewing tapes of her conversation well into the night.